Siren Beloved

Other Books By Lexi Blake

ROMANTIC SUSPENSE

Masters and Mercenaries
The Dom Who Loved Me
The Men With The Golden Cuffs
A Dom is Forever
On Her Master's Secret Service
Sanctum: A Masters and Mercenaries Novella
Love and Let Die
Unconditional: A Masters and Mercenaries Novella
Dungeon Royale
Dungeon Games: A Masters and Mercenaries Novella
A View to a Thrill
Cherished: A Masters and Mercenaries Novella
You Only Love Twice
Luscious: Masters and Mercenaries~Topped
Adored: A Masters and Mercenaries Novella
Master No
Just One Taste: Masters and Mercenaries~Topped 2
From Sanctum with Love
Devoted: A Masters and Mercenaries Novella
Dominance Never Dies
Submission is Not Enough
Master Bits and Mercenary Bites~The Secret Recipes of Topped
Perfectly Paired: Masters and Mercenaries~Topped 3
For His Eyes Only
Arranged: A Masters and Mercenaries Novella
Love Another Day
At Your Service: Masters and Mercenaries~Topped 4
Master Bits and Mercenary Bites~Girls Night
Nobody Does It Better
Close Cover
Protected: A Masters and Mercenaries Novella
Enchanted: A Masters and Mercenaries Novella
Charmed: A Masters and Mercenaries Novella
Treasured: A Masters and Mercenaries Novella, Coming June 29, 2021

Smoke and Sin
At the Pleasure of the President

URBAN FANTASY

Thieves
Steal the Light
Steal the Day
Steal the Moon
Steal the Sun
Steal the Night
Ripper
Addict
Sleeper
Outcast
Stealing Summer

LEXI BLAKE WRITING AS SOPHIE OAK

Texas Sirens
Small Town Siren
Siren in the City
Siren Enslaved
Siren Beloved
Siren in Waiting
Siren in Bloom
Siren Unleashed
Siren Reborn

Nights in Bliss, Colorado
Three to Ride
Two to Love
One to Keep
Lost in Bliss
Found in Bliss
Pure Bliss
Chasing Bliss
Once Upon a Time in Bliss
Back in Bliss
Sirens in Bliss

Happily Ever After in Bliss
Far From Bliss, Coming 2021

A Faery Story
Bound
Beast
Beauty

Standalone
Away From Me
Snowed In

Siren Beloved

Texas Sirens Book 4

Lexi Blake
writing as
Sophie Oak

Siren Beloved
Texas Sirens Book 4

Published by DLZ Entertainment LLC at Smashwords

Copyright 2018 DLZ Entertainment LLC
Edited by Chloe Vale
ISBN: 978-1-937608-87-3

Sign up for Lexi Blake's newsletter
and be entered to win a $25 gift certificate
to the bookseller of your choice.

Join us for news, fun, and exclusive content
including free short stories.

There's a new contest every month!

Go to www.lexiblake.net to subscribe.

Dedication

Special thanks to the people who make my writing life happen – Chloe Vale, the best assistant a writer could have, Shayla Black, my cohort and partner in crime, Kris Cook, the person most likely to hold my hand as I jump off the ledge, my kids, and my mom. I love you all.

2018 Dedication

Reading through this book again, I'm struck by how much of my own story is in here. There's a reason that I chose the name Lexi when I decided to branch out into independent publishing. Lexi is very close to who I was at her age—stubborn, loyal, insecure about some things and positively arrogant about others, afraid, so afraid that the world will take away the things she loves. I had a Lucas back then. From the age of twelve until I stood in front of our family and friends, finally smart enough to say I do, my husband did what he could to stay close to me. He became my friend so he could be there when I was ready to acknowledge what he knew when he stood outside the band hall and asked me to the Hawaiian dance at Hurst Jr. High—that we were meant to be together.

You are my Lucas and my Aidan, my Danny and Dev, always my Big Tag—my Richard. I love you far more now than I did then and will love you even more tomorrow.

Chapter One

"**I**'m waiting." Julian Lodge leaned back in his chair. Though he was perfectly still, he gave off an air of irritation that Lexi Moore couldn't possibly miss. "And you know I don't like to wait."

Lexi's head was pounding as Julian Lodge stared at her across his ridiculously expensive desk. He was giving her "the stare." She was sure he'd trademarked and maybe put a patent on it, because nothing in the world could be as intimidating as those silvery eyes staring holes through her body. Julian Lodge knew exactly how to intimidate a person. The only person who was worse was her stepfather, Jack Barnes. Unfortunately, he was attending this meeting, too.

"Do you have something to say for yourself?" Jack asked, disapproval dripping from every word. "Maybe an explanation of what you thought you were doing?"

She had lots of things to say for herself and to herself, but in the harsh light of day, she could only manage a weak, "I'm sorry."

Julian's fingers drummed along the surface of the mahogany desk where he kept a framed picture of himself and his two loves. Julian and Finn Taylor were resplendent in tuxedoes, and Danielle Lodge-Taylor was a vision in her white wedding dress. She hadn't been there. She'd given a pitiful excuse to not go to her friends' wedding.

God, she was running out of excuses.

"I don't know if an apology is going to work this time, Alexis." Julian's words felt like a hammer coming down.

Her stomach dropped. Was he really going to kick her out of The Club? How was she going to explain it to Lucas? Would Lucas even listen to her? Tears pooled in her eyes even as her head pounded. "I don't know what else to say. The truth is I don't remember much about last night."

She remembered starting in on the bottle of chardonnay and then switching to tequila. It had all made perfect sense at the time. She didn't recall much after a couple of hours with Jose Cuervo. She'd woken up in a suite above The Club to find her stepfather sitting in the living area waiting to give her the lecture of a lifetime.

"Would you like to see the tapes? I have them. Your father has seen them."

Yep, she was going to throw up. She didn't argue with Julian about Jack's title in her life. He truly had been her father for the last couple of years. Her biological dad had died before she'd been born. Her first stepfather had been great, but most of the time he'd been in her life he'd been sick. Jack Barnes was the first male in her life who had expended an enormous amount of his energy to protect her.

Lucas did, too. But she didn't have anything close to fatherly feelings for him, and she never had. "I'll pass on the entertainment. Why don't you tell me what happened?"

"Well, you showed up drunk at my club for starters."

Damn, she was in trouble when Julian used that voice. He had a strict policy of never allowing anyone more than two drinks in his bar. Julian Lodge ran the most infamous BDSM club in the south, and he ruled it with an iron fist. Consensual was Julian's first rule, and consent couldn't happen in his brain if the participants were drunk.

"How did I get past the bouncer?" There was security in The Club. One couldn't wander in off the streets and there were rules even about club members coming in.

Jack's eyebrows rose over his stern face. "You mean Martin?"

Damn it. Martin was always nice to her. He was the front desk guy. "Yes. Why did he let me in? Lucas wasn't with me."

Lucas acted as her Dom when they were in The Club. They had

14

started coming in roughly a year and a half before, when her curiosity finally overrode her heartache over the subject. Lucas had been the one to introduce her to the lifestyle. He was happy in The Club. Lucas was a true switch. He was happy playing the Dom and gained a great deal of satisfaction from submitting when the partner was right. Lucas hadn't bottomed in years, and that was her fault.

"You talked him into it," Julian explained flatly. "And you talked him out of a job. I fired him this morning."

"Julian, you can't do that." She leaned forward, pleading. She couldn't have cost that nice man his job.

He simply frowned. "Of course I can. It's already done. I gave him a nice severance package, but he proved he can't handle working here. He should have immediately informed me or Leo that you were causing trouble. As it was, you interrupted several scenes, and Leo was forced to pull you out of the Red Room."

She gasped, pure shock running through her system. The Red Room was an orgy room. What the hell had she done? She was going to be sick. If she'd allowed herself to be used…

Jack shook his head. "You didn't have sex, Lexi. That wasn't at all why you went in there. You aggressively tried to talk the women in the room out of having sex. You went on and on about how they should protect themselves and that the men in the room weren't worthy of them. I believe they found you highly annoying."

She let her head find her hands. She rarely drank, but she'd been talked into happy hour the night before. Who was she kidding? She'd been drinking a bit too much lately. Lucas was out of town, and she'd been at loose ends. It had been months since she'd been kidnapped, and she was having horrible dreams again. She'd wanted to find a bit of oblivion, but she'd found a ton of trouble. "Tell me I didn't drive."

Lucas would kill her if she'd gotten behind the wheel.

"You took a cab. I tracked down your car and had it brought to The Club," Jack said.

"Thank you." Her hands were shaking. Jack sighed and walked out of the room for a moment.

"These people pay enormous amounts of money to belong to this club, Alexis." Julian's dark hair was pulled back in a severe queue. He looked like a man who could deal with mobsters and win, which, according to her mother's stories, Julian had. She felt like a small, fluffy bunny in the presence of a leopard. "They do not expect to have to deal with my family issues."

Though he didn't say it, his meaning was plain. She wasn't allowed into The Club because of who she was, but rather who she knew. Julian considered her family because she was Jack Barnes's daughter and Lucas Cameron's…whatever the hell she was to Lucas. Julian carefully vetted the members of his club, but not so much the people he considered family.

Well, she'd shown him…

"Julian, I'm sorry. I don't know what else to say. If I'd been in my right mind, I would never have done anything like that."

"Yes," Julian said with an air of finality, as though she'd sealed her own fate. "I realize that, and I'm glad you realize it, too."

Jack strode back in the room. He had a mug in hand and held it in front of her. "Coffee. It'll help with the headache."

She reached out for it. It was warm against her hands. Frustration poured over her. She was stuck, and she wasn't sure how to get out. "Thanks."

It was right there on the tip of her tongue. She wanted to say, "Thanks, Dad." She wanted to, but she couldn't. Just like she wanted to say, "I love you, Lucas," and she couldn't force the words from her lips. All the men she'd ever said it to died or walked away, because in the end, they didn't want her love. She was trouble. So much fucking trouble.

"You're welcome." Jack took up his prior position behind Julian. He loomed over her like a big hawk staring down at something he wanted to protect. She always felt safe with Jack Barnes. It was precisely the reason she felt bad about letting the man down. When would she get her shit straight? She was twenty-five. It was way past time to know what she was doing in life. Most of her friends were getting married and settling down. She was adrift. She was utterly in a state of pause. Like the button on her remote was stuck.

"I'm terminating your rights in this club, Alexis." Julian pronounced her sentence with what almost seemed like sympathy coming from him. His voice was softer than she ever remembered it sounding.

She'd expected it, but the decision hit her squarely in the gut. This was the place Lucas felt most at home, and now she couldn't come here anymore. *Fuck.* She was going to lose Lucas. Her heart seized. She set the coffee back down on the desk untouched. She welcomed the physical pain her headache brought because it took her mind off the devastation Julian's pronouncement brought her. And yet she knew begging wouldn't work with Julian.

"All right. I understand." She managed to stand, though her legs were a bit wobbly. She had one thought in her brain at this point. Get out with some semblance of dignity. "I appreciate the time I had here, Julian. Jack, please say hello to my mother. Tell her I can't come down this weekend. I…I can't."

"Lexi," her stepfather said with a frown that told her how tired he was. He must have driven here in the middle of the night. "Sit down. I don't think Julian is done yet."

"Oh, I think he's done." Lucas's voice rang out through the room.

She turned back, and he was standing there in the doorway looking tired and unkempt. His normally perfect clothes were wrinkled, and his handsome face was marred with worry and no small amount of indignation. She'd seen this look on Lucas's face when he felt justice wasn't being served. She wanted more than anything to run to him and fling herself against his strong body. She wanted to bury her head in Lucas's shoulder and cry her eyes out. Lucas was her protector, her best friend, her whole stinking world, and now, as she sat looking at him, she wondered if she even deserved him.

"Lucas," Julian said, that single eyebrow arching. "I was told you and Finn would be at least another day in Chicago."

"Yeah, I bet you were," Lucas said, stalking into the office. He made a direct line for her. "You want to explain to me why you have my sub in your office without the courtesy of a fucking phone call? I had to find out from Finn who found out from Dani."

"Both of whom will get a stern talking to from me." Julian had gone positively glacial. "I didn't call you, Lucas, because she isn't wearing your collar. I called her closest male relative. It's what I do. Call me what you like, but I believe in the traditional ways. Jackson is her father. As she has no permanently contracted Dom, I called him in because she's in trouble. Would you prefer I simply shoved her on the

17

street? I don't do that with family. Alexis, would you have preferred I called in your mother?"

Dear god, no. That would be worse. "I don't suppose you could simply consider me an adult and just talk to me?"

An unamused chuckle came from Julian's mouth. "Heavens no, dear. After last night, I don't consider you a functional adult at all."

Well, she'd brought that one on herself.

Lucas's hand reached down to grasp her own. "Come on. We're leaving. If Julian can't honor my rights, we'll find someplace else."

Jack stepped forward. "You are not taking my daughter to another club, is that understood?"

Lucas's jaw settled in a firm, stubborn line. "She's mine, and I'll do what I think is best with her. I've taken care of her for years, Jack. Fucking years. So you will back off. She belongs to me. And I quit. You can find another goddamn lawyer, brother."

Whoa. She pulled away from Lucas. What was wrong with him? He loved Jack. He practically worshipped the ground the man walked on, and he was willing to walk away from him? Lexi shook her head. She couldn't allow that to happen. She'd already cost a man his job. She couldn't cost Lucas his relationship with Jack.

She looked at Julian, well aware that she was practically begging. "Please, let me make this up to you. I'll do anything. Don't let this happen."

Jack and Lucas were staring each other down. They looked like the same damn man, but at different stages of life. Jack had ten plus years on Lucas, but they had the same eyes and face, and the same stubborn glare.

"Well, I wasn't allowed to finish," Julian said with a sigh. The testosterone flowing around the room didn't seem to bother him at all. "I was about to map out a plan that would give you access to The Club again."

"She doesn't need access to a place that doesn't appreciate her," Lucas snarled Julian's way.

"Nor does she need someone who enables her every self-destructive tendency," Jack snapped right back. "I love you, Lucas. You're my blood, my brother. She's my daughter in every sense but biology, but I'm starting to wonder if the two of you aren't going to

18

be the death of each other."

Lucas's face went red. "You stay out of my relationship with Lexi!"

She moved between the two men. "Stop, please. Can we hear Julian out?"

Lucas looked like he was ready to continue the argument, but Jack took a step back. She put a hand on Lucas's chest and realized she'd brought him here. She'd brought him here with all the things she wasn't willing to say to him. She'd never told him she loved him with all her heart. After that terrible day when Aidan had left her, she'd shut down and simply accepted Lucas's love without giving him much back. The time had come to move past what she'd lost. She needed to decide if she was brave enough to try a real life with Lucas, and that included this club.

"Please sit with me." She knew how to get to Lucas. She softened against him. She put her arms around him and let herself sag into his strength. Just like that, the fight went out of him, and his hands found her hair.

"All right, baby. I'll listen, but I reserve the right to pick you up and walk out. We can find somewhere else. I can talk to Taggart. His club is private right now, but I think if I offer him free legal services, maybe he'll let us in. We all know that's one man who is going to need a damn lawyer." His words were soft against her ear, and he settled into the chair next to her. He held her hand as they looked to Julian. As always, Lucas was the strong presence anchoring her. He'd been her best friend for the majority of her adult life. He'd stood beside her when he wasn't even sure why she needed him. It was way past time to stand up and be brave, and that meant facing the music with Julian Lodge and her stepfather.

She wasn't so sure about Taggart welcoming them. He ran a security firm that Julian and Jack had funded. The man knew where his bread was buttered.

There wasn't anywhere else. This was home. She wasn't going to get kicked out of her home. "What do I need to do?"

Julian Lodge leaned forward and began to speak.

* * * *

Lucas kept his eyes on the road in front of him, though every other cell of his being was intently thinking about the woman in the seat beside him.

Jack was right, damn it. Lexi was going to be the death of him. Why had he left Dallas? He'd known she'd been on edge the last week. Why had he thought he could waltz off to Chicago and leave her alone with her demons?

"It isn't your fault, Lucas." Lexi sounded tired.

"I wasn't thinking it was," he lied.

She laughed, but it held not an ounce of humor. "Yes, you were. I can tell from the way you're holding the steering wheel. You're wondering why you left me alone. Let me tell you why. You left because you have a job to do, and it isn't babysitting a stubborn woman twenty-four-seven. I don't want a babysitter. I want a friend, and I need to be one, too. I did the crime. I'll do the time."

His fingers tightened on the steering wheel as he turned up Good Latimer. "Maybe I don't like the time you're going to do."

A slight smile played at her lips. Her black hair was glossy in the morning light. She was so ridiculously gorgeous to him. "What do you object to, babe? Sessions with Leo?"

Julian's verdict had been a strange version of parole with the possibility of a full pardon. Lexi was to enter into therapy sessions with Leo, and she had to be cleared by a Dom of Julian's choice. That was the part Lucas had vocally objected to. Unfortunately, Julian had proven far more stubborn than any judge Lucas had to deal with.

He frowned. "You know I don't care about the therapy sessions. I trust Leo. I have no fucking idea who this Master A asshole is."

"You obviously haven't been talking to Dani," Lexi replied.

Her eyes drifted closed as she relaxed back into the seat of the Lexus SUV. They had left her car behind. He'd have someone drive it to her place later. After last night, he wasn't letting her out of his sight for a day or two. It didn't matter what she thought or what Julian Lodge believed. Collar or no collar, she was his responsibility. He wasn't willing to let that go. No matter what Jack said, he was good for her. He had to be.

"What does Dani say about this guy, and why do you have to get cleared by him? Leo, I understand. He's a psychologist. But he's also the Dom in residence. Why can't he clear you on both?" Lucas asked.

The thought of Lexi in some unknown Dom's hands terrified him. His every insecurity was bubbling to the surface and had been since Finn had gotten the call early this morning. Lucas had gotten on the first plane back to Dallas.

She didn't open her eyes, merely talked and turned her porcelain skin toward the sun. He loved her skin. It was lovely, like the woman herself. She brought out his every protective and possessive instinct. "Supposedly he's a badass. He's become Leo's little protégé, and by little, I mean ridiculously big. He's as big as Leo, and one of the other subs said he's covered in scars, like he was wounded in battle or something. They say he's one tough son of a bitch. He's former Army, which is probably why Leo took to him. You know those military types. Dani says Julian brought him in a couple of months back. He's some sort of cowboy now. He has a ranch."

"Then shouldn't he be on his ranch rather than setting himself up to play with my sub?" Yes, Lexi brought out his possessiveness, and this Master A asshole was going to bring out his need to kick some ass.

"You know all the other Doms have day jobs. Leo is the only full-time Dom, and he never plays with anyone he's counseling. Dani says Leo is super high on this guy. He's supposed to be hard, but fair. I'm not worried about it. I can pass whatever test this guy tries to give me."

"You have no idea what he's going to do to you."

Her husky laugh went straight to his cock. *Fuck*. He hadn't had a moment of sleep in forty-eight hours, but one laugh from Lexi and he was like a bull in rut.

"I can imagine. The question is what's he going to do to you, babe?" she asked.

"Nothing, if he knows what's good for him."

Her eyes opened now, and she turned in her seat. They were so dark blue he could drown in them. "Lucas, have you thought about the fact that maybe we should find a Dom?"

Now there was a terrible feeling in the pit of his stomach. Had he thought about it? Of course he had. He found slight refuge in defensiveness. "I'm not Dom enough for you? Maybe Jack's right."

Her hand came out, stroking across the line of his jaw. "That's not what I meant, and you know it. You miss bottoming, babe. I know you do."

He'd given it up a long time ago. He didn't need it. He needed her. At one point he thought he could have both, but that had turned out to be a lie. Aidan had been the perfect solution to everything. He was gorgeous, and Lucas had been sure there was a spark between them. He'd felt it and he'd seen it plainly in Aidan's eyes that he had, too.

Aidan O'Malley had been dominant down to his bone, but he hadn't understood the lifestyle and certainly, in the end, hadn't wanted Lucas himself. One night. He'd had one night before it all fell apart.

It hadn't merely fallen apart. No, it hadn't been some random act that had blown up their lives. Guilt washed over him. He'd done that to Lexi. He'd upended her whole world and caused her fiancé to leave. He owed the woman he loved everything.

"I don't need it, Lexi. I need you. I need you so fucking much, but I can't seem to do it for you. I can't seem to find a way to be enough."

It was true. He wasn't what Lexi needed, and maybe he should honestly think about that. He was always the one to hold her while she cried, but eventually she would need more. She would need a real Dom. She would need someone who could give her everything.

"Stop this car right now, Lucas Cameron." Lexi sat up straight in her seat now, her jaw firming stubbornly.

Lucas pulled over. Now he'd pissed her off, and that hadn't been his plan. Damn it, he was fucking up again. "I'll take you home if you want."

"That is not what I want. I want you to look at me." She turned toward him.

Lucas shifted in his seat and faced the only woman he'd ever really loved. She'd been his friend, his heart and soul, his whole world since the day he'd met her, but he wasn't that for her. Her whole world had walked out the door when Aidan O'Malley left.

"I love you, Lucas Cameron."

His heart almost stopped. How long had he wanted those words? She'd never said I love you, not once. He'd waited to hear those words forever, but now he could hear the "but" somewhere in there like a jolt of poison waiting to kill his happiness. "You know I love you, Lexi. I've said it every day for the past couple of years. I've asked you to move in with me. I've asked you to marry me."

"But you won't sleep with me."

It was the only thing he'd withheld. It had been easier when she was in Austin. He'd known her for years, been in love with her for that whole time, but they'd gone their separate ways while she finished school and he started a career. He'd thought he would never have her, thought she was out of his reach. She'd been ready to get married and have a happy life in Austin with her fiancé, Aidan. He'd been the one to screw that up. Yes, it had been much simpler when all he had were phone calls and texts and long instant messenger chats on the computer.

When Lexi moved to Dallas, his life had become a testament to the power of patience. She slept at his place more often than not. He took her to The Club. He'd introduced her to the lifestyle. He'd given her more orgasms than he could count but taken none for himself because he refused to be her rebound man. He wanted more. He wanted forever.

"Marry me and we'll talk about it." He wasn't going to let her use him for sex.

She laughed. "God, you are exactly like your brother. Except I think he's smarter than you."

Jack went home every night to two subs who loved him and each other more than life itself. Jack had two gorgeous kids. Jack had a job that meant the world to him. Damn straight Jack was smarter than he was. "He got all the brains."

She reached up to touch his hair. "Not all of them. Lucas, I did something stupid last night, and I hurt some people I care about. I don't want to do that anymore. I need a solution, and it's not going to come with you compromising. You've done enough of that for me."

He felt like she'd kicked him in the stomach. This was the moment he'd been dreading for the last two years. She didn't need him anymore. That was why she was willing to say I love you. It was

23

a good-bye gift of sorts. She would steep it in all kinds of bullshit about how this was for him, but she was leaving. He didn't say anything. He couldn't. He kind of wished she would get it over with now that the moment was here.

"I love you, Lucas. I won't stop saying it. I've been selfish to hold it back. Selfish and afraid. I know if I had an ounce of sense, I would take what you're offering and run with it, but I think we would end up unhappy."

Bitterness welled. He'd done everything he could to prove how much he loved her. Why couldn't he be enough? "Yeah, unhappy. Really, I'm thrilled with the fact that you're breaking up with me. That's going to make me really fucking happy."

"Babe, what are you talking about?" Lexi put her hands on the sides of his head and forced him to look at her. "I am not breaking up with you. I could never do that. Ever. I need you, but I think we both need something more. I think we need to find a Dom. Even if it's only for play, we need to admit that you're missing something you crave. Come on. Let's see how things go with this Master A person. Maybe he has something he can teach us. I want what my mom has, and I can have that with you. But we need to move on. Aidan left us."

His heart ached, but he wasn't about to show it to her. He needed to be strong. "Aidan was never with me."

"Oh, my memory says differently. I remember a night when he was with you, and it was a beautiful thing."

Lucas couldn't remember it that way. "Damn it, he left you because of that night."

Her lips curled up in a sad smile. "Because he couldn't handle it. And he left *us*. That's the way I've come to think of it. It wasn't anything you did. He enjoyed what we did that night, and my only regret was that I didn't get to have you. Aidan was far too busy playing the Dom to let us be together. It was an amazing, beautiful night and I won't let Aidan's cowardice taint it anymore. I want to move past Aidan. I have to. It's killing me."

A kernel of hope lit inside Lucas. He pulled her into his arms, loving the feel of her against his chest. This was where he lived. "All right. We'll move past him. I love you, Lexi. I'll never love another human being the way I love you."

24

It was an easy thing to say since he'd only really loved once before, and Aidan was gone from him as surely as he'd walked out on Lexi. Aidan had left them alone and adrift. She was right. It was time to put the pieces back together.

"We'll meet this Master A, and then maybe we can decide what we want to do from there," he conceded. "But I still want to marry you."

She snuggled close to him. "And I still want to have wanton, disgusting, uncommitted sex with you."

He groaned. "You are so frustrating."

"I know." Her arms tightened around him. "You're right about the sex thing, Lucas. I want it to be special. I want it to be right."

He would make it right. And poor Master A had no idea what was coming for him.

Chapter Two

Aidan O'Malley ignored the searing pain in his lower back. He knew it, like all the other pains that plagued his body, would give over once it realized he wouldn't give in. He held his position, downward-facing dog, and sure enough felt the bunched muscles in his back ease.

"You are one tough motherfucker. You know that, right?"

Leo's voice rang through the small gym and brought him out of his almost meditative state. He brought his left leg up and patiently finished his sun salutation before turning to face one of his current mentors.

"For doing yoga?" Aidan grabbed the bottle of water he'd brought and took a long drink. "Most of my friends back home would think it was a pussy thing to do."

Which was precisely why they were no longer his friends. They had very small views of the world, in his opinion.

Leo laughed sharply, and his eyes drifted down to the scars that covered his legs. He couldn't see the ones on his back, but he was sure Leo was thinking of those, too. "Well, you weren't walking a year ago. I think you being able to bend your body like a pretzel is nothing short of miraculous. And they need to rethink their definition of pussy because those things are strong as fuck."

He bowed slightly to the man who had taught him how to "bend like a pretzel." Leo Meyer had been very good to him. He'd taken a desperate man and taught him to focus. If it hadn't been for Leo, he would have fucked up a long time ago. He would have gone after Lexi and Lucas and more than likely gotten his ass handed to him. Leo had been the one to preach patience. Julian had been the one to demand it. And Aidan had learned that timing was everything.

It had been Julian who requested his presence here today. Though Julian's "requests" were always couched in perfect courtesy, Aidan knew an order when he heard one. "So, do you want to clue me in on why I'm here? I'm not scheduled to work until next weekend."

"Get dressed. We're having breakfast with the boss, and he's not in a pleasant mood. Oh, and to top off the beginning of what looks to be an interesting day for you, both of your bosses will be joining us."

Aidan stopped in the middle of pulling his shirt over his head. *Damn it.* Jack Barnes was here. He should have dressed better. He should have brought along his computer so he could show Jack the monthly numbers. He'd kept ultra-careful records since that first business meeting with the man he hoped would be his father-in-law— and his brother-in-law. Damn, it was still weird to think that way. Jack was Lexi's stepfather and Lucas's half brother. He needed a road map to figure out all the familial reasons he needed to watch his step around Jack Barnes. He only needed instinct to realize the man was dangerous in every way.

He had to find a way to make Jack understand he'd screwed up with Lexi and Lucas before, but he wouldn't again. He loved them. Both of them. He would do anything for them. How did he explain that when he'd been excellent at making them think the opposite?

Leo shook his head. "You're panicking. I can feel it from here."

Fuck yeah, he was panicking. This was the most important thing in the world to him. Aidan pulled the T-shirt over his head. "So now you're psychic, too?"

Leo slapped him on the back and started walking down the corridor. "Well, according to my mother, anything is possible. Even aliens. You need to calm down. You've proven yourself to Jack. He wouldn't have gone into business with you if he was planning your murder."

Aidan pushed the button to the elevator. He wasn't so sure about that. If Jack Barnes thought he could make an enemy's life wretched hell on earth by going into business with that person, he would likely sign the paperwork with a smile on his face. Jack Barnes was known for playing long games when it came to revenge.

Leo shook his head and proved to Aidan that he might be a mind-reader. "He's not playing games with you. You're about to find that out once and for all. Lexi had an episode last night."

Now that was a kick in the crotch. His carefully constructed walls threatened to crumble at the mere mention of her name. He forced himself to breathe. "What happened and where the hell was Lucas?"

It wasn't fair. He knew it. He'd left Lucas to pick up the pieces, but damn it, Lucas was supposed to take care of her. He could still remember Lucas's emerald eyes staring a hole through him as he vowed to take care of the woman they both loved. Aidan had been walking out at the time.

"Lucas had business in Chicago. He was there with Julian's partner, Finn. I believe he was doing some business for Barnes-Fleetwood. There's a chain of gourmet groceries Jack's negotiating with now that he's been able to up his production."

He knew all about the deal. He was the reason Barnes-Fleetwood was growing. He'd added his herd to theirs and was now toeing the company line on organic cattle ranching. He wasn't the only one. There was another ranch in South Texas that was adding to the company and their product. Between the Willow Fork ranch, his own, and the Rycroft Ranch in Broken Bend, they were able to offer a lot of product. Aidan's brother Bo had been against it, but he hadn't been left the family ranch. "What happened to Lexi?"

Leo watched the floors going by. "Apparently a good portion of Napa Valley, and then she chose to spend the evening with Jose Cuervo."

Fuck. She was a terrible lightweight when it came to liquor. The elevator door opened, and Leo led him through the doors to Julian's penthouse. Aidan could hear Julian's low growl.

"That's ten for you, little one. That is gossip, and I don't care that she's your friend. I don't allow gossip, and you know it." Julian was sitting at an elegant table growling into his cell phone.

Jack Barnes sat beside him, thoughtfully sipping a cup of coffee. The breakfast in front of him looked untouched. That was not so with the third member of this particular breakfast club. He'd met Ian Taggart briefly when he'd gone through the application process to work at The Club. The massive blond man ran the security firm that vetted all of Julian's employees and club members. He'd heard Taggart didn't mind getting his hands dirty, and from the rumors about his stint in the Green Berets and the CIA, Aidan didn't discount it for a second. Taggart's plate was nearly empty and he took a second one from the server, plowing into another round of pancakes and bacon. Jack gestured that Leo and Aidan should join them.

Julian continued his apparently contentious conversation. "Excuse me. What did you say to me? For your information, Danielle, the stick up my ass has served me well over the years. I will not be removing it, but I might have something to shove up yours when you return from class."

Leo smiled as a well-dressed servant placed a plate of bacon and eggs and pancakes in front of him. "Sounds like Dani's in trouble."

"There's a lot of trouble going around today," Jack said, frustration evident in his tone. "Dani called Finn when she found out about what happened last night. That's why Lucas showed up this morning when he was supposed to be in Chicago. Julian considers it gossiping. I believe Dani is arguing that she was talking to one of her husbands about a dear friend."

"This has been going on for twenty minutes," Taggart said. "How exactly does he think he's going to keep gossip out of his club? Clubs run on gossip."

"Danielle, you know the rules of this club," Julian was saying into the phone. "A very bratty 'I'm sorry' isn't going to do it. And while we're at it, Finn is due some punishment, too. He passed on your snippet of information to Lucas, and Lucas nearly disrupted my plan."

Aidan felt his heart start to race as he had a sudden suspicion why he had been called in. Was it really time? He felt like he'd been waiting for years.

29

"I love you, too, little one. And I am going to deeply enjoy spanking that gorgeous ass of yours tonight." Julian's normally placid face broke into a grin. "I'm glad you're looking forward to it. Make sure our Finn knows he's in trouble, too. Good-bye, Danielle." He set the cell down and turned to Leo. "Make sure I have two whipping chairs in the dungeon tonight. My subs require a bit of public punishment."

"Julian, I'm glad you have something to look forward to. Could we move on? This is serious." Jack leaned forward and stared at Taggart. "You're satisfied there's nothing in O'Malley's background that I should know. No drugs? Nothing wrong with his ranch? I know you did a background check on him before I offered the partnership, but this is more important than money. This is my family. I want to be absolutely sure."

Jesus. Had Taggart been following him? How long had that been going on? He'd been put through the full McKay-Taggart treatment when he'd approached Julian in the beginning. "I don't do drugs."

Taggart ignored him. "Aside from the occasional beer, he's perfectly sober. Dude doesn't even take the pain pills he's been prescribed. The ranch is full of cows and cow shit and a baby brother who needs to get his head out of his ass. I don't like a couple of his employees, but you won't let me get up close and personal with them."

Jack sighed. "We can't randomly snatch people off the streets and give them lie detector tests."

Taggart shrugged. "And that's why we fail. One little lawsuit and Julian flips his shit."

Julian eyed his security head. "It was a big lawsuit, Taggart. However, I'm unconcerned about Aidan's employees. If I had you run deep checks on everyone you thought was shady, I would be broke." He turned to Aidan. "I apologize. Our Mr. Taggart is on the paranoid side. It actually makes him quite good at his job."

"He's been following me?" Aidan wasn't sure what to think of that.

"Nah, I made Adam do it. His sense of smell was utterly destroyed by the amount of body spray he wears. I'm pretty sure he owns stock in several men's cologne makers." Taggart was known for his sarcasm. His eyes turned sharp and all that intimidation was turned on Aidan. "I'd like to know why you've been seeing Karen Wilcox though. She's going to be trouble."

Whoa. Someone *had* been following him. "Karen is an old friend. When I first got home from the hospital, I couldn't drive myself around and my brother isn't always the most reliable person in the world. I had an appointment and no one else could take me. She offered."

"You dated her in high school." Taggart watched him like a lion ready to pounce if the time was right. "She married an older gentleman and stuck it out until the old man died."

He shook his head. "There's nothing going on. I don't have feelings for her anymore. I honestly haven't looked at another woman since the moment I laid eyes on Lexi. Like I said, Karen dropped me off at my therapy appointments a couple of times and we went to some business functions together. There's no connection beyond that."

Taggart leaned back, apparently satisfied for the moment. "I believe you. But you're wrong about the woman in question. Adam thinks she's interested in you, and according to his report, she's got the crazy eyes."

Crazy eyes? He kind of thought her eyes were normal, but he hadn't really looked at them in a long time. He was too caught up in Lexi's eyes, in eyes so blue he got lost in them. In the emerald green of Lucas's eyes.

"She's Aidan's problem, then. Crazy eyes and all," Julian replied, waving the issue off.

Jack looked at Leo. "All right, I'm comfortable that Aidan's clean and he's not playing around. But I need to know something from you, too. Is he ready for this?"

Fuck yeah, he was ready. He wanted to shout it from the rooftops, but that might prove to Jack that he wasn't ready. He sat calmly and tried to give off an air of confidence. He was confident. He was prepared. He'd been ready for eighteen months in his heart. His body finally had the discipline to catch up. He'd been studying under Leo for the past six months. He'd worked with several submissives, and each one had claimed he was an excellent Dom. He

31

was ready to move on to someone he genuinely cared about.

Leo paused in his wolfing down of breakfast. "He's absolutely one of the best students I've ever taught. I would trust him with my own sub."

Jack's eyes rolled. He looked so much like Lucas at times like this, it made Aidan's heart hurt a little. "You don't have a permanent sub. And this is my stepdaughter we're talking about. I have to make sure. My wife is already going to have my head for this. She doesn't exactly like you, Aidan."

"I'm supposed to make sure she doesn't put out a hit on you," Taggart added helpfully. "But what she doesn't know is my brother, Sean, would shoot you for free. He's got a thing for Abby. She's kind of his type." When he realized Jack was staring at him, he put a hand up as though trying to show he was harmless. "I didn't let him or anything. And Abby merely curses O'Malley's name. From what I can tell she hasn't actually tried to hire someone to murder him."

"That's good to know," Jack said with a frown.

Aidan leaned Jack's way, trying to get this conversation back on track. "I understand, sir." Abigail Barnes was a bridge he would have to cross when he got to her. If she didn't shoot him first. "I promise you that I will do whatever it takes to win Lexi's mom over."

At one point, she'd been an ally. Abby Barnes had been thrilled when he'd asked Lexi to marry him. She and Lexi had planned that wedding, their heads together as they looked at the bridal books. He'd been on a plane to South Carolina the day he was supposed to get married. His honeymoon had been spent at Fort Jackson getting his ass handed to him when he should have been in Hawaii with Lexi and Lucas. He should have married Lexi and worked Lucas into his life, but he'd been too scared.

His mind didn't even cringe now at the thought of Lucas. At the time, he'd been so bound by convention that the night he'd spent with the two of them had seemed like a direct line to perdition. Now he'd seen hell, and damn it, he wanted heaven.

Jack Barnes looked like he had known a bit of both, too. "Just watch your balls, son. I'm afraid my wife won't hesitate to cut them off and she won't need to hire someone to do it."

Julian smiled, a bright, open smile Aidan wasn't used to seeing on the Dom's face. "She took Samuel's, after all."

Jack shook his head. "You were easier to deal with when you didn't have a sense of humor."

"Well, Jackson, you are being a bit gloom and doom about this whole thing. I, for one, am glad Alexis gave me the perfect opportunity to fix her. She and Lucas have been in limbo for far too long. Now she can face Aidan and move on—with him or without him. It's up to Aidan, but I'm doing it for Alexis and Lucas. Never forget that." Julian turned to Aidan, and his previous happy expression was suddenly dark and dangerous. It reminded Aidan of his reputation as a man who didn't mind doing the dirty work. "If you hurt them again, I assure you, no one will find the body. I personally don't mind getting my hands dirty and Mr. Taggart hasn't killed anyone lately."

"Not that you know about," Taggart replied with a smile that showed a lot of teeth. It was probably how a shark smiled.

"Exactly my point." Julian nodded at his pit bull/security head. "If Aidan screws up no one will find his body."

He believed Julian. He'd learned a few things about Julian Lodge, and he didn't want to fuck with the man. "I'm in this for the right reasons. And I have no intention of allowing either one of them to move on without me. We're going to be together. I'm going to make this work."

Julian nodded and turned his attention back to his eggs. "See that you do, then. Lexi has an appointment with Leo this afternoon. If he clears her for play, you can begin tonight. The punishment is public, you understand?"

And just like that, his cock got hard. Fuck, he would have to watch that. The thought of Lexi bound and waiting for his discipline was an image that tightened every muscle in his body. "And Lucas?"

Julian studied him for a moment. "Lucas isn't being punished."

"You don't want Lucas involved?" Now Jack's green eyes pinned him as well. "I thought you had pushed past your problems with bisexuality."

Taggart frowned. "I thought he was into the lawyer dude, too. They're kind of a matched pair. It won't work if he breaks them up. I should know. I've got two of my own who can't figure out how to

33

fuck a girl without the other one in the room."

"Whoa. You misunderstand me. I wanted to make sure Lucas is okay with all of this." He felt like someone was shining a bright light in his face and interrogating him.

"Lucas signed off," Leo assured him before turning back to Jack. "Trust me, we've worked through this in session. He's good to go."

Leo's sessions usually involved getting him to talk while they worked out. Aidan had found himself pouring his heart out to the man before realizing it was a "session." He'd rapidly realized that Leo was an odd psychotherapist, but an effective one. "I'm comfortable with it, Jack. More than comfortable."

"He is." Leo smirked. "He's all about the butt sex now."

And he was a sarcastic one. He didn't miss the quick fist bump Taggart gave Leo. Aidan turned to stare at him in what he hoped was an intimidating fashion. Julian and Jack were already there.

Leo simply shrugged and grinned. "Hey, it's totally masculine. It's cowboy butt sex."

Julian snorted, but Jack merely rolled his eyes. "Didn't you fire that asshole?"

Julian sighed and sat back. "More than once." Julian went back to being the jovial host. "Excellent. If you're ready, then we can proceed. You may punish Alexis after I get through with my naughty subs. Oh, and add some extra licks for her language last night. Is there a reason all the women in my life are concerned with sticks being up my ass?"

Jack broke into a long laugh. "I can think of a couple, old friend."

"I suppose you can, Jackson." Julian looked at Jack. "It's going to be okay. Have I ever let you down?"

Jack sobered quickly. "No. Not once. It's not you I'm worried about."

The big cowboy finally picked up his fork, and Julian began talking about innocuous things. Aidan sat back and promised himself he was done with letting the people he loved down. He'd lost Lexi and Lucas. He'd lost his music career. He'd damn near lost his life. He stared down at his left hand. It didn't work the way it used to. He couldn't handle a guitar anymore, but he could wield a paddle and a whip. He could work his ranch and bring in money. He could give

Lucas and Lexi what they needed.

It was time to take his life back.

* * * *

Lexi relaxed back in the comfy chair Leo kept in his office. Despite being The Club's resident leather-clad Dom, his office was an oasis of Zen. He kept bamboo plants around the space, and it was painted in soothing, muted colors. There was a fountain on the wall that made the whole thing look like a waterfall. Everything about the office said calm, cool, sane.

Yep, Leo was a shrink.

And she had to convince him she wasn't crazy.

"I'm not crazy, you know," she said, hating the silence.

Leo, on the other hand, seemed perfectly willing to let it go on forever. She felt stupid the moment the words left her mouth. Yeah, that was the way to work it. He'd never heard those words before.

"I know." Leo sat back in the chair across from her, negligently planting one leg over the other. He was dressed casually, and his hair was still wet as though he'd recently come from a shower. He was ridiculously handsome, with long dark hair that reached his shoulders and piercing blue eyes. He had a military bearing that no amount of letting his hair grow out could cover. He reminded her of...nope, she wasn't going to go there.

"Then why am I stuck in Shrinkville?" Sarcasm was a familiar hideaway.

"I prefer to think of this as two friends talking a few things out."

Yeah, she wasn't buying that. "Two friends, where one has the power to shut the other one out of a place that's incredibly important to her. I don't think there's a balance of power here."

He pinned her with what she was coming to think of as his shrink gaze. It was slightly different from his Dom gaze. The shrink gaze made her feel dumb. The Dom gaze made her feel like a dummy who was about to get her ass whipped. "Is it? Is The Club important to you? Or is it just Lucas?"

Wasn't that a question she'd asked herself a lot in the beginning? She'd been curious but unsure of what she wanted. Aidan walking out

35

on her had made her question a lot of things. "When I started coming here, I came because Lucas loved it."

"Was that the only reason?"

Honesty. It was all he would accept, and she'd known Leo for too long to expect to be able to lie to him. He was known as a human lie detector. Nothing got past those blue eyes. "No. I was curious, but I wasn't in love with the idea. Lucas and I met at my stepfather's ranch. We quickly became friends, best friends. I relied on Lucas like I've never relied on anyone else. After we became closer, I wanted to be in every part of his life. He loved this place, so I decided I should give it a try. I came because I needed him, and I was worried if I didn't come with him, he would meet someone."

Leo nodded as though pleased with her answer. "I can see where that would worry you. Do you feel more secure in the way Lucas feels about you now?"

She felt a smile cross her face. Lucas was her anchor. "I feel secure with Lucas."

Those eyes of his widened expectantly. "But?"

There was always that nasty "but." "But I have to wonder if I'm what Lucas needs."

"In what way?"

Oh, so many ways. How did she even start to count them? Lucas was a professional. He was an up-and-coming lawyer. She worked in a gallery because she couldn't make herself do what she truly wanted to do. She settled on the obvious. "Lucas is a switch. I can't top him. I don't even want to, Leo."

"Of course you don't. You're a sub, sweetheart. At least you are when it comes to sex." He leaned forward. "Would it help at all to know that I fully believe Lucas would bury those needs in order to be with you?"

Lucas had already given up too much for her. "No. I don't want Lucas to compromise himself for me."

Leo laughed, a warm sound. "I sometimes forget how young you are, then you say something like that and I'm reminded. Much of life is about compromise, but that word is anathema to the young folks."

"I'm not exactly a baby. I'm twenty-five and, quite frankly, I've been through enough stinking trauma in my life that I'm practically a walking tabloid. First, I get my poor mom kicked out of town by simply being conceived. I had to watch her scrimp and fight for everything she gave me. When we finally find a comfortable place, my stepdad gets cancer, and I have to watch her lose him. Then she finds a crazy threesome, and my new stepdad gets shot by my grandma, who has a heart attack and dies on the spot. My fiancé leaves me, but only after telling me I'm a freak and then I lose—well, I lose my damn mind." God, she'd almost said it. She couldn't say it. Her heart pounded as she shoved the memory aside. She forced herself to continue. "It didn't help that last year some asswipe kidnapped me to get to Lucas. For once I would love to be kidnapped and nearly killed on my own merits. I can be a bitch, you know. I get fired all the time."

He laughed out loud. "I know the feeling. You've been through a lot. I get that. What I want to know is how playing with Lucas helps you deal with that."

This whole conversation was starting to irritate her. She'd thought this would be the easy portion of her penance. Taking a few licks from the mysterious Master A was starting to look like a breeze compared to dealing with Leo. "Shouldn't you be the one telling me that? Isn't this like your specialty?"

"I would rather hear it from you."

"Fine." She groped for words. How did she say this without sounding like a lunatic? "Look, when I'm here, I don't have to think. I don't have to worry. I don't even have to be me if I don't want to. That came out wrong. I don't have to be the me I have to be all day."

"I understand that. Your mask can come off. We all feel like that. Contrary to popular belief, I think being able to feel safe enough to be the person we enjoy being is the number one reason people get involved with the lifestyle, but I think it's more than simple pleasure for you. I've watched your sessions with Lucas."

Damn him. "Lucas can be intense."

"Lucas isn't the intense one. You push him. There have been times you've pushed him to the point that I was ready to stop the scene. Have you ever used your safe word?"

A stubborn hostility settled over her. She hated the judgment in his voice. "No. I haven't had to. Lucas wouldn't hurt me."

"Oh, but you would hurt yourself, and that's what worries me. Do you think you're the first sub I've seen who uses physical pain to relieve emotional pain? I don't have a real problem with it if it works and it's done in a safe fashion. I don't know that Lucas is the right Dom for you. Lucas would do anything to give you what you need, but he doesn't stop when you go too far. Watching the two of you can be painful at times. You push Lucas to dominate you. Yet when he tries to actually dominate you, you shove him back. You pick the scenes, am I correct?"

Lexi shrugged. She didn't see anything wrong with that. She was the one getting her ass whipped. "I have certain things I like. Lucas indulges me."

"Lucas is never honestly in control of those scenes and that worries me. I don't know that he would stop you even if he thought you were going too far. He would simply go over the edge with you."

"Don't be a drama queen. I'm not going over the edge of anything, and I'm certainly not taking Lucas with me."

The shrink's face suddenly became a Dom's face. His jaw firmed, and an almost icy atmosphere emanated from the man. "If you aren't going to take this seriously, then we have nothing further to talk about."

She sniffled. She was doing it again. She was pushing away the people who gave a damn because it was easier than dealing with her own shit. "I'm sorry. This is hard to talk about. I'm not trying to drag Lucas down with me. I love him. He's the best thing that ever happened to me."

Leo relaxed. "I would like to talk to you about your fiancé. You mentioned him before. Why did you cancel your wedding?"

"It didn't work out." She said it as politely as she could, but she wasn't going there. Aidan was in the past.

It wasn't like she still felt him next to her at night. It wasn't like she longed for the way she'd felt when he pinned her and spread her legs. Aidan had been so overpowering and dominant that she'd never been able to think of anything but him when they made love. Had sex. It couldn't have been love on his part or he wouldn't have left her. He wouldn't have forced her to choose between him and Lucas.

I am not living this freaky life with you, Lexi. I can't

38

believe you got me to do that last night. I...my father is a freaking church elder. What the hell would he think?

Why does it matter? She'd asked, trying to keep her voice low. Lucas had still been asleep. *Why does it matter what anyone besides the three of us thinks?*

Welcome to the real world. I have a career, and it doesn't include fucking your best friend. I'm a country-western musician. Do you know any bisexual country stars? Do you know what it could have cost me? What it still could cost me if anyone ever finds out? Choose, Lexi. Him or me.

She tried to shake the memory off. It was the last thing she needed. It was time to move forward, time to invest in the future, not mourn the past. "Aidan and I didn't work out. I'm okay with it. I've accepted the fact and I'm ready to move on. Lucas and I are right for each other."

She hated the hesitation in her voice. She loved Lucas. She loved him so much her heart ached with it, but she did wonder if they were right. She had caused Lucas a lot of trouble. Wasn't it only a matter of time until he figured out she wasn't worth it?

"What just went through your head?" Leo studied her for a moment. "I would like to know."

She was stubbornly silent.

He leaned forward, his eyes earnest. "Lexi, have you ever considered the fact that I can help you? Have you thought about the fact that you might need to talk about these things?"

Talking to Leo could get her in trouble. "You'll say that I don't belong here. You'll decide that I'm crazy."

Leo ran a hand through his hair as he sat back. "I thought that might be the reason. Listen, I can think you're a little crazy and not kick you out of this club. Unlike some of my colleagues, I recognize that certain people live in a different reality. As long as it doesn't threaten their enjoyment of life, why is it wrong? Let me share something personal with you, and maybe you'll feel more comfortable with me. I was raised in Colorado, in a town called Del Norte. My mom still lives there. It was me and my mom and my brother. My father, whoever he was, ran out before my brother was born. My mother is clinically insane. She firmly believes that my brother and I are the offspring of her encounters with aliens."

She wondered how many people knew this about the perfectly put-together Dom. Leo Meyer was always in control. "That must have been rough on you."

He smiled, perfectly open. "I had a lovely childhood. My mother is a wonderful woman. With the singular exception of her insistence that I needed beets on a daily basis, I couldn't have asked for more in a mom. She is an incredibly loving woman. She made sure I got everything I needed, though she rarely had enough for herself. She raised me to be a gentleman. She was funny and taught me how to fish and hunt. She was upset when both my brother and I joined the Navy, but she wrote both of us all the time. Here's my point, my mother has a different view of reality than most people do, but she is capable of giving and receiving love. That is what constitutes real sanity in my mind. Why do you think I only practice here? I'm on the outside of my profession in this belief, but I stand firm. Loving other people, treating them with love and true kindness and having a heart that is open to accepting the love given to us—this is far more important than an arbitrary reality. Can you truly accept that Lucas loves you?"

She didn't try to stop the tears in her eyes. She let them fall. They felt strangely good, purifying almost. "I want to."

He reached out and held her hand. "Then that's a good step. We can keep talking. I'm going to allow you to meet with Master A because I truly believe you need this. I believe Lucas needs it as well. The Master has said he is willing to include Lucas in the session if you would like. Julian is negotiating the contract with Master A. I assure you that he'll put in clauses to protect you. You and Lucas will have a chance to read it and sign off on it. You understand that everyone in this club has your best interests at heart, right?"

She did know that. Her stepfather loved her. Julian did, too, in his strange way. She belonged to Jack's family and was friends with Julian's loves. She was Julian's family, too. "I know they do. I just worry about how they might show their love. They can be a bit overwhelming at times."

Leo's grin spread across his face. "See, pure sanity right there. Keep that in mind, and we'll all get through this. Let's meet here at this time tomorrow, and we can talk through your experience tonight."

Leo bounced on to his feet and walked to his day planner. He made a note while she got out of her chair.

"Leo?"

"Yes?"

"Is that stuff about your mom true?" It seemed too perfect. It had been exactly the right thing to say to her.

He turned a picture on his desk around and showed her. There was Leo and a man who looked slightly younger, but awfully like him. In the middle of the men was a petite woman with her steel gray hair in a long braid. There were mountains behind them, and they smiled for the camera. "This was taken when my brother was last on leave. My mom's new boyfriend took it. Now there's an insane person. Well, he's from the next town over. Everyone in that freaking town is butt-fuck crazy. I'm totally moving there one day."

Lexi took a deep breath. Maybe everyone was a little crazy. Maybe she did need to talk. Not about everything, but some of it. She did feel better. She walked to the door and started to open it.

"And, Lexi, one day we're going to have to talk about it."

She turned at the dark sound in his voice. "Talk about what?"

"What you lost. You lost something, and it was more important than a fiancé or your sense of security. What you lost haunts you every moment of the day, and it will continue to do so until you talk about it. I'll be here when you're ready."

She walked out the door, her sense of calm utterly blown. She would never be ready to talk about it. Not ever.

Chapter Three

Aidan stood next to Julian, looking out over the dungeon. Preparations were being made. All over the atmospheric space, the staff was cleaning and checking the equipment for safety. Julian was still dressed in his day suit, but Aidan knew that soon the businessman would trade in his thousand-dollar tailored suit for a set of leathers. Aidan would do it, as well, with one exception. He would cover his face with a mask. Neither Lexi nor Lucas would recognize his ravaged body, but they would probably still remember his face. He'd like a chance to work on them before he got slapped or punched or walked out on.

"You practiced?" Julian asked.

Aidan nodded. "Yes. I worked with the six-footer, but I would prefer to use the four-footer. It's more accurate."

"I think you should consider something a bit more creative in your punishment this evening. The whip can be intimidating, but it's not very intimate. I believe Lexi will be perfectly amenable to a whip. After all, she and Lucas perform such scenes every weekend. She takes the whip, cries, he holds her, and they begin the cycle again. I didn't bring you in so they could add a third person to a cycle of behavior that isn't working for them." Julian slanted him one of those glances that made him feel like he was five years old and being called to the principal's office. "Have you given any real thought to this?"

He got Julian's meaning. *Come up with something fast, or I'll call this off.* Luckily, he had a fantasy in his head that had been playing there for months. It was more like an apology and an attempt to bind them all together. It was what he should have done that night two years before. "Edging. I'll start with edge play and some spanking. I'll have her begging by the end, and I'll make sure Lucas is involved."

Julian nodded his assent. "Excellent. That sounds much more interesting."

Aidan's blood thrummed through his veins. Edging? Could he handle that? He was the one on edge, and had been all day. He glanced down at his watch. Two hours to go.

Leo strode into the room. Like Julian, he was in day clothes, but unlike his boss, he stopped and talked to practically everyone in the room.

"Such a chatty Dom," Julian said with a long-suffering sigh. "Leo! I don't have all day."

Leo grinned and shook hands with one of the cleaning staff before his long legs ate the distance between him and Julian. "Of course you do, Julian. You're the boss. You have all the time in the world."

Julian didn't seem to care. "Naturally. Now, tell me if Lexi is going to be here tonight."

Aidan felt his gut tighten. He hadn't considered the possibility that Leo wouldn't clear her for play. "Lexi is sane. She's not crazy."

"Oh, she's buckets of crazy," Leo announced with a laugh. "Seriously, girlfriend has some problems, but nothing that would keep her from being here."

He took a deep breath and relaxed. He could handle that. Leo thought everyone was crazy in their own unique way.

"Did she open up to you?" Julian asked.

"In a sense," Leo replied. "Did she get to the heart of her problem? No. It will take more than a simple conversation to get her to give that up."

"Give what up?" Aidan asked. "What do you mean by 'the heart of her problem'?"

Julian turned to Aidan and seemed to consider whether or not he should talk. "I believe Alexis is hiding something. I don't know if Lucas knows her secret, or if she's kept it completely hidden. Jackson and Leo believe this as well. I haven't asked Mr. Taggart to look into it because I don't want to upset her. I would rather she tell us."

"You didn't have a problem setting him on me," Aidan replied.

Julian nodded like he was glad Aidan understood. "Absolutely. You're not important here. According to Jackson, she was sad and somewhat depressed by your departure, but she didn't go into a deep depression until several months later. She was in a car accident in Austin. Lucas was the only one she called. Shortly after, she left her job at the newspaper and moved to Dallas. From what I can tell, she's stopped writing altogether."

That made his heart ache. Lexi was always working on something. She carried a notepad in her overblown bag so she would always have paper. She even kept a dream journal because she said she got story ideas while she slept. He could remember all the times he would walk in with her coffee in hand to find her furiously writing. He loved those mornings. He would sit and strum his guitar, writing songs while Lexi worked on a new story. Lucas would show up on the weekends, and they would sit outside when the weather was nice. Just the three of them. They wouldn't talk. They had simply enjoyed each other's presence.

He couldn't play guitar anymore. His fingers didn't work that way. He'd accepted that. But, by god, he would never accept that Lexi couldn't write.

"What happened?"

Julian's shoulders moved up and down in a negligent shrug. "I don't know, but I doubt it's the car accident that truly troubles her. The other driver was at fault, and he walked away injury free. He was drunk. He pled out and served a little time in jail. He was caught violating his parole about six months after he got out and was sent back to serve his full sentence. So sad."

Leo's eyebrows rose on his head as he stared at Julian. "That's what happens when a man gets a private investigative team following him twenty-four-seven. I bet Taggart had fun with that one."

"I didn't force him into the bar, Leo. I believe that was someone Ian hired. He does like to spread cash around to young ladies trying to pay their way through college. I merely made sure Ian's men called it in."

He kind of loved Julian Lodge in that moment. Still, he'd spent enough time in a hospital bed that the thought of Lexi being in pain fucking killed him. He should have been there when the accident had happened. He should have been the one she called, and then he would have called Lucas. He would never leave Lucas out. He knew now that he needed Lucas. "She was okay? What do her medical records say?"

Julian's mouth turned down. "I asked her about it. She told me to butt out. As she is not my sub, I have respected her wishes up to this point. If I do something like have Ian's company hack her medical records, she won't trust me. This is all about trust, Aidan. I'm risking Alexis's trust by bringing you in, but we've reached a point where it's worth the risk."

Leo slapped Aidan on the back. "I think it will work. She seems more open than she has in months. Of course, I don't expect it to be perfectly smooth, but I think eventually she'll realize that both she and Lucas need you. You should probably start getting ready. Won't be long now."

He said good-bye, trying to process everything he'd learned. As he reached the elevator that would take him to his room, his cell phone rang. He punched the button code for the hotel portion of the building and pulled his phone out of his pocket. *Dwight.* He sighed. He was about to get a lecture. It played around in the back of his head that Taggart hadn't liked some of his employees. Had one of them been Dwight? It was hard to believe. He'd been in the service with Dwight.

"Hey, man, how is the ranch?"

Dwight Creely was his foreman. He'd also been Aidan's friend in the Army. They had been in the same squad in Iraq. When Aidan had been injured, Dwight was the one who sat by his bedside. Dwight had taken some heavy fire during the mission that almost cost Aidan his legs, but he'd put it aside to check on his friend. When they were both discharged, Dwight had followed Aidan back home to help on the ranch Aidan had inherited, much to Bo's never-ending dismay.

It didn't escape his attention that Taggart had also mentioned Bo was a difficulty he had to address.

"Well, the boss is gone, so Bo is trying to run the show." The complaint came out as a low rumble.

He should have expected it. Bo hated the fact that their father had left the ranch to him and only left Bo some cash. He'd been ready to sign over a portion to Bo when Bo had walked out of the lawyer's office and threatened to sue and hadn't said a word to Aidan for a month and a half. He was at a loss. He knew Bo hadn't gotten a fair shake, but he needed to keep the ranch whole if he was going to make it work. Bo, for his part, had made a nuisance of himself around the ranch, fighting with Dwight at every turn.

It looked like baby brother was at it again.

"Put him on his ass," Aidan said. It was what he would do. He'd been forced to, as though it was the only way to prove to Bo he was still a man. Even when he'd been on crutches, learning to walk again, his brother wouldn't let up. He was a constant pest buzzing in his ear.

"As long as I have permission, it will be my pleasure. But seriously, Aidan, it would be better if you came home. Bo isn't the only one causing trouble around town. Karen is telling everyone that the two of you are back together and getting married."

He nearly threw the phone. Karen Wilcox was rapidly becoming a pain in his ass. She'd been his high school girlfriend. It had been a natural connection in a small town. She'd been the head cheerleader, and he'd been the quarterback. Aidan had done what he'd always done—he had played the role designated to him. When he'd left for college, she'd almost immediately married another man. Karen's husband had been older and established, with money to burn on a young trophy wife.

By the time he'd come home, broken and battered, Karen's husband had died, and she'd been left little money in his will. She hadn't decided to visit Aidan's convalescent bed until the day it was announced he'd inherited the ranch. That day she'd been full of heartfelt concern for his injuries and talked about how much she would miss his father now that he was gone. Karen had hated his father. He hadn't bought her crap back then and didn't buy it now.

"Goddamn it, I haven't touched that woman. I have no interest in touching that woman." He was lucky apparently Taggart had done what Julian had told him to and stayed away from the people on the outer edges of his life or he would have discussed this with Jack.

Dwight sighed. "I know that, but the people around here are starting to talk. You know how it is here. People expect things. She's hinting at a spring wedding."

He'd escorted her to exactly two events, both charity gatherings where he'd networked all night long. He'd made it plain to her that they weren't dating. When she had tried to come on to him and invite herself in, he'd been gentle and gracious about turning her down. It looked like he was going to have to be a bit more forceful. "I'll talk to her when I get home, but that could be a week or two."

There was a long pause. "Damn it, Aidan. We need you here. What the hell is so all-fired important in Dallas?"

"Lexi." He let the name drop like a jewel, his voice getting soft. He steeled himself because he wasn't hiding anymore. Aidan O'Malley was done playing roles other people tried to force him to play. "Lexi and Lucas. I'm getting them back."

A low whistle came across the line as the elevator doors opened, and Aidan started walking down the hall to his room. "Damn, Aidan, that's going to cause a stir in this town. I don't know that Deer Run, Texas, is ready for you and your, uhm, partners. Maybe if it was two hot chicks you were trying to bring home, it would be, you know, eccentric. They would say your time in Austin corrupted you. You know the church ladies here like to blame everything on marijuana and Austin."

"Let them," Aidan said sharply. "I don't care. I love Lexi and I love Lucas, and I'm not hiding it or pretending it's less than it is. If the citizens of Deer Run, Texas, can't handle it, then they can go to hell."

He was damn sick of trying to live up to other people's expectations. He'd lost the best thing in his whole damn life because he feared the potential fallout. He knew what real pain was now, and he knew that the only thing that healed it was genuine, pure love for another human being. He'd been lucky enough to find two soul mates. He wasn't letting them go because society deemed he was only allowed one. The world could go to hell as long as he had Lexi and Lucas in his life.

"Well, I admire you for your conviction, Aidan. I hope it doesn't bite you in the ass in the end." Dwight was silent for a moment and then seemed almost hesitant. "Are you sleeping okay, buddy?"

He stood beside the door to his room and felt his soul sag. He didn't even like to think about sleep. When he slept, he was back in hell. "Sure."

"That doesn't sound reassuring."

He sighed and decided that honesty was the word of the whole damn day. He didn't like talking about how he'd been injured, mostly because he couldn't remember anything about the day. "Lately, I can't seem to stop dreaming about it."

"The doctors said you wouldn't be able to remember that day, Aidan."

"Well, they also said I wouldn't walk." They had been firm on that point. He'd been stubborn, and exactly six months after he'd been sentenced to life in a wheelchair, he'd stood up and walked. He'd walked because he loved them. They would never know it, but Lucas and Lexi had been his crutches, the very thought of them spurring him to move. And they were going to be his reward. "It's nothing, really. Just flashes of the team and the firefight. I don't even know if what I'm seeing really happened. Probably not."

But he wished it would go away. Every night, it was the same dream. Darkness and then that terrible sound. In the dream, he rushed out to see what was happening, and he felt the bullets hit him, agony overtaking him. Then Dwight looking down at him and he couldn't move, couldn't talk, couldn't breathe. He wanted it to stop. He wanted to dream about his loves, not that terrible day.

"The dreams are coming even when you take your sleeping pills?"

He groaned and wished Dwight would leave him be. "I didn't bring them with me. I'm trying to get off of them."

He hated the fact that he didn't sleep well without them. He was going to break free of those pills. It was all a matter of discipline, but he knew Dwight disagreed. There was a long pause, and he was happy when Dwight didn't argue.

"How long will you be gone?" Dwight asked.

"Like I said, a week or two. Hire some more hands if you need it.

The money is there. And tell Bo to keep his hands off the emergency funds. I'm not paying for his drinking binges." Taggart had been right about one thing. His younger brother was a pain in the ass.

"Will do, boss. Tell me something. Have you given any thought to bringing Lucas and Lexi here?"

He sighed. He would love that. "Only if I can figure out a way to drag them."

He hung up his phone, opened the door, and started to get ready for the most important night of his life.

* * * *

Dwight Creely shoved his cell in his back pocket, cursing under his breath as he did it. He'd thought he could get Aidan to come home. Aidan had explained to him how important these two people were to him. He understood that. When they were in the Army together, he'd talked about his ex-fiancée and their best friend. It was only after the "incident" that Aidan admitted he was involved with Lucas, too. Something had changed after Aidan had gotten out of the hospital. He had purpose. First, he'd fought hard to get back the use of his legs, and then he'd thrown himself into the ranch.

Dwight had stayed close, managing to get himself hired as the ranch's foreman. He'd known a bit about ranching having grown up in Wyoming. His uncle owned a ramshackle ranch where Dwight had spent a couple of years after his father kicked him out. It was a stroke of luck since he needed to stay close to Aidan. He had to keep a watchful eye on the big bastard or everything could fall apart.

"Hey!" Bo O'Malley swung down from the horse he'd been riding. It still surprised Dwight how much the boy looked like his brother. Well, he looked like his brother before he'd gotten shot up in Iraq. Bo was a younger, slightly thinner version of Aidan, with sandy hair and a square jaw. "Have you talked to Aidan? Did you tell him Karen came around again? She tried to get me to tell her where Aidan went, but I didn't think that was such a great idea. I don't know what he's doing in Dallas, but I bet he doesn't want Karen around."

Dwight hated Bo. Every word that came out of the younger man's mouth was like nails on a chalkboard. Bo had been given everything, but he whined about how his brother didn't pay enough attention to him. *Spoiled fucker*. It was fun to come between him and his precious brother. A few words here and there and both brothers thought the other hated them. It was so easy. It also made him glad he'd never been saddled with a sibling.

"I talked to him a couple of minutes ago. He's pissed at you. He says the paperwork you did sucked, and he won't let you near the business side of the ranch again." Aidan had said nothing of the sort, but those two didn't talk, so there wasn't a lot of worry that they would find out about his lie. They would simply yell at each other about other things, never getting to the heart of the matter. "You need to watch yourself. I think he's close to getting rid of you. The only reason he's kept you around is he doesn't have money for new hands. You have to understand, your brother is trying to make this place work again. If you get in the way, he'll cut you loose."

"He can't do that." Bo's jaw went rigid, his face flushing with obvious emotion. "This is my home. He can't kick me out."

Actually, Aidan had said exactly that when he'd suggested kicking the annoying pest out. But he wasn't about to admit that to Bo. "Look, you have to see where your brother would be pissed off at you. He got the ranch, but you took all the money. He had to sell out a piece of his ownership to Barnes-Fleetwood to have the cash to operate."

Bo's stare had gone stubborn. "He didn't have to do that. I offered to buy shares a couple of months back."

And Dwight had convinced Aidan that Bo would cause trouble. It had been easy. Bo had been pissed about the terms of the will. He'd been making trouble. Now he was more reasonable, but Dwight still wanted to keep them apart.

"And Aidan doesn't want you to have anything to do with the business end. He wants to keep the ranch together in one piece. He's never going to share it with you. Not knowing how useless you are at anything but manual labor."

Bo's face fell. He was an easy mark. One minute he was all sad puppy dog, and the next he was pissed-off boy. It was a turbulent combo that Dwight had used to his advantage. "Well, if he wanted me to do the fucking paperwork, he should have taught me how. Screw

50

this. I'm going into town."

Bo stalked off, leading the horse toward the stables.

That was a good thing. If Bo was out getting drunk, he wouldn't notice that Dwight was gone. Aidan needed to come home where he could watch him.

He sighed as he entered the house. He needed a plan. He wouldn't be so fucking worried if Aidan had taken his sleeping pills with him. Those pills kept him from dreaming. When he didn't take them, he dreamed about what had happened the day he was injured.

And that was precisely what he was trying to stop. If Aidan ever remembered what happened to their squad, Dwight's life would be over. He had to get Aidan home and get him back on his pills.

Maybe a little chaos was in order. What if Aidan had a reason to do just what he'd said? What if he needed to bring Lexi and Lucas back home to Deer Run?

He sat down at the computer in the office and in a few moments pulled up information on one Alexis Ann Moore. He wrote down her address and printed out a map to her house and one to the club where Aidan was staying.

Then he gave old Karen Wilcox a call. *Chaos*. That girl knew a thing or two about chaos. She was exactly what he needed. Well, Karen, and a high-powered rifle. He'd have Aidan back in Deer Run in no time at all.

* * * *

Lexi adjusted her bustier and stared at herself in the mirror. She saw a woman closing in on thirty and utterly unsure of her place in life. What the hell was she doing? By this time in her life, her mother had a career and was raising a child. Sure, she hadn't planned on giving birth to a bastard daughter, but she'd done it with grace and pure stubborn will. Lexi would have done anything to…

She took a deep breath. *Not going there tonight*. Tonight was about the future, not the past. She had to move on so she and Lucas could be happy.

"You're so fucking gorgeous."

She smiled at Lucas in the mirror of their room at The Club. He

51

was heartbreakingly handsome in nothing but a pair of boots and leather pants. His gloriously cut chest and that ridiculous six-pack were on display. She loved his movie star face, and that silky black hair completed the perfect picture of masculine beauty that was Lucas Cameron. "I'm glad you think so."

"You're always fucking gorgeous to me."

She sighed and turned to him. She was wearing nothing but a bustier and a black thong. Lucas had seen her like this a hundred times, and yet he'd never been overwhelmed by her. She had to think that maybe her charms weren't what pulled Lucas in. Maybe they had simply been close for so long that she was a habit for him. "That's what you always say, babe."

His face turned hard, and he was on her in an instant. He put one hand on her waist and another behind her neck, pulling her close. He pushed his crotch at her so she couldn't miss his erection. His cock was long and hard and insistent. "I want you. I want you every minute of the day and twice as much when I'm sleeping. There isn't a second that goes by that I don't dream of shoving my cock deep inside you."

His lips hovered right over her mouth. She could feel the heat of his breath mingle with hers. His emerald eyes bored through her. He was so frustrating. She'd wanted him forever, and he'd held her off. God, she wanted that to change. She wanted to be with Lucas in every way possible. "I want you, Lucas."

"Tell me you love me."

That was easy. Now that she'd made the decision to be brave, it was a simple thing to tell him the truth. "I love you, Lucas Cameron."

"I love you, too. Do you understand why I've waited? Why I've forced both of us to wait? It has nothing to do with how much I want to have sex with you. I want this to be forever, and you haven't been ready for that. Tell me something, baby. If we had slept together when you first asked me to make love to you, what do you think would have happened?"

She leaned into his strength. She remembered the night so well. It had been about a month after she'd been released from the hospital. She'd gone to Dallas to see Lucas because she couldn't seem to move forward. She'd thrown herself at him. He'd kissed her and held her and he'd gotten her off with his hands. He'd shoved his fingers into her pussy, his thumb worrying the nub of her clit. He'd put his tongue on her and made her quake as she came. But when she urged him to come inside, he'd said no. She remembered how pissed off she'd been at the time. She'd flown into a rage and called him all sorts of names. She'd even flung a coffee mug and caught him on the shoulder. He'd taken all of it, and when she'd calmed down, he'd held her hand.

Do you feel better now, baby? Can we go to bed?

He'd held her all night, and in the morning they were friends again. She'd left her job in Austin and moved to Dallas shortly after. What would have happened?

"I would have walked away," she admitted. "I wasn't ready. I probably would have avoided you."

He turned her face up and kissed her nose, a gentle touch. "I know. I couldn't risk that. I couldn't handle it if you weren't with me. I'll take your friendship if I can't have more. I was always willing to do that. I haven't been celibate since I met you, you know that."

She smiled up at him, relieved to still be close to him. She let her hands wander across the strong muscles of his back. Things were changing, and she was ready for it this time. "I know you have horrible taste in women."

He laughed, pulling her close to his heart. "I have not been picky about women or men, because I've only ever loved you and—"

He paused as though shocked he'd been about to say the name.

"Say his name, babe. He's not exactly Satan, you know. He's a man who was too stupid and uptight to be able to accept the love that was handed to him."

Lucas took a deep breath. "I've only loved you and Aidan. Everyone else was just a body in a bed. I slept with people who didn't want more from me than sex. But you should know that for the last year, I haven't slept with anyone. After what happened with Jeremy, I couldn't touch someone else. I thought you were dead when I walked in that fucking cabin."

Lexi tightened her arms around him. Almost a year before, Lexi had been kidnapped by a man who wanted revenge on Lucas and Julian. She'd survived the experience because Finn Taylor had shot the man before he'd managed to kill Dani, Julian, and herself. When Lucas had found her, she'd been drugged to unconsciousness. She'd come to in a hospital, and the first thing she'd seen was Lucas sitting next to her bed. He'd fallen asleep in a chair, his hand tangled with hers.

"It's over." She'd been holding on for far too long. It was all over. The stuff with Aidan was over. The accident was over. The kidnapping was over. It was past time to move on. "We're together now, and that means you have to find a way to sleep with me. I know it's going to be hard, but I'm demanding sex, and I won't take no for an answer."

His hand was suddenly in her hair, pulling her head back, and a hard look fell on his face. Her pulse started to race.

"You'll take what I give you. And I assure you, I have a lot to give." He pressed his erection against her belly, rubbing himself against her. "But you'll beg me for it first."

She curled her lips up. He wanted to play? She could do that with him. "I've been begging for a long time, babe. Begging never got me anywhere with you."

"Because you're a greedy sub. You want everything, but you don't want to earn it. Let me tell you something, baby, that's about to change. Our play is about to change. I told Julian I want in on your punishment. You want to see what it would be like if we brought in a Dom, well, we're going to find out. Julian says this Master A is hard, but fair. I've negotiated terms with him through Julian. He tops me, but we both top you. He won't make a move sexually unless I indicate it's all right. You have your safe word, and I expect you to use it if you need to."

"Would we want that?" This was the only part that made her nervous. Could they bring this other man into their sexual relationship? Lucas was bisexual. He would enjoy having a man now and then, but could she really share him? It had seemed natural with Aidan. She'd loved them both, but a stranger?

The hand on the back of her head eased, and he was back to tender, his role tossed away the minute she faltered. "Not if you don't want it. Not at all. If you want to walk away, we'll do it. Baby, this is all about you."

But it wasn't. It couldn't be. It had been all about her since Aidan had left, and she needed to give back to him. "Let's give it some time and see what happens. I want you to know, though, that our relationship is the most important thing to me."

He gave her a soft smile. "Me, too. You're always the most important person in the world to me."

There was a light knock on the door, and when Lucas opened it, Leo walked in.

"It's time, you two. Julian is almost finished with Dani and Finn. Master A is getting ready. He would prefer to not meet you beforehand."

She thrust her hand in Lucas's, and he immediately threaded their fingers together. "We're ready."

She walked beside Lucas, nervous, but sure that this was the right path. They needed to break free. Lucas led her from the private room Julian had designated for their use for the evening into the dungeon.

Julian's dungeon was a rich mix of torture and elegance. She'd never been in another dungeon before, but she couldn't imagine one quite like The Club. The four-inch heels she wore clicked neatly against the hard wood of the floor. She normally didn't wear heels, preferring comfortable shoes, but the sexy stilettos did something for Lucas. Aidan used to love her legs in heels. He loved her in a pair of red shoes and absolutely nothing else. He would prop her ankles up against his shoulders and press his dick into her pussy.

Why couldn't she get Aidan out of her head? Maybe it was this Master A person. She wondered what his real name was. Probably Adam or Alan. She wished it was Barney. Then he could be Master B, and he wouldn't make her think of Aidan at all.

"Julian's been having a fun night." Lucas pointed out the front of the raised stage where Julian held his public punishment scenes.

There was a St. Andrew's Cross and various torture devices across the stage. Julian was already deep into his scene. Danielle Lodge-Taylor and Finn Taylor were strapped to side-by-side whipping chairs, their naked asses in the air. Dani's was a delicate pink, but Finn's had a red sheen to it.

"Why is he always harder on Finn?" Lexi asked, shaking her head. Julian could be slightly brutal with his male partner. She turned her face up to see if Lucas was outraged by the treatment of his friend.

He was staring at the scene almost in rapture. She followed the line of his sight. He wasn't watching Dani. He was staring at Finn, and it had nothing to do with whether or not he found Finn attractive. He was watching the way Julian struck Finn's flesh with the flogger. He was watching the way that line of red lashed across Finn's skin.

Lucas's eyes had an almost dreamy quality to them. Her heart clenched. How long had it been since he had gotten what he needed? How long had he suppressed his own needs for hers?

He came out of his trance and looked down at her. "I'm sorry. Did you ask me something?"

She managed to not smile at him. "I did, babe, but you got a bit distracted by the show. I asked why Julian is so hard on Finn when he barely spanks Dani."

His face softened, and his hands found her hair again. His voice was quiet in deference to the scene. "He needs it. Finn enjoys the pain. It frees something in him. You should understand that."

"You are never that hard on me, Lucas." Lucas had never broken her skin, but she would admit that sometimes the pain allowed her to cry about things she wouldn't allow herself to release. She always felt unburdened after a session.

"You don't need as much pain as Finn. And don't get pissy at Julian for treating Dani differently. They aren't the same. Julian might be punishing them, but I assure you they enjoy it, too. The real punishment comes later, when he doesn't allow her to come. That's when Dani will feel the burn." Lucas whispered in her ear, his breath a soft caress. "I'm afraid you might be in for a bit of that, too, baby. The word edging came up in my negotiations with Julian."

Lexi groaned. She hated that. Edging. Edge play. It sometimes referred to a variety of play that tested the boundaries—blood play, knife play, wax play. That wasn't what Lucas meant. He knew her hard boundaries better than she did. He was referring to the practice of keeping a sub right on the edge of orgasm and pulling back every time. It was frustrating, and Lucas could never do it. When she pleaded and begged, he would take out the vibrator or dildo and get her off quickly, as though he couldn't stand to hear her frustration. More than once Lexi knew the other Doms had taunted him for his lack of control. She had to hope this Master A was a softie.

Finn was counting out his punishment in a strong voice. The

crowd watched in rapt attention, but she couldn't get her mind off the coming scene. Her heels gave her a little more height, and Lucas hunched over so it was easy to whisper to him.

"Why didn't Master A negotiate the contract directly with you?" It was odd. Julian might sit in on contract negotiations, but he rarely butted in. She should have been there, but she preferred to leave it to Lucas. She'd had to work this afternoon despite her hangover. Her boss hadn't been happy with her, but she'd let it all slide away the minute she entered The Club.

"I don't know. I suppose because he doesn't consider me your permanent Dom because you aren't wearing my collar. Possibly Julian did it because Master A is new. Julian is such a control freak. He considers you part of his family, and he's trying to look out for you."

And she was fond of the man, too. Over the years, Julian had proven to be an amazing friend to her family. She stopped watching the scene in front of her. A flash of heat sparked across her skin, and she was utterly certain that someone was watching her. She glanced around the crowd.

"What's wrong?" Lucas asked.

"I don't know. I just…feel like someone's watching."

She heard him chuckle in her ear. "Well, baby, that's what happens when you're a gorgeous woman wearing next to no clothing. People tend to watch."

But it was more than that. She looked to the left of the stage. Everyone else in the room was watching the punishment scene playing out, but one man faced the opposite direction of the stage. One large, incredibly built hunk of masculinity was staring right at her. His dark eyes were visible under the mask that covered the top half of his face. He looked like a man perfectly capable of all manner of dirty deeds.

"Oh, god," she groaned. "I think that's Master A."

Lucas followed her line of sight. Suddenly she felt his hand tighten on hers. "Holy fuck, look at that."

He was amazing. He was at least six foot five, maybe six. Lucas was tall, but this man had a couple of inches on him. He was corded with thick muscles, every inch of skin seemed sun-kissed, but

57

something was wrong with it. Not wrong, exactly, but white wispy lines marred his physical perfection. Scars. He was covered in scars.

"What happened to him?" Lexi heard herself ask. She couldn't take her eyes off him.

"Some sort of accident." Lucas's voice was hushed, smaller than it had been before, as though he was worried the man across the room might be able to listen in. "He was in the Army. He was injured in Iraq. The way Leo explains it, he's lucky to be alive."

Something about the huge man called to her. Seeing that man standing and staring so intently in their direction made her feel nervous. She wasn't scared of him exactly, but she wasn't calm at the thought of meeting him.

"Why the mask?" She wanted to see his face. All she could see from here was the hard, unrelenting line of his jaw. His hair was cut so short she couldn't tell if it was blonde or brown. Everything about him—from his stare to his stance—seemed severe and unmoving. And then the corner of his lip ticked up slightly. It wasn't much, but that tiny smile caused a dimple to form in one cheek.

Beside her, Lucas's breath hitched. She knew why. It was the same reason her own heart had skipped a beat. Aidan had the most perfect dimples. They had teased him about his smile. But Aidan was utterly unlike the man in the mask. Perhaps he'd been as tall, but Aidan had been lean. This man had at least fifty pounds on Aidan, all of it muscle. Aidan had been a slave to his music, not the gym. Aidan had been all-American handsome. This man looked like sin.

He was a stranger, nothing more. And one she didn't have to see again after tonight if she chose not to.

Still, when he smiled, he would be glorious.

"They're done," Lucas whispered in her ear as Julian began taking his loves off the chairs and preparing their aftercare.

It was time. Master A was already supervising the change of the scene in a deep voice. Nothing at all like Aidan's musical, lyrical voice.

She wouldn't hear that voice again.

"Are you ready?"

She turned a smile up to the man who was her future and nodded her assent.

Chapter Four

Lucas felt his cock pulsing as he walked Lexi toward the stage.

What the fuck was he doing?

He needed to keep it together. He needed to pretend like he wasn't responding to the man in the mask. He didn't want to. He wasn't going to get involved with another man. He was with Lexi. Lexi was the only person who mattered now.

But god, that fucker reminded him of Aidan. It was the smile that did it. Aidan had the sweetest "aw-shucks-ma'am-weren't-nothing" smile on the planet. He would look at a person, that one lip would tug up, making the smile all the more perfect for its lopsided nature, and Lucas couldn't help but melt a little. Aidan was masculine perfection, and when he sang, no one could help but stop and listen.

God, as much as Lucas loved Aidan, he hated him now. Lucas hated him for the coward he was. He hated him for showing Lucas the edge of heaven and walking away. And he hated Aidan for leaving Lexi. So many times, he'd wondered if she wouldn't have been happier if she'd gone with Aidan.

She certainly wouldn't be in this position. Even though Aidan hadn't acknowledged it, he'd been the dominant partner. Aidan had been indulgent, but when he'd put his foot down, Lexi fell in line. So had Lucas, for that matter. He'd enjoyed having a partner to curb some of Lexi's more wild tendencies. If Aidan had been around, Lexi wouldn't have gotten into this trouble.

Dani winked at Lucas as she was carried off the stage in Julian's arms. The curvy blonde looked perfect cuddled against her Master's chest. Finn walked behind them, his body covered in a robe. Lucas remembered a time when all of Julian's aftercare, including sex, occurred right there on the stage. Not anymore. He jealously guarded both Dani and Finn.

Lucas shook Finn's hand. He felt a bit guilty. He was the reason Finn's ass was red as hell. "Sorry I got you got in trouble, man."

Finn's face was still flushed. "No way. I wouldn't have missed that for the world. Julian has gotten to be a big old softie since we got married. Now I know how to get him to give it to me good. The next time I need it, I'll gossip a little. I moaned and cried enough that he won't even withhold sex. I'm looking forward to the evening."

Lucas only half heard what Finn said because Lucas was staring at Master A. Two club employees were moving the whipping chairs off the stage in favor of a padded sawhorse. Finn waved good-bye and jogged after his lover and their shared wife.

"What are they doing?" Lexi's voice had the slightest shake to it. She hated the sawhorse. He would never put her over one.

"I'll find out." He gave her hand a squeeze.

Lexi preferred the comfort of the whipping chair or the St. Andrew's Cross. When he'd started playing the role of Lexi's Dom, he'd introduced her to all of the equipment in the dungeon. Some of it hadn't appealed to her at all, and he'd never pushed her on it. He had the handcuffs he'd had made for her. They were lined with faux fur so her wrists never chaffed. He pulled them out as he approached Master A.

The enormous mountain of a man picked up a strap and tested it against his own hand. He had a table full of torture implements. None of them were the ones Lucas had brought.

"There seems to have been a miscommunication, Sir." He was exceedingly polite. He was suddenly intensely aware that he'd agreed to sub for this man. At the time, it had seemed like an afterthought, something incidental. BDSM scenes required a chain of command.

When he'd signed his name to the bottom line of the contract, he'd been thinking more of Lexi than himself. Now, as Master A turned and his dark chocolate eyes pinned him, it seemed pretty damn serious.

"What's wrong, Lucas?" His voice was like gravel, as though something had damaged it, but a lyrical quality still held. Up close, his scars were like rivers crossing his powerful chest. Some were thick and wove across his skin, others a mere whisper, but together they made a map of the man. "Why aren't you waiting with Lexi?"

Lucas felt that voice deep inside him. It was much more than mere sexual attraction. He could be sexually attracted to any number of people. He'd learned to ignore it entirely. His cock didn't have the best of taste, but it had stopped ruling his life long ago. This was more. This was the instant, soul-deep recognition of someone he knew could top him. Master A was one hell of a Dom.

But he wasn't Lexi's Dom. He might be for the evening, but that was Lucas's full-time role. Though he'd signed over control of the punishment to Master A, surely the man would take advice from the sub's permanent Dom. "We need to move that sawhorse out of here. Lexi prefers a whipping chair. Actually, it would be better if we used a whip. She's comfortable with a St. Andrew's Cross."

There was a long pause as Master A stared a hole through him. There was no hot dimple in his cheek now. There was only a simple stony silence emanating from the man. Lucas fought not to fidget under his stare. This was how he'd felt when he'd done something stupid at the ranch and Jack wanted him to know he was a dumbass.

"So, should I set up the whipping chair?" he asked. Master A was obviously not amenable to the cross for some reason. He silently cursed himself. He should have tightened that contract, but he hadn't been the one negotiating. He placed a lot of trust in Julian, especially when it came to contracts.

"You should take your place beside Lexi. I'll let you know when I need your help. We'll be using a sawhorse. If Lexi has a problem with it, she can use her safe word. Leo is waiting in case she requires assistance off the grounds."

Lucas felt his face flush. Bastard wanted to play rough? "So, it's your way or the highway?"

Master A took a slow step forward, his boots thudding across the hard floor of the stage. "Yes, it is, sub. Welcome to D/s. I was told you weren't a tourist, but every word that comes out of your mouth is proving to me that you are."

His heart started to pound. He hated someone questioning his seriousness. Years and years he'd spent under his father's disdain. He'd been compared to his siblings and found lacking in every way possible. Lucas had never been good enough for the great Senator Allen Cameron. Looking down on him was the one button sure to set him off, and Master A had firmly pushed it. "I've been in the lifestyle for years, asshole."

He'd been in the lifestyle since the day he'd met his half brother, Jack Barnes. Everything about his brother's life fascinated him, including his D/s relationship with his lovers, Sam Fleetwood and their wife, Abigail Barnes. Lucas had emulated his brother from the day he'd met him.

Master A's head shook. "No, you've played at it for years. You're no Dom or you wouldn't be over here telling me what she will or won't accept and expecting me to change my plans for her. You agreed to allow me to top both of you, and yet you're making demands. Here's the bottom line. She will accept her punishment meted out my way with respect to her hard limits, or she will leave. And you will cease cursing at me, or we'll have some trouble, you and I."

He started to move forward, ready for a little trouble, but before he could make the first move, Master A had a hand in his hair. That big hand pulled back, drawing Lucas close enough that he could feel the heat pouring off the other man's body. Master A towered over him, and at Lucas's six foot one, that wasn't an easy feat. He'd rarely met a man who could utterly overpower him.

Master A's voice was a low, gravely growl in his ear. "Don't test me here, Lucas. I don't want to start this way. I want it to be easy with us. We should be partners in her pleasure, but I'm the Dom, and I won't accept being treated like your lackey. I am not some hired hand brought in here for your convenience. I'm here for a reason, and I won't allow you to disrespect me."

Put like that, it did sound bad. He had signed the contract. It was reasonable for Master A to expect that he wouldn't have to deal with a bratty switch. He was close enough to see that Master A's hair was a sandy color. It was cut in a close-crop military style that highlighted the Master's roughhewn bone structure. His face was marked, a long jagged line running from under his mask down to his neck.

"I'm trying to look out for her." He didn't want to start this out on the wrong foot, but he needed the Master to understand what his place was.

The hand in his hair softened, and the tension ratcheted down. When Master A spoke again, it was in a cajoling tone. "I know you're doing the best you can, but this isn't your strong suit. You're a nurturer. You're the one to take care of all the small details that make a life run smoothly. You're smart and strong, and you'll do anything for someone you love, but not this. You're too soft for this. I can give her what she needs. I can give you what you need if you let me."

He wanted to take a step back. It seemed this Master had done a lot of homework on him. Master A sounded almost as though he admired Lucas. It wasn't something he was used to. Lucas had been admired for his money and his connections. He'd been looked up to for being one of the Camerons, even if he was the black sheep of the political family. Only Lexi and his small, cobbled-together family ever admired him for what he could do, for the care he gave to the people around him. The stranger had seen far too much of him.

"What's wrong?" Lexi's voice pulled him out of his panic. He looked down at her, so beautiful and vulnerable.

Master A's hand came out of his hair, and he felt strangely cold as the large man stepped back, taking his body heat with him. It had been oddly comforting to be held like that. It had been so, so long since he'd felt like someone else was in control and he could relax.

"There's nothing wrong, Lexi," Master A said. He could see their small encounter wasn't completely lost on the Dom. The big Dom was sporting an impressive erection in his leathers. Apparently Leo had been right. Master A liked it both ways. "Lucas and I were having a slight disagreement over the equipment we'll use for this evening's scene. We've settled it now. Go back to your place and get into slave position. I'll call on you in a minute."

He saw the moment they got into serious trouble. Lexi's eyes flared, and her hands came up on her hips. The world moved in a strange slow motion as her gorgeous, painted red mouth came open.

"Fuck you. I'm not getting on that sawhorse. It's uncomfortable. And what right do you have to put a hand on Lucas?"

The room seemed to go ice cold as all that intimidation turned on Lexi's petite, curvy body. Master A stared at her for a moment. The room went deadly quiet as though the crowd realized the scene had started without the traditional opening. Everyone was watching as the universally acknowledged problem child of The Club turned her bratty mouth on the new guy.

Even Lexi seemed to realize she'd gone too far, but she held her ground. His girl wouldn't sweetly apologize. Not to a Dom she hadn't felt had earned her respect.

"Lucas, I need to know if you're in or you're out." The words rang from the Master's mouth and seemed to swell in the otherwise silent room.

Master A hadn't turned to him. Those cold eyes held Lexi in their snare like a cobra waiting to strike at a pretty bird he'd caught in a trap. But he understood. He was the one who was really trapped. He could take his girl and leave this world they had come to love. He and Lexi had played at the edges of this particular ocean, but they'd never waded into deep waters. He could scoop her up and walk away and never know if they could have been happy if they had only learned how to swim.

Or he could do what every switch had to do from time to time. He could gamble and give up control and hope that he found paradise for his trouble. Lucas Cameron might have grown more stable and settled in the past few years, but he hadn't forgotten what it meant to take a risk.

"I'm in."

* * * *

Lexi realized she was in serious trouble the minute the words left Lucas's mouth. Hell, she'd realized she was in trouble the minute she opened her mouth. What was she thinking? She knew damn well how to behave in a dungeon, but something about this Master made her want to push him. *Damn it*. She'd been this way all of her life. She had to push. She thought about taking a step back, but before she could make her feet move, Master A had her in a fireman's hold.

"Hey!" She shouted as her world upended. She turned her head up to throw a desperate look Lucas's way.

Lucas stood there, a stony cold look on his face. In that moment, he was all Dom, and she'd never seen him look hotter. There was a confidence about him she had rarely seen when he was around her. Lucas was utterly in command at work, but his surety faltered when she walked into the room. Even when he performed a scene with her, she knew he worried about her comfort. He didn't look worried now. He looked ready.

Her heart started to pound as Master A turned, and she lost sight of Lucas.

"I need a chair, Lucas." The words came out of the Master's mouth like a judge delivering a sentence.

"Yes, Sir." Lucas's words were silky smooth. There was not a hint of hesitation now. She could hear him moving to do Master A's bidding.

"What do you think you're doing?" she asked, though she was a bit less hostile now. She'd fucked up. She was glad Julian wasn't around to witness it, though Leo would probably tell him. Tears pricked her eyes. Damn, she was proving to Leo she couldn't handle the lifestyle. "Look, Sir, I'm sorry. It was wrong of me to be rude to you, but I was merely pointing out that Lucas and I had a plan for tonight."

Reason. She could reason with him, surely. It worked on all the men in her life. Of course, usually she was looking at them instead of trying to plead her case to a group of back muscles. The muscles were unbelievably tight, but his skin—oh, his skin had been decimated in his lower back. It was a mess of white, puckered flesh, and she could see both neat, surgical lines, and jagged edges. She reached out to touch the mass of scars, but she was jerked back over his shoulder and set on her feet before she could make it. She wobbled on her heels, but Master A's big hands held her shoulders.

"I don't think you understand how this is going to go, sub. I am the Master, and you are the one being punished. I won't put up with a spoiled princess telling me how her punishment will go. It will go the way I say it will go. First, you will pay for the insult to me, and then we'll proceed to the sawhorse."

"I don't like the sawhorse." The words came out breathy and small, because she was beginning to understand that this was serious.

Master A didn't look like he was planning on giving in. And she hated being called a spoiled princess, but a part of her worried that he was right. The last few years, she'd allowed herself to become spoiled and dependent. She'd fled from everything that hurt her. She'd hidden. She'd let her stepfathers and Lucas coddle and provide for her so she didn't have to face the truth.

Master A didn't flinch. "I don't care. Lucas has done the best he can, but the truth is he wasn't trained to be a Dom. He might enjoy it from time to time, but he prefers bottoming. You require a firm hand. If you don't want it, then you're free to leave. No one is holding you against your will. This is all about consensual play, so you have to make the choice. Do you want the session to continue?"

She hated this part. This was the part that she'd never understood. She had to make the choice, and she couldn't put it off on anyone else. She wanted for him to simply do it. Then she could blame him later, but that wasn't what The Club was about. She'd been coming here for over a year, and she finally had to decide to make the choice—stay and put herself in the hands of a stranger, or go and never know what it was like. And then there was the fact that Master A was right. Lucas needed something she couldn't give him.

She cast her eyes down submissively. How bad could it be? "Yes, Sir."

"Then strip."

Lexi's eyes came up. She was never naked in The Club. Oh, sure, she wore some really skimpy outfits, but she'd never been fully unclothed before.

"You're beautiful, baby. Show them." Lucas's hands were suddenly on her shoulders, a welcome warmth.

With shaking fingers, she started to undo the clasps of her corset. She swallowed, thinking about everyone in the crowd. Suddenly Master A's hand came out, cupping her cheek, enveloping her. His dark eyes were really brown, not black, and there was a heat in them now that was absent before.

"It's only us, Lexi. Don't think about the audience. It's you and Lucas and your Dom. You don't trust me yet, but you will. Now take off your clothes and show your Dom that gorgeous body. Lucas wants to show you off."

There was a husky chuckle, and Lucas's hands slid around her waist, covering her own. "I do, baby. I've always wanted to show you off."

Lucas undid the next hook, and the rest of the world seemed to fall away. She could feel Lucas's heat at her back, and Master A's hot eyes on her body. She felt lovely all of a sudden. Lucas wanted to show her off? It was common in The Club for a Dom to show off his sub, but Lucas had never asked. He was probably afraid to. She let her head fall back against Lucas's shoulder, giving him free access to undress her. If this was his fantasy, then she would make it a good one.

And was it truly only his fantasy? She knew it was a trick of the imagination, but if she closed her eyes, she could turn Master A's deep, husky voice more melodic, a slight bit higher. She could make him less muscular, and if his hair was longer and more sun-kissed, he could be Aidan. She could pretend for a moment that Aidan was with them again, and they were complete.

Longing swept across her soul as Lucas slipped the corset off, baring her breasts. Cool air wisped at her nipples, tightening them. She wondered what Master A was seeing. She knew her own body. It was bigger than perfect, more hourglass than was fashionable. Her breasts were large, and she thought they were already sagging a bit. Her hips were far too big, and she didn't like to think about her ass.

"Touch was allowed in our contract. I'm going to touch you now." Master A's voice had gone to a deep, seductive grumble.

Now her nipples peaked, and it had nothing to do with the cold and everything to do with the magnificent man in front of her. He was scarred, but there was no denying his appeal. He exuded masculinity, and it called to her. She might have hesitated, but Lucas was behind her, kissing her neck. His hips were moving gently against the small of her back as though he couldn't help himself.

"That is if Lucas isn't planning on prematurely ejaculating all over you," Master A said dryly.

She felt Lucas smile on the nape of her neck. He kissed her one last time and then stepped back. "I make no promises. I've waited a long time for her."

The Master inclined his head politely. "And I'm honored to be a part of it."

She stood still, expecting his hands to come out and grab for her breasts, but he touched her face. With a single finger he traced the line of her jaw from below her ear to her chin. Lucas's hands were on her waist. He slid his fingers under the sides of her silky thong and pushed them off her hips. He helped her balance as she stepped out of them and faced the Master without a stitch of clothing on. Master A ran his hand across her cheek and nose and through her hair, like a blind man memorizing the planes of her face, experiencing through touch.

He moved his hands down to her neck and shoulders. He caressed her arms, and his fingers tangled with hers. He turned her palms up and examined her fingers, touching the deep calluses she bore on her right thumb pad and the middle finger beside her nail. The damn finger was grooved because she'd spent so many years holding a pencil, and then a pen. She'd switched to a laptop, but the indention had never gone away. He pulled her writing hand into both of his, and suddenly she felt precious. She was enveloped in his warmth and care. She stood before the man utterly naked, and he was fascinated with her hand. He couldn't know how that hand was a symbol of everything she was and everything she'd lost.

When he pulled it to his lips, she shuddered as he kissed her skin. It felt, for the briefest of moments, like he was worshipping something infinitely precious and worthy.

He wasn't anything she'd expected.

She turned her eyes to find Lucas standing at Master A's side. There was no jealousy on his face, only a slight, indulgent smile.

"She's beautiful, Lucas," the Master said, gently allowing her hand to drop.

"She's the most beautiful woman in the world." Lucas had said it so many times, but this time, with both their eyes on her, she believed the words.

"I agree," Master A said, and that glorious dimple made an appearance. "Unfortunately, she's also a bit of a brat. What do we do to bratty subs in The Club, Lucas?"

Lucas's smile became distinctly predatory. "All manner of dirty, nasty things, Sir."

Master A sat down in the chair Lucas had provided. He stretched his long, strong body in that rinky-dink folding chair and patted his lap. "Why don't we start with the basics? Over my knee, sub. You owe me ten for cursing and another five for questioning me."

She took a deep breath. She was almost dizzy from the quick change. One minute the men were soft, sweet, and worshipful. Now they were ready to spank her. She suddenly remembered the crowd. *Damn*. She was in front of fifty people buck naked and about to get a spanking that, if she suspected right, was not going to be anything like Lucas's. And yet she found herself placing her body over Master A's lap. She closed her eyes and hoped she would survive the experience.

Chapter Five

Aidan nearly sighed as Lexi placed her soft, sexy body over his knee. His dick was an iron poker pressing against his leathers. He'd been rock hard all day, but his erection reached epic proportions the minute they had walked into the room.

She was shaking slightly as she positioned herself facing down over his lap. Such a sweet bundle of femininity. He'd seen her insecurity when he'd ordered her to strip, but he couldn't resist. It had been so long since he'd been close to her, his skin against hers. He needed to see her again, all of her. She was as perfect as he'd remembered. Glorious, round breasts tipped with dusky pink nipples. Generous hips he'd loved to grip as he'd fucked into her tight pussy. If they had been alone, he would have ordered her to spread her legs and present her pussy to him. An image of that one perfect night flooded his brain. He'd shoved his cock into her wet pussy and pulled out to offer Lucas a taste. Lucas had bent down to put his mouth on Lexi, but Aidan had stopped him. He'd pressed his cock to Lucas's mouth and shared the taste of their lover.

Oh, he wanted that again, but he had to prove himself first.

He caressed Lexi's silky skin. She'd been a perfect brat, thinking she could control her own punishment. Julian was right. She was in dire need of some correction. He brought his hand up and smacked that gorgeous ass.

Lexi yelped, but he was merciless. Her pretty legs kicked, and she clutched his ankles. He spanked her over and over, never losing count. He watched her porcelain skin flush a pretty pink as he struck in a pattern, never hitting the same spot twice. After he reached a count of ten, Lexi seemed to calm, her body softening and hanging over him, limp as a doll. He could hear her crying, and everything in him wanted to pull her up and hold her, but she needed this. She needed the discipline and everything that came after.

He slapped her ass, carefully remembering every bit of his training. The last few months had been a nonstop mixture of getting reacquainted with ranch work and learning how to be a Dom. He'd spent every hour of the week working the herd he'd inherited from his father and the weekends learning what he needed to know to get his loves back.

Julian Lodge and Leo Meyer had made sure his training was thorough. There wasn't anything, and he meant anything, he could do to Lexi and Lucas that he hadn't had done to him. He knew that Lexi's ass was stinging. He brought his hand down one last time, and it was done. Now was the part he'd wanted to get to all along.

He smoothed his hand down her spine. "You did very well, Lexi."

She sniffled but didn't move under his hand. He took it as his cue to help her up. She was soft, almost boneless in his lap as he arranged her so she sat cuddled in his arms. Lucas walked up behind him and stroked her hair. Tears streaked down her face, but she seemed calmer now. He'd never gotten the whole "getting spanked" thing, but damn if it didn't work for Lexi. She tilted her head up and those dark blue eyes pulled him right in. She was so fucking gorgeous. All he wanted to do was bend his lips to hers and kiss her. There was a watery smile on her face as he realized she wasn't looking at him. Lucas bent down and brushed his lips against hers.

"You were great, baby," Lucas said.

She practically glowed under his praise. Her grin turned slightly devilish. "Thanks, babe. It takes true talent to get your ass whipped."

"Step back, Lucas." He nearly winced at the harsh edge of his voice.

Lucas merely winked at Lexi and did as he was told. He took it as the confidence of a man who was certain of his place with a woman. Lucas wasn't jealous of him, but oh, he was getting jealous of Lucas. And Lexi, now that he thought of it. He was jealous of their ease and comfort with one another. Julian had been right. They needed a Dom. He needed to make sure he was the Dom they wanted.

"Now, we can start things properly." He shifted her off his lap. No kiss for the man who'd given her the spanking, but he still had a job to do, and Lexi still had some punishment coming. "Find your position, please."

Lexi sank gracefully to her knees in front of him, and her head was lowered, sending her long, glossy black hair cascading down her body.

He turned slightly to bring Lucas into his line of sight. He cocked a single eyebrow, sending Lucas the question he shouldn't have been required to ask.

Lucas's face lit with surprise. "Really?"

Lexi might not be the only one with a red ass. "You signed the contract, sub."

A light stain crept up Lucas's neck. Aidan might have worried, but there was a slight smile playing on Lucas's lips, and there was no mistaking how his cock responded. That big cock was straining against the leather of his pants as Lucas gracefully stepped around him and sank to his knees beside Lexi.

He had to catch his breath. This, this was what he'd longed for. Why had he wasted all that time? They were gorgeous sitting there together, their dark heads bowed in submission. It was a precious gift, one he'd thrown away before. He wouldn't make the same mistake again. He stood and placed a hand on each bowed head. Both of his subs had dark hair. Lucas's was black as night, while Lexi's seemed like it was threaded with wisps of auburn. They were so alike and yet so very, very different.

He looked up because he had a job to do. The crowd was waiting. Leo stood close to the stage, arms across his chest. He was standing in for Julian because Julian had come to think of Lexi as a daughter. Julian had told Aidan he had zero desire to see his "daughter" naked.

Jack Barnes had felt the same way. He wasn't in the dungeon this evening. So it was Leo he looked to when he went into his punishment protocol.

"Master Leo, this woman belongs to me by right of contract. She has broken the rules of this club and seeks to make reparation. Will you accept?"

Leo's head nodded. "I speak for Mr. Lodge. We will accept her apology should she make it with an open heart."

Aidan reached down and drew Lucas up, presenting him to the crowd. "This is my partner. He will aid in her pain and pleasure. Lucas, prepare her."

He felt Lucas flinch, but then Lucas straightened up, standing tall. His shoulders squared; his jaw firmed. He went from sub to Dom in an instant, a chameleon as always. Lucas was very good at taking on the roles needed to please those around him. One day, Aidan would prove to him that he didn't need to take on roles. One day, they would all be together, and Lucas could simply be Lucas.

But for now, Lucas played his role to perfection. He had Lexi on her feet and bound to the sawhorse. Her gorgeous ass was in the air. The pink hue of her flesh there called to Aidan. He checked the knots Lucas had tied and found them to be expertly done. Tight, but it wouldn't cut off her circulation. Lexi rested her head down on the padding of the bench, her eyes closed, her expression beatific.

It was time to start.

Aidan walked to the table and pulled out his first implement. He knew from talking to Leo that she'd never taken this particular torture.

He picked up the small plug and the bottle of lube. He watched Lucas's eyes widen as he walked toward the sawhorse.

"Are you serious?"

"Don't question me, Lucas." He sent him a look that had those green orbs sliding away from his face. "Hold her cheeks open. Lexi, you are not allowed to talk unless it is to use your safe word."

She shuddered underneath him, but kept her mouth closed. Lucas's hands came out and parted those lush cheeks. He stared down at that beautiful asshole. *Shit.* He had to get himself under control. It was cute and perky, if an asshole could be described as perky. He dribbled lube into the crack of her ass. This was what he'd gained by tossing aside his so-called morality. He'd gained the ability to enjoy his loves on every level. His sex life with Lexi had been nice before, but it had been very vanilla. What he wanted now was different. He wanted no boundaries.

He took his time, massaging the lube onto her rosette before he pressed his pinky finger in. The tight muscles of her anus tried to keep him out, but he wasn't going to allow it. He worked his finger back and forth. Lexi whimpered a little. The sound went straight to his dick. Aidan finally pressed the finger in. He looked up and Lucas was watching, his green eyes dark and lustful.

"Join me."

It was all Lucas seemed to need. Lucas's pinky joined his. He pressed in, first to the knuckle. Lexi groaned, but didn't say a word. Her ass wriggled as though she was trying to accommodate them. Finally, Lucas's finger slid in past the tight ring, joining Aidan's.

Fine trembles crept across Lexi's skin. Aidan and Lucas found a rhythm as they fucked Lexi's asshole with their fingers. When Lucas pressed in, Aidan pulled out slightly. They both massaged her anus, opening her, and all Aidan could think about was replacing those fingers with his cock. He'd been inside Lexi many times, but he'd never taken her ass. He'd never shared that with her because he'd had a stick up his own.

After a moment's sweet play, he looked to Lucas. "Get the bullet. Strap it on her and then take your position in front of that lovely mouth."

Lucas pulled his finger out and rushed across the stage. He quickly washed his hands and came back with the small egg-shaped vibrator and a washcloth. Aidan pulled his finger out and allowed Lucas to wash him while he stared at that hungry asshole. It was tight again, but he would fix that. While Lucas strapped the vibrator around Lexi's hips, Aidan prepped the plug. He lubed the small, hard plastic plug and lined it up to Lexi's anus. Lucas stepped around to his position, and his hand quickly found Lexi's hair. He smoothed it back.

"Press back against me, Lexi," Aidan ordered, pushing the tip of the plug just inside the rosy pucker of her asshole. She moaned, but did as he asked. He fucked the plug back and forth until it finally slid deep inside her. He held her cheeks apart, admiring how the plug looked. His heart was racing. Every inch of his skin tingled with want. He traced the line of her spine before placing a lingering kiss on the small of her back. "Very good, sub. I think they enjoyed that. They loved watching me and Lucas prepare that virgin ass to take a reaming. One day you'll take a cock up that little hole to please your Masters, won't you?"

Her voice was quivering and breathless. "Oh, yes, Sir. If that pleases you, Sir."

God, she was so submissive. Why hadn't he listened when she'd tried to talk to him about this? Why the fuck had he walked away? It was everything he could hope for. "Now it would please me to torture you. Think about the plug in your ass while you take a cock in your mouth. Lucas, fill her up. She's your toy. Fuck her mouth."

* * * *

Lucas stilled at the Master's command.

Lucas, fill her up. She's your toy. Fuck her mouth.

Well, not everything. His dick stood straight up, straining at his leathers, practically bursting the seams of his pants. Master A wanted him to fuck Lexi's mouth here?

He looked down, expecting to see Lexi's worried face. Those bright blue eyes stared up at him, but the smile curling her lips was seductive, not worried. His cock pulsed.

She licked her lips like she was anticipating a treat. "You better do what the big, bad Dom tells you to, or you might find something shoved up your ass, too."

There was a loud smack as Master A slapped her ass and Lexi gasped, though she didn't lose the devilish grin.

"You are not allowed to talk." Master A stood ready to swat her again. He towered over Lexi's form. His dark eyes shifted to Lucas, and Lucas couldn't help but remember what it had felt like to stand next to Master A when they had pressed their fingers into Lexi's tight hole, opening her up and preparing her. He'd liked the image of their hands working together. *Partners in her pleasure.* That's what

Master A had said. Lucas loved the sound of that. Could this man be the one? Ever since Aidan had fled like the coward he was, Lucas couldn't get it out of his mind. He wanted what his brother had. He wanted his girl and his best friend, lovers all.

"Lucas, I gave you an order." There was no give in the Master's voice. It left no room for doubt or indecision. He'd made the decision when he'd signed the contract to bottom for Master A. He'd given over power to a man Julian trusted. Hell, even Jack had signed off on this plan. His hands went to the ties on his leathers.

He felt the Master's and Lexi's eyes on him as his cock burst free. If he wasn't careful, the damn thing would sing a hallelujah chorus. A whole fucking year and all he'd had was the comfort of his hand. He pressed the head of his dick to those luscious lips of Lexi's. Her tongue darted out, and Lucas thought he might come right then and there.

Smack. "You're a tease, sub." Master A had a fierce grin on his face. He was obviously enjoying the play. "Let's see how you like it. Lexi, you are not allowed to come. Trust me, angel, you don't want to know what will happen to you if you do come."

Master A flicked on the vibe and a low hum started. Her eyes opened wide, and Lucas almost felt sorry for her. Almost. He was far too busy pressing into her hot mouth.

"Open for me." He almost didn't recognize the guttural sound that came out of his mouth. So long. He'd wanted her for so long. She had become his whole damn world. She was so important to him that he'd been afraid to take her. But there was no room for fear in this place. There was only pleasing the Master, and when the Master was a good one, a sub's pleasure wasn't far behind.

Lexi's mouth opened obediently. She sucked the head of his cock inside, her tongue swirling, drawing out the arousal there. He steadied himself on his feet. Her tongue felt so good, lapping away at him.

"Deeper," Master A ordered.

The Master was watching the scene with heated eyes. His hand clutched the remote to the vibe, but his eyes were focused on Lucas's cock sinking into Lexi's mouth. The fact that Master A was watching made Lucas's cock lengthen further. It reminded him of the last time he'd had a cock in his own mouth. Aidan's big dick had been covered in Lexi's cream, and he'd licked it off. He'd taken Aidan's cock to the back of his throat and swallowed every bit of semen Aidan had spewed.

Lucas shoved another inch between Lexi's lips. He smiled down at her. They might have lost Aidan, but they had each other. His hand sank into her silky hair. Why had he worried? Her tongue worked around him, and he gave over. She was his. She would always be his. They would make it work.

She whimpered around his cock, the vibration making his balls ache with pleasure.

Master A put a hand on her back. "Oh, is my angel feeling the burn? Are you close? Don't come. I'll get out the paddle, and you won't be able to sit down tomorrow. You suck that cock. You take him deep."

Lexi's mouth opened a bit more, and Lucas was able to sink in all the way to his balls. She surrounded him. Her mouth pulled as her tongue lapped, and Lucas lost it. He held her head gently and started to fuck that gorgeous, red-lipped mouth of hers. He thrust in and pulled out. Lexi moaned around him, and he noticed that Master A had his hand between her legs. The vibrator hummed, and Lexi's eyes were wide and desperate. She had to be going crazy. She was such a responsive girl. It never took him long to get her off. Between the plug in her ass and the vibe on her clit, she had to be close. Now Master A was pushing his fingers into her cunt, probably seeking her G-spot. There was no way she could hold out.

"You feel so fucking good, Lexi." He pumped into her, his cock pulsing. His balls drew up, and he felt his blood racing through his system. He looked at Master A, their eyes meeting, and Lucas saw it.

Such a small thing, but then he'd memorized the man's body. He'd had one night in paradise, but he'd loved Aidan for so long before then. The mask had slipped slightly, and his eyebrow was visible. So was the scar Aidan had gotten at the age of seventeen. He'd told Lucas the story over beers one night while they waited for Lexi. Aidan had been playing at a bar. Aidan had lied to get the gig.

She sucked at him, pulling his cock to the back of her throat and swallowing. The soft heat of her throat did him in. He pulsed and came as he watched the man he thought he'd never see again.

The bar fight had resulted in Aidan damn near losing his left eye. Master A's eyebrow was creased with a perfect crescent-shaped scar.

Aidan.

Lucas's mind whirled as he pulled out of Lexi's mouth. He took a step back, trying to understand what the fuck was going on. One moment the world had been close to perfect, and now he didn't understand a damn thing.

Aidan's eyes—yes, he could see that plainly now—were on him. "Lucas, take over for me here."

Lucas didn't move. He looked down at Lexi. Her eyes were closed as she concentrated, probably trying to hold off the orgasm that was coming.

"Lucas!"

Lucas turned to the man who had once completed their threesome and then torn them apart. A bitterness welled up inside him. Aidan thought he could play a game with them? A sick feeling hit the pit of Lucas's stomach. This betrayal could go far past Aidan playing a trick.

"Does my brother know you're here?"

Aidan stopped. Lucas knew the minute his face fell that he'd been right. There was a long moment of silence.

"Yes."

Lucas simply turned away and began working on Lexi's bindings. Her eyes were open and questioning.

"You can talk, baby," Lucas said, his voice flat and emotionless. "We're done here."

The Master drew himself up to his full, intimidating height. "Lucas, stop it right now. You signed a contract. Do you really want to put your rights at this club in jeopardy?"

"What's happening?" Lexi's hands came free. Lucas wished he'd brought a shirt or a freaking robe with him.

"Get behind me, Alexis." He pulled her off the sawhorse and unhooked the vibrator, tossing it away.

Aidan O'Malley seemed a bit miffed his game was up. He invaded Lucas's space, but Lucas was done being intimidated by him. He wasn't sure what Aidan was doing here, but he was done.

"This club can go to hell for all I care now. And so can my

brother and Julian." Lucas turned to Leo, whose eyes were grave.

People were talking now. There was a hum in the crowd. Despite Julian's disdain for gossip, The Club thrived on it. They would be grist for the gossip mill for years after this, but it didn't matter.

"Lucas, please." The Dom was gone. Aidan seemed to almost deflate.

Lucas felt Lexi's hands on his waist, tightening. "Who is he?"

Aidan pulled the mask off his face, and for the first time, Lucas truly looked at the man. He looked older and harder, his once stunning face now hard as granite. He was still a beautiful man, but he'd changed, and there was no doubt that he'd been through an enormous amount of pain. *What the fuck had happened to Aidan?*

"Lexi, I came back to fix things." Aidan tried to take a step toward them, but Lucas merely moved back.

Lexi curved around Lucas's body, straining to see what was going on. "Oh, my god. Aidan?"

Lexi took off. One minute she was on the stage behind Lucas, and the next she was pushing her way through the crowd. She didn't seem to care that she wasn't wearing anything. Lucas started to take off after her, but a big hand pulled him back.

"Lucas, please listen to me," Aidan said, his gravelly voice deep and pleading.

He pulled away. "Yeah? Like you listened to me? I believe both Lexi and I begged you to listen, and what did you say? You said you didn't want this fucked-up life. I believe you called me a queer."

Aidan paled visibly. "That's not true. I said I wasn't gay. I would never have used that word."

"Yeah, well, you made yourself plain." Lucas started to walk past him, but he got in the way again.

"Lucas, I was wrong, so fucking wrong—"

Leo placed a hand on Aidan's shoulder. "He's done for now, Aidan. Let him go."

Lucas strode off the stage after Lexi. He tried not to think about the sorrow in Aidan's eyes.

"I love you, Lucas."

Yeah, he wasn't going to think about that, either.

Chapter Six

Lexi slammed into the private room, wishing she'd thought about picking up her damn clothes. At least she could have held them in front of her. As it was, she'd run through the club, pushing her way through the crowd with her boobs and ass hanging out. Did she even have a shred of dignity left? God, did any of it matter? It felt like the walls were closing in on her.

Aidan was here.

What the hell had he come back for?

Bitterness welled up inside her as she kicked out of the heels she'd been wearing. Mere minutes ago they had made her feel feminine and sexy. Now they hurt her feet and made her feel like a fucking idiot. She looked at herself in the mirror. Her mascara was already streaking. She'd been so happy for a moment. She'd had Lucas, and it had been perfect. She'd adored the way he filled her mouth. She'd reveled in his masculine taste. It had been all the more perfect for the man behind her.

Master A had tortured her in the sweetest way possible. She'd felt a real connection to him. He'd called to her, with his damaged face and body. He'd been a true Dom, and the sub deep inside her responded. She'd pushed, and he'd been an unmovable brick wall. It totally turned her on. As she'd lain there, bound and helpless, she'd wondered if he was the one who could complete her and Lucas. She'd had no doubt in her mind that this was what they needed.

It had all been a lie. Like everything about Aidan.

"Lexi, please put on some clothes."

She started and practically jumped into the robe sitting on the counter at the sound of her stepfather's voice. She wrapped the white silk robe around her body and turned to face the big cowboy who was averting his eyes. Jack Barnes sat in one of the elegant chairs, a glass of Scotch at hand. Normally, her big, strong stepfather was a comforting presence, but not today.

He'd told her he was leaving. It seemed to Lexi like he'd been lying to her a lot lately.

"You knew."

He took a long drink of that Scotch. "Yes. I'd like a chance to explain."

"Really?" Lexi asked, her arms over her chest. Her stepfather was dressed in his usual jeans and western shirt. Somehow he managed to be more powerful in casual clothes than most men were in thousand-dollar suits. She wasn't intimidated by it this evening, though. "I would have enjoyed a chance to decide whether or not I wanted to perform several sexual acts in public with a man who ripped my heart out. Guess we can't always get what we want. You tell me something, Jack Barnes, did my mother know?"

Tears welled in her eyes at the thought of her mother being in on this—plot, scheme—she had no idea what to call it. Her mother had been her rock for so long, but now she had a new family. It struck her forcefully that even her mother had left her behind. Abby Barnes had Jack and Sam, and now little Olivia and Josh. Maybe her mom didn't need her anymore. Maybe she was a reminder of how crappy Abby's life had been because she'd had a kid at the age of seventeen.

"No, she doesn't know, and she might divorce me when she finds out." Jack's hands tightened around the glass, and his face was flushed. It was the most emotional she could remember seeing him aside from the joy he had on his face when he was with his family. Now he looked haggard and worried. "If it makes a difference to you, Sam doesn't know, either. I couldn't tell him because he can't keep his mouth closed around Abby."

Good for Sam. "Well, at least one of my mother's husbands isn't a bastard and a half."

Jack's eyes came up. "Lexi, please hear me out. Aidan came to me a little over six months ago."

She held up a hand. The last thing she wanted to hear was Aidan's story. She didn't want to know what he'd been doing during the time he'd been gone. She didn't want to know what had happened to him. God, she didn't care how he'd gotten those scars. They covered his body. If he'd been a car, she would have wondered if anyone had survived the wreck. She forced herself to be strong. "I don't care."

"I find that very hard to believe. You were ready to marry this man."

She remembered that quite well. She also remembered how it felt to call all the people she'd invited and tell them the wedding was off. She'd burned her wedding dress one night on the barbecue grill while she made her way through a bottle and a half of Pinot Noir. "And he dumped me three weeks before the wedding. You know, Jack, usually the family of the dumped girl doesn't invite the man who humiliated her to abuse her in a club."

"He didn't abuse you. I made damn sure he was properly trained, and Leo would have stopped anything that could have possibly hurt you." Jack's voice was annoyingly calm.

The door slammed open, and Lucas was there, his eyes immediately finding her and honing in. He strode inside and gathered her close, his scent and touch so familiar and comforting they brought more tears to her eyes. Lucas was her touchstone now. Sometimes Lucas was the only thing in the world that seemed real.

"Baby, we're getting out of here, and I swear we'll never come back." He buried his head in her hair, his mouth close to her ear. "I'll quit tomorrow, and we can go wherever you like. If you want to, we can pack up and move anywhere. I have a lot of money saved up."

It was a sweet gesture, but not really practical. Lucas had worked his ass off for his career. He couldn't leave it all behind because she was pissed. Of course, she'd left her career behind, but that was different.

"I would greatly prefer you didn't quit, Lucas." Jack's voice held a wealth of weariness.

Lucas's arms came down, and he turned to his brother, his expression changing from tender to angry bull in an instant. "You son of a bitch! You planned this."

Lexi put a hand on his chest. The last thing she needed was a Jack/Lucas throwdown. She was fine with fighting with her stepfather, but she couldn't stand the thought of Lucas going toe-to-toe with his brother. Jack was the only family Lucas had. She didn't want to be the reason Lucas lost him. *Damn it.* She hated being reasonable. "Stop. Let's hear him out."

She owed that much to Jack. The man had made the last few years infinitely more comfortable for her. He'd never turned her down when she needed a favor, and he always seemed to care. If something had changed, she wanted to know.

Reason didn't seem to be something Lucas was interested in at this point. "We don't have to hear him out. He's a manipulative son of a bitch who can't keep his goddamn fingers out of other people's business. I know exactly what's going on here. Do you really hate the fact that I'm with her so fucking much that you need to bring back the jerk who broke her heart?"

Jack blanched, the blood leaving his face in an instant. "Lucas, how can you even think that?"

Lucas stood tall, his shoulders thrown back. There was a blank expression on his face that told her he was feeling inconsequential. It was the same look he had when he talked to his father. "I'm not so far outside the tabloids, am I, Jack? You can't forget how you met me. I tried to blackmail you. I was known as a drug user and a queer. I'm the black sheep of the family. Guess I'm not great son-in-law material."

She flinched. Jack couldn't think that, could he? When Lucas had met Jack, he'd been the darling of the tabloids. Lucas had been young and lost. His father had cut him off. Lucas had lashed out by being the baddest boy around. But Jack knew it was an act, right? Since Jack took him under his wing, Lucas had blossomed into the most responsible man she knew. Lucas was the one who took her car in for service and fixed things in her apartment. Lucas brought her lunch when she forgot it and took care of her when she was sick.

"Lucas is good for me," she said, holding on to him.

Jack ignored her, choosing to stare at Lucas. "What the fuck are you talking about? You're my brother. Don't you ever fucking talk about yourself that way. You're the black sheep? Hell, son, I'm the bastard Dad swept under the rug. You never used a drug once in your damn life. I don't care how many tabloids you showed up on trying to get the senator's attention. I love you, Lucas. I am proud of the man you've become. I would be thrilled if you would marry Lexi. I'll open my wallet and pay for the whole damn thing. I'll write you a blank check, but that won't happen because you need him."

"We do not need him. He walked out on her." Though Lucas's words were stubborn, she felt a bit of the fight go out of him. His shoulders relaxed slightly. Jack had said the right thing.

Jack deflated, the righteous anger leaving him like a balloon that had been popped. "Oh, brother, he left you, too. I know the whole story. He told me everything, and he didn't leave out a single bad thing he did. He left both of you, and you haven't been the same since."

The room seemed to calm, and Lexi was finally able to ask the question on her mind. If she knew one thing in the world, it was that Jack Barnes loved her mother. "Why would you risk pissing off Mom?"

"First because I love my brother." Jack's lips pursed, and he sighed, a long, sad sound. "But mostly because you need help, baby girl, and this was the only way I knew to give it."

"Help? I'm fine." She was. She was making it just fine.

Jack's head shook. "No, you're not. You drink too much, and you've utterly given up on your dreams. You're a writer, a good one, but you haven't written a word in years. You're wasting your life. You've had three jobs in two years. I can't stand it. I worry about it all the time. I know I'm not your father, Lexi, but I swear I love you like you were my own. If I thought rehab would fix you, I would have you hauled to a clinic."

She huffed, utterly shocked at the accusation. Sure she'd had some trouble with jobs, but it wasn't her fault all her bosses had been jerks. And she didn't want to write. It wasn't like it was a crime or something. "I am not an alcoholic."

Her stepdad stared at her. "That's why you're not in rehab, but can you honestly tell me you haven't been drinking too much? Can you tell me you aren't using a bottle of wine to dull whatever pain you're in?"

It was only one glass to help her sleep. That was what she'd told herself, but then one became two, and three. All so she wouldn't dream about it at night. The nights with Lucas were easier. She didn't want him to suspect she was drinking too much, so she curbed it. She kept it to one, but when Lucas was gone, sometimes she lost count, like the night before.

"Lexi?"

Lucas's quiet question made her want to retreat. She stared at the floor so she didn't have to look at Lucas.

"Damn it, Lexi." He pulled her close.

Suddenly it was all too much. Between Jack and Lucas, she felt so small. They were in control of their lives, and she wasn't. She was drifting. She knew it, but she couldn't stand the thought that she was some fuckup they needed to take care of. She was such a screwup that apparently they needed to bring in yet another man to spread the load of taking care of her.

Lucas looked so hurt as she pushed him away, but she couldn't stand to be coddled at that moment.

"Don't. I just need some time," she muttered, grabbing her bag. "I won't go far. I'll head up to the suite, but I need to be alone. And I promise not to fall into an alcoholic haze. Tell room service not to deliver. I'm sure I can't be trusted."

"Alexis," Jack began in a tone that let her know he was reaching the end of his patience.

It didn't matter. Her patience was a live, frayed wire waiting to explode. She needed to get out of here. She had zero intention of staying in The Club, but she wasn't about to let them know that. She needed to be alone.

"I'll talk to you in the morning. I...I have to go." Lexi fled the dressing room like the devil was after her.

* * * *

Lucas slumped down on the small sofa and let his head fall into his hands. How had the night gone so fucking wrong? One minute it was perfect bliss, and the next it was an avalanche of their old baggage hitting him squarely in the nuts. Now Lexi had retreated. Not exactly how he'd seen their first real sexual encounter ending.

"Here, drink this." His brother pressed a glass of Scotch in his hand.

The irony was not lost on Lucas. "Pot, meet kettle."

He still took a swig.

Jack sat back down. "It's not the same, and you know it. And you know she's out of control. She has been since that goddamn car accident."

"What do you know about that?" Lucas stared at his brother, willing him to change the subject. Jack could be a manipulative SOB when it came to his family. He often knew things about Lucas's life and his job before Lucas knew them. It was one of the many things he admired about his brother. Did Jack know something he wasn't telling? Lexi had been adamant about not talking about what happened that night. He thought she was wrong not to talk about it, but she wouldn't listen to reason. It would almost be a relief if Jack had found out.

Jack's mouth became a flat line of frustration. "I know hospitals are a bitch to get information out of. I even tried bribing some people to get records. Julian could do it. He could have Taggart's hacker get in. He could do it himself if he wanted to. You know he's got shit on every power player in Texas, but he's gone all ethical on me. He'd change his tune if it was Dani or Finn. But I have my suspicions."

Lucas couldn't confirm or deny Jack's suspicions. He'd been sworn to silence. And he wasn't sure Lexi could handle being confronted with the truth right now. "I never should have left her alone."

Jack shook his head. "You can't be with her twenty-four hours a day, seven days a week. I meant what I said. I would love for you and Lexi to get married, but I don't think it can work unless you two deal with Aidan."

He took another drink. Now that he was calm, he knew his

brother had his best interests at heart. Of course, Jack didn't always go about serving those interests in the way he would prefer. "Is that why you brought him back?"

Jack's lips quirked up slightly. "I didn't go looking for him. He came to me. He'd been discharged from the Army."

Lucas had to take a long, deep breath. Aidan had gone into the Army? He'd obviously seen some combat. God, he couldn't imagine fun-loving, creative, playful Aidan with a gun in his hand. Aidan had always been very alpha male, but he'd preferred his music over anything else. Why had he done that?

Guilt gnawed at Lucas because deep down he knew the reason. Aidan had escaped. He'd needed to prove he was still a "man" after the night he'd spent with Lucas. That one night seemed to have ruined a lot of lives.

"I think you need to talk to him," Jack said slowly, as though he wanted the words to permeate Lucas's thick brain.

He nodded. He did need to talk to Aidan. Lexi could probably use some closure, too. "I get that, but don't you think that maybe Leo's office would have been a better place for a therapy session?"

Now his brother smiled outright. "Hell, no. I think, in this case, a scene was the only way to go. Did Aidan fuck up? He wasn't supposed to tell you who he was until you were comfortable with him again."

"He has a scar over his left eye. His mask slipped."

"Yeah, it's the little things that trip you up."

"I'm still pissed at you." Hearing Jack say he was all right with him marrying Lexi went a long way to mending the fence, but they still had some problems. "You should have told me."

"Yeah, because then you would have been totally reasonable about it. Neither one of you has said his name in years, and yet he's always there between you. I could plead his case for him, but in the end, you need to talk to him." Jack leaned forward, his face serious in the low light. "Look at me, Lucas. I love you, brother, and I love Lexi. I wouldn't do this if I didn't think it was important. I wouldn't allow him close to my family again unless I was damn certain that boy had changed. I believe in him. You need to make that decision for yourself, though. But you think about it. I believe in you, too. I'm a damn good judge of character, and I don't hand out second chances like they were candy. I gave you a second chance, and I've never regretted it. I never will. You talk to him, and maybe you can come to the same conclusion that I did."

"What's that?"

Jack leaned in. "That life is far too short to waste on grudges. Love does not come along often. When it does, you can't throw it away because it isn't perfect."

Lucas felt his fists clench. "That was what Aidan did."

"I know. He knows. Don't make his mistake," Jack said. "You and Lexi are an awful lot like me and Sam. You two are halves of a whole. I knew it the minute I saw you two together. You're too alike. Just like me and Sam. If Abigail hadn't come along, we would have gone on, but we wouldn't have been complete. We wouldn't have found the love that was always there. Abby made that possible. I believe Aidan can do that for you and Lexi. Tell me something. Was he selfish tonight? Did he use the two of you?"

"No. He brought us together." But he could have. Aidan could have ordered them to pleasure him, and they would have. He and Lexi had both been under his spell from the moment he took charge. He'd called Lucas his partner when he didn't have to. Lucas had signed up to bottom for him. Aidan could have shoved him to the side and taken Lexi for himself. Yet, he'd given Lucas his fantasy.

"He loves you." Jack's tone was quiet, almost tender.

"He told Lexi he loved her, too. He left her." Lucas didn't like the way he was already softening. Already, he felt the need to talk to Aidan. Why couldn't he be a ruthless bastard? Why couldn't he be cold? Aidan had walked out on them, but was Lucas able to turn away without a second thought? *Fuck no.* He was sitting here, wondering what had happened and how Aidan had felt when he'd been injured. Had he been alone? Had he been scared?

Fuck.

"Talk to him." Jack stood, and he held out his hand, pulling Lucas up and enveloping him in the type of bone-cracking, backslapping bear hug he'd missed for the first twenty-three years of his life. Lucas gave in. He couldn't withhold his affection from the man who had given him his new life. Without Jackson Barnes, he wouldn't have become a lawyer. He wouldn't have met Lexi. He wouldn't be a man.

He was going to have to talk to Aidan.

"You're an asshole," he said as he finally pulled away.

Jack grinned. "You know, I get that a lot. Good luck, Lucas. I'm heading home. I have to talk to Abby before she hears the story from someone else. I might be sleeping in the barn for a week or two. If you need anything, please call. At least Sam will still be able to answer the phone. There are a lot of nice things about sharing a woman. One of us is usually in good with the wife. Good night, brother."

The door closed behind Jack. Lucas picked up his shirt and shrugged into it. He couldn't help but look in the mirror. He could still see hints of that scared, desperate boy who had first walked into this club all those years before. He had walked in, determined to blackmail his brother, but what he'd found was something like salvation. Was that how Aidan had felt when he walked through the doors?

Jack was right. If anyone understood the value of a second chance, it was Lucas Cameron. But he was going to make damn sure Aidan O'Malley deserved one.

Chapter Seven

Aidan toyed with the beer in front of him. He knew he should be packing and getting ready to go home. He had his answer, but he sat at the bar, unable to force himself to leave. He heard people whispering all around him. It didn't matter. He'd fucked everything up, again.

Leo had tried to talk to him. He'd growled enough that Leo had finally given up. The last thing Aidan wanted was a coaching session.

What exactly had he thought would happen? Had he thought they would be okay with him walking back into their lives? And he hadn't exactly walked. He'd ordered and spanked his way back in. He'd deceived his way back in. But, damn it, it had seemed like the only way to do it. If he didn't know deep in his heart that he was the best thing in the world for them, he would sacrifice and walk away. He'd been half afraid he'd look them back up and find they were married and happy without him.

He wasn't going to give up. Deception hadn't worked. He didn't like to think of it that way. He liked to think of it as easing back in. Well, easing back in had blown up in his face. He needed a new plan because this was the most important thing in his life. He wasn't about to give up now.

His cell phone vibrated. He pulled it out, half hoping it was Lexi calling to scream at him. He'd listen to her. He would let her rage at him because he wanted to hear her voice. He would have let Lucas beat on him just to feel his hands again. Aidan groaned as he saw the number. His brother.

"What?"

There was a momentary pause. "Well, ain't that typical. You leave me with all the work and then act like I'm the one in trouble."

And it was exactly like his brother to try to turn everything around. "Look, Bo, I've already talked to Dwight. He said you were busy causing trouble."

"What? Motherfucker. He ain't even here, Aidan. He left the ranch early this afternoon."

That wasn't what Dwight had said. Bo wasn't exactly known for his honesty. "Where did he go?"

His brother huffed over the phone. "I don't know. It's not like he tells me anything. He's a fucking asshole."

Bo pretty much thought everyone was a fucking asshole. Aidan felt unaccountably tired. "Was there something you wanted, Bo?"

"There are a lot of things I want, but I'm not getting them, am I? I called because I thought you should know something, but now I think you deserve everything you have coming your way. Go to hell."

The connection was cut with a brutal click. Aidan let the phone fall from his hands, not caring when it fell to the floor. It didn't matter. If it rang again, it would be one more person who wanted to tell him what a failure he was.

Aidan closed his eyes and shut out the world. Music, sad and sweet, flowed through his brain. Just because he couldn't play anymore didn't mean he didn't write in his head. He heard a single guitar, plucking gently, the sound as lonely as he felt.

He could see the song in his head, but none of it mattered since the people he'd wanted to play for were gone.

"How about some water, Bill? I think I can handle this particular confrontation without liquor."

He opened his eyes, turning because he knew the sound of that voice, deep and always with a hint of sarcasm, like the owner never took the world too seriously. It was deceptive, that voice, because he

91

happened to know that Lucas Cameron took everything he loved with an almost worshipful reverence. Lucas Cameron knew how to love.

But he had the distinct feeling he might find out Lucas Cameron didn't love him anymore.

He took a long drink. Lucas might not need liquid courage, but he sure as hell did.

"Why?" Lucas asked the question without inflection, as though the actual answer was meaningless to him.

Lucas didn't look at him. He kept his expression bland as he faced forward, but Aidan couldn't help but stare. Lucas was lovely to him now. He'd fought the attraction before because it had seemed the final nail in the coffin of some perfect, vanilla life he had planned. Now he let himself stare. Lucas was a testament to masculine beauty. His pitch black hair fell over his forehead, tumbling almost over his eyes. In the past, Lucas had kept it shorter, but Lexi had always begged him to let it grow out. It looked damn good on him. Aidan wanted to reach out, but he had some explaining to do first.

"Why am I here?"

Lucas sighed softly. "We can start there."

It was time to tell him the truth. "I came back because I love you and Lexi. I came back because I need you so fucking much."

"And you decided this when?" There it was, that sarcastic edge. Lucas was good at putting on fronts.

He needed to get past the mask. Honesty was his only weapon. "The day I nearly lost my legs."

Lucas turned, and his eyes flared with shock. Aidan was almost certain he saw concern there. "What happened?"

"I don't know," Aidan said quietly. "It's all a jumble. I was with my squad. We were on a security detail. We started taking some heavy fire. I know this from the report that was filed by a friend of mine. We were the only ones who survived. I woke up in a field hospital, and they told me I wouldn't walk again. And I realized as I was lying in that bed that it wasn't the worst day of my life."

Those emerald eyes of Lucas's shimmered slightly with unshed tears. "Don't you fucking say it."

"The worst day of my life was the day I walked out on you and Lexi."

Lucas slammed off the stool. "Fuck you, Aidan."

He watched as Lucas stormed off. He was patient. If Lucas wanted to fume for a while, that was perfectly acceptable because at least he felt something. He'd seen it in Lucas's eyes. He'd been moved, and it wasn't all anger. Julian and Leo had spent hours and hours the last several months teaching him how to read body language. Lucas's entire body was bunched up. He was one huge ball of emotion. He could see it plainly. Anger was at the forefront, but there was more there.

Lucas made it to the door that led back to the hotel section of The Club before turning on his heels and stalking back.

"You think you can waltz back in here and give me some sob story, and I'll fall down on my knees and be grateful you're back?"

"No." He was going to let Lucas get it all out. He knew he deserved it. "I know I have a lot to make up for."

"You can't make up for it," Lucas shot back. "You can't. You left us. You're the one who turned away. You joined the Army? What is wrong with you? I respect anyone who wants to serve this country, but you're not a soldier, Aidan. You're a fucking musician."

He held his hand up. "Not anymore."

Lucas swallowed whatever he was about to say. He reached out and grabbed Aidan's hand. It was his left hand. It was missing two fingers, but only his middle finger and thumb still had any real agility. He'd joked with the doctors that at least he could hitch a ride and flip someone off, but he would never play guitar again. The muscles in his hand still worked, but they were far too stiff to play with any accuracy or real rhythm.

"Was it worth it? Did it make you forget what happened?" Lucas asked.

Aidan forced himself to smile. Arguing with Lucas would get him nowhere. "No. Like I said, I woke up in that bed, and all I wanted was the two of you. I called."

Lucas's face went white. "I know. You think I'm not feeling that right now? You called, and I hung up on you."

He finally did what he'd wanted to do for years. He cupped Lucas's face and let himself feel that skin against his hand. "I deserved it. I would have hung up on me, too."

Lucas pulled away, but not after his eyes had closed slightly as though he reveled in the contact. He took a step back, those emerald eyes hooding as he looked down. Aidan had put a shirt on, but he knew Lucas was remembering the scars on his body.

"I should have…it doesn't matter now. I need to understand why you're here and what you want. I need to know why you didn't simply talk to me. That whole deception out there in the dungeon doesn't help your case."

Aidan eased back onto his barstool. "I think it does. I know the lifestyle you've always wanted. You want a ménage, and you want a Dom."

A bitter huff came out of Lucas's mouth. "Yes, I believe I mentioned that before. That conversation didn't go well."

"I know. I was an ass. I didn't really get it. I was surprised at how much I enjoyed our night together. God, the word enjoy cheapens it. I loved it. It was the closest I've ever felt to anyone, but it was counter to everything I'd been taught. I understand more now. I get it."

"Just like that?" Lucas held his hands out, obviously waiting for a much better explanation.

"Fuck, no," he replied. "Not just like that. I had to go through a lot to get here, but I did it, and I'm standing and walking because I love you and Lexi. I'm not going anywhere. I'll be here at this club every day until you listen to me. I'll let everything else go, the ranch, my brother, my friends, none of it matters if I can't prove to you and Lexi that I'm the man for you."

"It's going to take something more than you lying to me."

Aidan sat forward, unwilling to take on that sin. "I didn't lie. I followed every rule and code of conduct this club has. I trained and was approved by both the Dom in residence and the owner. I've spent countless hours training."

"I bet you did. That must have been fun."

That lurid huff in Lucas's voice got his back up. "No, sub, it wasn't fun. You will respect me while we're in this club. Or have you forgotten the contract you signed?"

Lucas leaned in slightly. "I signed that contract under false pretenses. I would never have signed a contract with you, Aidan."

That hurt but he had to keep going. "Nevertheless, you signed it, and you owe me the respect you would give any Dom. As for having fun, I suspect you're accusing me of cheating on you and Lexi. I haven't put my dick in anyone the entire time we've been apart. Can you say the same?"

Lucas's eyes came up. "Are you kidding me?"

"I have been utterly faithful, even when I was walking away."

"I don't understand you." Lucas scrubbed a hand through his hair, his frustration easy to read.

"You will. Please give me a chance."

Lucas's cell phone trilled. He pulled it out. "Lexi." He turned away, leaving Aidan feeling left out. When he finally turned back there was a stricken look on his face. "Lexi was supposed to go up to our suite."

Aidan knew exactly what was coming. Lexi had always been a hellcat. She'd never taken anything lying down. "She left, I take it?"

Lucas nodded. "She went home, but someone broke in. She says it's bad."

He hopped off the barstool. This he could handle. "Then we should go get her and bring her back to where she's supposed to be."

Lucas sighed. "It's not that easy with Lexi."

Aidan felt his blood start to pump again. Lucas was the one he had to play slow and easy. Lexi was a different type altogether. They had always been fiery. Lexi liked to yell and fight, and submit as sweet as a kitten when he'd finally won the battle. "That's what I like about it, Lucas. And she will do what I say in the end. I promise you."

He could have sworn Lucas breathed a sigh of relief as they started for the parking garage.

* * * *

Lexi kicked at her sofa. It was in utter ruins. It was the perfectly awful end to a perfectly awful day. And now her damn head was pounding. *Fuck.* She shouldn't have called Lucas, but it had been instinctive. Something bad had happened, and she pulled Lucas in.

That might have been a mistake because this time he was going to kill her. She went into the bathroom and quickly brushed her teeth. Maybe he wouldn't notice. She'd only had three shots of tequila.

95

She'd been so pissed off at her stepfather and Aidan and Julian. Even Leo had been in on it. She'd meant to go up to the suite, but she hadn't been able to force herself inside. Aidan was obviously staying in The Club, and he probably had the damn key to the place. He seemed to have taken over everything else. The last thing she'd wanted was another confrontation with him. She'd gotten dressed and walked out of The Club. Her anger had been brewing, simmering right below the surface. Her stepfather's accusations had really pissed her off. She'd decided to show him. She was an adult, not some kid. If she wanted a drink, she could have one. She'd stopped at a bar across the street from The Club before hopping on the Blue Line and heading home.

Then she'd walked up to her apartment only to find someone had kicked the door in and trashed the place. They'd taken a knife to her couch and smashed her TV. The mirror in the entryway was broken and her plants were all over the floor. She hadn't thought at all. She'd immediately called Lucas. Maybe she should have called the cops and left Lucas out of it.

Her hands were shaking. All of Jack's words were coming back to her now. Was she self-destructive? She looked in the bathroom mirror, the one that was still in one piece. There were dark smudges under her eyes. She hadn't even bothered to clean herself up. When had she let everything go? When had she stopped caring? Lexi quickly washed her face, trying to forget. She knew the day it had happened. It was burned in her brain, but knowing didn't seem to stop her.

Maybe she did need rehab.

"What the hell? Lexi?" Lucas's voice rang out and there was the fine-tinged edge of panic in his tone.

"I'm fine," she called out.

She took a towel to her face. The bathroom door swung open. Lucas wasn't a great believer in privacy these days. When had she gone from being a partner to being a burden?

"What are you doing here? Where are the cops? What the hell happened?" Lucas spat the questions out like a rapid-fire pistol, his hands cupping her shoulders. He looked her over as if discerning whether or not she was physically fine.

She let her eyes slide away from his, hoping he didn't see too much. "I came home and found it like this."

"And you decided to hang out? What if they had still been here?"

She heard another voice coming from her living room. This one was deep and authoritative. "Yes, I need you to send the police to the address I gave you. My girlfriend's apartment has been broken into."

"I'm not your girlfriend!" she shouted at Aidan. What was he doing here? She'd left The Club to get away from him and now he was standing in her apartment?

Lucas stood in her way, shaking his head. "That's not helpful."

"Maybe, but it's true." The fact that Aidan was here in her apartment made her restless. He'd never been in this apartment. He wasn't a ghost here, and now she would be able to see him here.

Suddenly Aidan was standing in the doorway, his big, muscular body taking up all the space. He seemed even bigger as he stared down at her, a stern frown on his face. She could believe the man in front of her had been a soldier.

"Would you have preferred I announced to the 911 operator that my submissive's apartment had been robbed? I chose to forgo an explanation of D/s relationships in favor of something she would understand."

He said it in an even voice that set her teeth on edge. He was calm and collected, cool and attractive, while she looked ghastly from crying and drinking—over him.

"I am not your sub. I'm Lucas's sub."

Aidan stood there, an immovable object. "And Lucas belongs to me, according to our contract. He signed over rights to top you. Or are you going to give up your membership to The Club and force Lucas to find someplace new, someplace less safe? Perhaps you can convince him to give up BDSM all together, and he can live a half-life. Is that your choice, Alexis?"

"That was rough," Lucas muttered under his breath.

Aidan turned slightly toward Lucas. "Yes, I believe I mentioned this would get rough. She won't have it any other way."

She pushed away from Lucas. It sounded like the two of them had been discussing her. She damn straight didn't like that. It felt like betrayal. "What are the two of you talking about?"

"It means that Lucas and I are of the same mind. It's far past time you got yourself together." Aidan held up a small white piece of paper. Her blood went cold as she realized what it was. "You overpaid, angel. A shot of Patron at The Club only costs twelve dollars. And this is far inferior. Though it looks like you bought in bulk."

Lucas turned her back around, and his face had flushed, his brows coming together in a *V*. "You promised me."

She shook her head. She ignored the way her heart had clenched when Aidan called her angel. That had been his pet name for her. "No, I didn't. I promised Jack, but it's not a big deal. I'm fine. Jack is overreacting."

"Jack is scared for you, and so am I." Lucas dropped his hands, and his jaw tightened as he turned from her. "I'll pack a bag for her."

"I'm not going anywhere," she said as Lucas brushed by Aidan. He didn't stop, but Aidan slid into his place, his broad shoulders forming a wall she couldn't get around.

"Are you going to make this easy on me?"

"Not on your life, asshole. You get out of my apartment, and maybe I won't tell the cops that I think you did this." She felt overwhelmed. He took up all the space in her tiny bathroom.

If he took her threat seriously, it didn't show. His face never changed from the stony expression that seemed to be his norm now. "You're welcome to try. Let me give you the lowdown on how this is going to go. You're going to be given one of two choices. As always, it's up to you. You can come back to the ranch with me and spend the next few weeks drying out and dealing with your issues, or Jack is prepared to have you committed to a rehab facility."

She had to force herself to breathe. "He can't do that."

"Oh, I assure you that with your stepfather's money and Julian's influence, we can get just about anything done. If you make the wrong choice there is a very nice rehab center in Malibu. I've got Mr. Taggart on speed dial and he'll be more than happy to collect a bonus check for carrying you onto that plane and ensuring you make it there. You'll be on a plane tonight, and you won't see the light of day for twenty-eight days. Lucas will be miserable. Your mother will be heartbroken. Are you willing to be the cause of that?"

She was willing to be the cause of his broken nose, but she doubted that he would take that well. Frustration welled. She took a step back, but stumbled, her balance fleeing in an instant. Before she could hit the tiled floor, Aidan scooped her up in his arms.

He stared down at her. "Damn it. This is serious. You can't go on like this. How many did you have?"

"Shouldn't you know? You snooped through my purse." She didn't like the way the room was slightly off-kilter, or the way his arms held her so securely. She felt delicate against him. He was so much bigger than he had been. Aidan had been gorgeous before, and the scars had taken some of his beauty, but whatever he had been through had left a solid alpha male in the place of a lovely boy. This new Aidan could prove as dangerous as the last.

"I read the amount. With the tab as big as it was, I figured it was more than one. Now, I want to know how many."

"Three," she admitted.

"This ends, Lexi. One way or another, this can't go on."

"That's not for you to say." But the words sounded stupid coming out of her mouth. She knew she was on the edge of something really bad. She was hurting the people she loved. She was acting irrationally, but it didn't matter. She couldn't tell him he was right. "You can go to hell, Aidan."

"Already been there, angel. I have the T-shirt to prove it." There was a smile on his face, the dimple she'd always loved on display. How had she missed it? His hands tightened on her as though he didn't want to even contemplate letting her go.

"Lucas won't let you do this." Lucas had his own money and his own connections. They were nothing like Jack and Julian's, but he would fight for her. The thought crossed her mind that maybe he shouldn't. Maybe he would be fighting for her by laying down his arms. Maybe he should force her into a situation where she had to face her problems. She didn't seem capable of doing it on her own. She hadn't even really wanted the tequila. She'd simply wanted to shoot everyone the finger.

Aidan's mouth turned down. "Don't do this to him. I'm begging you, Lex. Don't make him choose. It will kill him."

It would. Lucas had already made hard choices for her. He'd kept her secret even though she knew it had cost him. Ever since that terrible day in the hospital after her accident, Lucas had been lying to everyone around him. And she'd seen this man who was her best friend, her soul mate, die a little every day because Lucas wouldn't let her down. She, on the other hand, had been dragging Lucas down ever since that day. She was on the ledge, and all Lucas could do was jump with her. What if Aidan could pull them both back?

And yet she couldn't lie down.

"Fuck you."

He started to walk out of the bathroom with her nestled in his arms. "Oh, angel, I assure you, that will happen."

Her pulse jumped at the thought, and it wasn't all about anger. "Let me down."

Her feet thudded to the floor. Aidan didn't let go until she was balanced. She settled on the carpet, hating the fact that she was cold without the heat of his body against her.

"We'll stop by The Club before we leave." Aidan looked down at his watch. "It's only nine-thirty. We can be in Deer Run by one."

"I'm not going anywhere with you," she said, stubbornness settling over her like a warm blanket.

His eyes narrowed to strips of deep brown. "I'll be on the plane to California with you, and I'll be waiting when you get out. I know I walked out on you once, but I won't do that again. I'm here, and I'm going to be here as long as you need me."

Fine words and ones she'd once prayed she'd hear. But she couldn't trust him. Not again. "I don't need you."

His arms crossed over his ridiculously muscular chest. She couldn't help but remember how defined that chest had been. "You need me. Lucas needs me. And god knows I need the two of you. This is the way it's going to be, angel. I'm the Dom, you and Lucas are the subs. We're going to my ranch, and we're spending the month there."

She laughed out loud. "Not going to happen. I have a job, you idiot."

He was obviously unmoved. "Take a sabbatical. This is too important. Everyone who gives a damn about you has signed off on this plan. Do you really want to let them down?"

"I'm not going to do something simply because you say I

should." How dare he? She found herself getting in his space, puffing herself up. She wished she hadn't worn flats because she was way too short to do what she wanted to do, which was to spit in his eye. He wanted to put her in a corner? He would find out that she fought her way out. "And don't you try to guilt me into anything, you motherfucker."

"No, I can proudly proclaim I never did that," Aidan said with an oddly soft smile. "Now, I have fucked a guy. It was amazing, and I wouldn't take it back for the world. He's the love of my life, along with an incredibly obnoxious raven-haired beauty. They're my whole fucking world."

He wasn't winning her back with praise. "Good for whoever. I don't care. I'm not leaving Dallas. Call whoever you want. I'm staying here. You can have fun in Deer Run, and if Lucas wants to go with you, good for him."

The thought of Lucas leaving her tore her heart out. She would be alone. For the last two years, Lucas had been her heart. What the hell would she do if he gave up on her?

"So stubborn. It won't come to that. I love you enough to piss you off, Lexi. I'm back. I'm sorry I left, but I won't leave again. I'm in control. You can relax because I won't let you fall, angel. I'm here for you and Lucas. I'm strong enough for all of us. Lucas can do what he does best. He can make our lives easy. You can be the creative, crazy, talented woman you are because I'll take care of the big stuff and Lucas will take care of the little stuff. You're free, Lexi. You're surrounded by the men who love you."

But she wasn't surrounded by all of her men. One of her men wasn't here, and he never would be. The day of the accident swept across her brain like a wasp itching to sting. She wouldn't think about it. Damn it, she would not think about him. Tears filled her eyes, and she had to get out of here. She couldn't stand here with Aidan. She couldn't stand here when Aidan didn't even know what they had lost. She pushed past him and ran for the door.

She flung it open as she heard Lucas call her name. It was followed by Aidan barking at her. She didn't care. It only mattered that she got the hell out of there before she flung herself at Aidan and confessed every secret she had. He didn't deserve to know what had happened. He'd left, and she'd been alone with only Lucas to count on. Lucas had been there during the worst time of her life. Lucas had been the only person in the world she'd told what had happened to her. Lucas had kept her secret even though he thought she should have told her mother. Her heart picked up double-time at the thought of her mother finding out the secret she'd held so close to her heart. She didn't want her mother finding out how weak she'd been.

She started toward the parking lot, stumbling as she reached into her pocket for the keys to her car. She had no right to drive, but it didn't matter. If she went out in a blaze of glory then maybe she could see...

She stopped, a chill going through her. Had she really thought that? Had she really thought about dying?

Then it didn't matter because a crack split the air, and she fell back as the blood began to flow.

Chapter Eight

Aidan heard the sound, knew exactly what it was, and panicked. His mind immediately went to another place. He could smell the scent of gun oil and feel the street under his boots. *Fallujah. Watch your step. Mines everywhere.* He could feel the buildings shaking from the bombs dropping. He would hear the sound, and then the dark sky would light up briefly as the world shook. The dark of the night was punctuated with the staccato rhythm of high-powered rifles banging through the air. He could see them going off all around him. At first they looked like the fireflies that lit up the night by the pond on his ranch, but then he remembered.

God, he was so fucking scared. Why wouldn't the dog stop barking? He was on the ground dying and the dog kept barking. It would be the last sound he ever heard.

"What was that?" Lucas's voice yanked Aidan out of his memory. "Are you okay?"

He was sweating and shaking, and for a moment he'd been back in that hellhole looking up at the sky, knowing it was the last time. What had happened? Gunshot. He'd heard a gunshot.

"Did a car backfire?" Lucas asked, looking around. "Where's Lexi?"

Aidan ran for the front door. That hadn't been a car backfiring. He knew the difference. Someone was shooting, and Lexi had stubbornly walked outside. He hadn't thought anything of it at the time. She'd needed a bit of space because he'd pushed her, but then he'd heard that sound.

"Lexi?" Lucas shouted her name. Aidan could feel him following right behind.

Lexi's body was crumpled on the ground outside of her first-floor apartment. His heart threatened to burst. He went down on his knees and gathered her into his arms.

"It hurts like a motherfucker," Lexi said, holding her arm. She turned her face up to Aidan. "I think someone shot me. Why do people always try to kill me? I'm a nice person. I give money to starving babies and properly tip my hairdresser. Why am I the one everyone tries to kill?"

"Where are you hit?" Lucas knelt in front of them both.

Aidan could see what he was doing. He was shielding her with his own body.

"It's my arm. It's nothing big, just a scratch."

"Come on," he said, lifting her up. He needed to get them both inside where he could protect them.

The night cracked around him again, and Aidan ducked, covering Lexi and trying to pull Lucas down, too.

"Son of a bitch," Lucas yelled, and he took off.

He watched in openmouthed horror as Lucas ran toward the tree line of a nearby park. What the hell was he doing?

"Lucas, get your ass back here!" Aidan moved quickly. He hoisted Lexi up and had her inside the house as quickly as his limbs would move. He settled her on the couch and handed her his phone. "Call an ambulance. And tell the cops your break-in has turned into something worse."

Lexi tried to get up. She winced as she moved her arm, but her eyes were wide with panic. "Lucas is out there."

"Yes, and I'm going to get him." He was painfully aware that he hadn't heard anything else. There had been no third shot, but that didn't mean he was going to calm down. He couldn't calm down until Lucas was safe and over his fucking knee getting the living daylights spanked out of him.

God, he wished he had a gun. During the time he was in the Army, he'd gotten used to the feel of a gun in his hand. On the ranch, he never went without one. It made him feel safer, but Julian didn't allow them in The Club. He should take stock of the situation, but Lucas was out there and having god only knew what done to him. He didn't have time if he wanted to save Lucas. He took off running toward the park. He stayed close to the building at first, but then there was no cover to be had. Aidan simply ran. The moonlight illuminated the night, and he saw a shadowy figure standing next to one of the largest of the trees at the edge of the small park.

Lucas turned his face to Aidan. He was pale in the moonlight. He pointed to the cigarette butts on the ground around him. "At least we know he smokes."

Aidan reached out and grabbed Lucas's arm. He started back toward the apartment building. The sound of sirens in the distance let him know the cops were on their way. At least the impending arrival of the police should scare off whoever had shot at Lexi.

"Hey," Lucas protested and dug his heels in.

He turned, his body humming with adrenaline. "Don't. Don't you fucking try me right now, Lucas. I've been through enough that I'm seriously thinking about starting your punishment right now, and if you keep on pushing me, we'll be in the middle of the spanking of a lifetime when the cops get here. Do you really want that?"

Lucas stared at him for a moment, but when Aidan started to walk again, he went along with it.

Two hours later, Aidan was beginning to calm down. Lexi's left arm had been grazed by the bullet. The paramedic had taken care of her, cleaning and dressing the wound and flirting outrageously with her to the point that Aidan had been forced to stare the man down. She hadn't needed to go to the hospital, which was a damn good thing since he wasn't about to let her ride alone with the handsome paramedic.

The police had taken statements and promised all sorts of investigation, but he'd overheard them talking about the fact that gang violence was on the rise. It sounded like a way to get out of work to him. First, Lexi's apartment had been broken into and then someone had taken a shot at her. He didn't see how those two things weren't connected and could possibly both be random.

There was only one thing to do. He paced as he considered how to deliver this particular news to his wayward subs. They sat on the couch, Lexi slumped against Lucas's shoulder. Lucas had fussed over her the whole time the cops were around, obviously preferring to leave the police business to Aidan. He stroked Lexi's hair as Aidan paced, but Lucas's eyes followed him every step he took.

"So, now that we're calm again, would you like to explain to me why I'm being punished?" There was no real heat in Lucas's words, merely curiosity.

Aidan felt the heat, though. Now that all the paperwork crap was over, he could finally get back to being mad. "You ran toward the maniac with the gun, Lucas."

His brows went up. "Well, when you put it that way, it doesn't sound like a smart thing to do."

"Asshole." Lexi gently punched at him. "You scared the crap out of me. Don't ever do that again."

Lucas sighed. "I wasn't trying to get shot. I was trying to catch the guy."

"The guy with the gun." He felt like that should be pointed out over and over again until Lucas truly got the point. He would never forget the terror that had overtaken him when Lucas had run off. "You made yourself an enormous target when you should have been in this apartment, protecting Lexi."

Now Lucas's face flushed, and his eyes lowered slightly in apology. "I am sorry about that. I thought you would protect Lexi."

He hadn't been thinking at all. "It is my job to protect both of you."

"No, it's not. Not anymore." Lexi's pretty face was scrunched up in a stubborn pout.

"And you," he began, because she wasn't off the hook either. "You're due some punishment, too. Your stubbornness caused this."

Her lips formed a mulish line before she spoke. "Did not. My stubbornness doesn't even own a gun. My stubbornness is a pacifist."

He would have smiled, if he wasn't still coming down from the wretched adrenaline high of almost seeing the two loves of his life get cut down by gunfire. "If you had stayed in the apartment, you wouldn't have been a target. You would have been safe and surrounded by me and Lucas when we left."

"Great. Then you and Lucas could have been shot."

Finally she got it. "Yes, a much more acceptable conclusion."

Lexi sat up, wincing a bit as she did. "That is not a good conclusion. That is a sucky conclusion."

"Lexi, stop," Lucas ordered, his voice going hard. She sat back. "Aidan is right. We would much prefer to get shot than watch it happen to you. For the time being, you don't go anywhere alone."

"Says the boy who chased after the guy with the gun," she muttered under her breath.

Lucas reached out and stroked her hand with his. "Well, last year you got in trouble because of me. I can't let that happen again."

"You're talking about what happened with Jeremy?" Aidan asked. He'd heard the story from Taggart when he'd been briefed on what had happened to Lucas and Lexi in the time he'd been gone. A former submissive of Julian's had tried to drug Lucas, though Taggart had used the term dumbass douchebag. When he'd been found out, Julian had tossed him out. Jeremy Walker had blamed both Julian and Lucas for his misfortunes, and he'd gone after their women. Only Julian's partner, Finn, had been able to save them. Aidan had nightmares about what could have happened to Lexi. Like he needed another nightmare.

"Yeah," Lucas said, his face falling. "He wanted to hurt me. He kidnapped Lexi and pumped a bunch of drugs through her system. He was going to kill her. I thought he had when I found her."

Lexi's hand curled over Lucas's.

"It wasn't your fault." He believed that. If anything, it had been his because he had been in Iraq getting his ass blown off. It was honorable to serve his country but not when he hadn't made any arrangements to keep his loves safe. They had been all alone. They had been without a Dom. Now that he truly understood what they needed, he felt the heavy weight of guilt. He should never have left them. He'd allowed his own need to be accepted by society in general to outweigh the love in his heart. "Lucas, you did the best you could. I'm very proud of you."

He could see the way Lucas relaxed. Praise meant a lot to him. Lucas wanted to please. He needed it. He needed this whole D/s thing. It completed him in a way Aidan couldn't have imagined before he'd gotten involved in the lifestyle. Lexi needed it, too. She would fight him, but she needed it.

"Lucas," Aidan began, "we need to get your punishment out of the way. Present yourself to me. Count of twenty."

He heard Lucas's intake of breath. It was sharp and shocked, and yet his skin flushed with arousal. There was a lot Lucas needed that he had never gotten. It was the true beauty of the power exchange.

"You don't have to," Lexi said.

He felt every muscle in his body still. Lexi had an enormous amount of influence over Lucas. She could guilt him into almost anything. Would she? She'd always been incredibly sweet, a thoughtful, caring woman. Had she changed in the years they had been apart?

A seductive smile curled her mouth up. "You don't have to take any punishment from him, but I kind of think it would be hot. Not that I like Aidan. He's still a dick and a half, but you might like it, babe. And I would love to watch you."

Aidan's heart swelled. She was a bitch to the end, but god, she was a loving one. His Lexi would never judge or hold another human being to some meaningless standard. She'd given Lucas permission to be who he was.

"Well, I did sign a contract." Lucas stood, and his hands were on his pants. He pushed his leathers down to his knees. He turned and presented his ass to his Dom.

It was all Aidan could do not to drool. Lucas Cameron was masculine perfection. His cheeks were muscled. He had a tan line that spoke of his modesty. Aidan liked it because he didn't want anyone else looking at what he considered his. Lucas was his. Lexi was his. He could handle people looking at their bodies in a club where everyone knew the rules, but the private thing had its glories, too.

"Count it out, sub."

"Yes, Sir."

Aidan began. His hand rained down on the cheeks of Lucas's ass. Lucas's voice rang out. There was no small amount of pride in his count. Aidan pulled his hand back, loving the feel of the crack on Lucas's flesh. His ass took a pounding with grace and glory. His flesh pinkened up beautifully.

Lexi leaned forward, watching as he struck Lucas's cheeks over and over.

"Fifteen." Lucas's ass actually wiggled a bit as though he was trying to tempt him in.

God, he would love that. He could still remember the tight clench of that gorgeous asshole on his dick. Lucas's ass had been the tightest hole he'd ever sunk his cock into. But he had a point to make. He slapped that ass again and again until Lucas finally called out, "Twenty."

He stopped and realized his breath was choppy. His cock was at full-mast, straining against his pants.

Lexi's eyes had glazed over. She was watching Lucas's exposed flesh with a diligence that made Aidan's breath catch. She was so submissive. Maybe not all the time, but she liked it when it came to sex. Why hadn't he listened to her in the first damn place?

"Is that all, Sir?" Lucas asked with perfect politeness, as though he was asking about the weather, not as if his Dom wanted to further torture him.

Oh, Aidan wanted more. He wanted to lube up his cock and sink it into that hot hole while Lucas fucked the hell out of Lexi's pussy. He wanted to fuck his subs until they couldn't move anymore, and then he would sink into the bed with them and sleep with his limbs tangled in theirs. But he hadn't earned it yet.

"That is all, Lucas. You did well. Now, get dressed. It's a long way to Deer Run, and we have to stop by The Club to pick up my things."

Lucas straightened up. He buttoned his pants and then held his hand out for Lexi to take. Lexi stared at him for a moment.

"You really want me to do this?" she asked.

Lucas's hand tightened on hers. "I do, baby. Please. I want to try this."

Her eyes filled with tears, and it struck Aidan that the only reason he was getting a second chance was because Lexi loved Lucas. It didn't matter why. His heart ached, but it truly didn't matter. It only mattered that he had the chance. He would make it right.

Lexi allowed Lucas to draw her up. "All right then. No rehab for me. We'll try the BDSM approach to fixing a fucked-up chick. Should be fun." She turned to Aidan. "Not that you'll have any fun. I know my safe word, and I intend to use it."

She flounced away, walking to the door and standing there.

Lucas picked up the bag he'd packed for her. "She hasn't joked like that in a very long time. Thank you, Aidan."

Tears pricked at Aidan's eyes. He might be the bad guy, but he felt pretty damn good in that moment.

* * * *

Lexi sighed as Aidan pulled his truck into The Club's parking garage. They were heading to Aidan's hometown in a few minutes, and there was absolutely nothing she could do about it. Lucas had set a course, and she would follow it. He needed this and that was why she was going along with the plan. It had nothing to do with the way her heart sped up when Aidan looked her way.

There was no question about it. Aidan O'Malley was infinitely more dangerous now. The pretty boy was gone, and in his place was a man who knew how to take control. He'd mastered Lucas. The spanking he'd delivered to Lucas had gotten her wet and twitchy in a way she'd never been before. Watching Lucas submit did something for her. They had sat together, waiting for Aidan's judgment, their fingers tangling like flowers growing together in the sunshine. Plot twist—Aidan was the sun.

She had to stop thinking that way. He would walk out on them the minute the going got tough. Lucas was the one she could count on. It was just that he'd looked so fulfilled as he took that punishment. Lucas's joy was what had her thinking about Aidan.

It wouldn't come to anything. Lucas had spent his whole life without discipline. His parents had utterly ignored him. He hadn't had anyone who cared until he'd met Jack. Lucas had a skewed view of life, and so did she. Everyone except her mother had died on her. It made a person think.

That was why they needed a Dom. It didn't have to be Aidan.

"I can't go," she said suddenly, her mind catching on a problem. "I have to be at work tomorrow."

It was Friday. They had an opening on Saturday. They would need her to do the grunt work that any monkey with half a brain could do. Someone needed to make a Starbucks run. Someone had to convince the gallery owner's wife that her face didn't look like a weird piece of plastic someone had applied blush to. That last part was the hardest part of her job because that woman had had way too much surgery. Still, it was her job, and she was paid very little money to do it.

"You're fine, Lexi." Lucas sat in the passenger's side seat and sent her a smooth smile. "Everything's been taken care of."

"Really?" She had to ask because her boss was an asshole with a two-by-four shoved up his anus.

"Yes, I called and quit for you," Aidan said flatly.

"See, no problem." Lucas slid a hand around her shoulder.

"You did what?" She was well aware that her screech reverberated through the cab.

Aidan brought the truck to a stop in front of the valet station. Even at this time of the night, there was a well-dressed young man eager to help. "I quit for you."

Lucas slipped out of the cab as the valet opened the door. He turned and held his hand out to assist her. "Don't be upset. You were three months in. It was only another week or so before you quit or got yourself fired. Aidan merely upped the timeline."

She allowed Lucas to guide her out of the truck. It was pretty judgmental of them. Sure, she'd had a bunch of jobs in the last two years. She hadn't found the right place. It didn't give Aidan the right to quit a job she loved. Except that she kind of hated it and *had* been thinking about quitting. The only reason she hadn't was the way her stepfather had groaned when she told him she needed a reference.

She could write.

The idea teased at the back of her brain. Lately, the stories had started to return, but she didn't deserve them.

"Oh, Lexi!" A curvy blonde rushed toward her, encasing her in a bear hug. "Are you okay?"

She hugged Dani Lodge-Taylor. Julian and Finn's wife was one of her closest friends. "I'm fine. I take it Aidan called Julian."

"Yes, he did and then I called in McKay-Taggart." Julian stepped up with Finn by his side. He looked her over as though assessing what damage had been done and what he needed to do about it. Finn shook Lucas's hand and asked how things had gone with the police.

There were three other men with him. She recognized Sean Taggart. Before the group had built their own club, they'd spent some time in Julian's and she'd gotten to know the former Green Beret. When he'd hung around The Club, he'd spent as much time in the kitchens as he had the dungeon floor. If she remembered correctly, the man could cook.

The other two were strangers. Sean Taggart looked an awful lot like his older brother, but he smiled more. He was infinitely more approachable than Ian.

She briefly studied the other two. One was dressed in jeans and a T-shirt, the other in slacks and a button down. Both were built, their clothes not able to hide the fact that these were dudes who spent time at the gym. She finally allowed her gaze to find their faces. Twins. Superhot twins. Given the air of authority they gave off, Lexi couldn't help but think of them as gorgeous Dom Ken dolls.

"Is this the pretty princess we're supposed to protect?" the one in the T-shirt asked. He was a flirty one.

Lucas actually stepped in front of her, his chest puffing out. Lexi couldn't help but grin a little. She thought he might do that gorilla-chest-thumping-thing. It was sweet.

Then she looked at Aidan and was pretty sure he was about to kill someone. When had he gotten so intimidating?

Julian's hand was already out, waving off the tension. "Don't you two start. Aidan, I called Ian. He's unavailable tonight. His brother came out and offered me an alternative. You had to know I would call my security team."

"I'm glad Big Tag is locked in Sanctum listening to hair metal," the guy in the slacks said. "I would hate to have missed out on this. I love close cover work."

Sean Taggart sighed. "We're not supposed to talk about that. And we were always going to place you two with Mr. Lodge. We've been training the Dawson brothers specifically to handle things like this for Mr. Lodge."

"McKay-Taggart is growing," Julian explained. "It's good for my investment, not good for my personal security needs. This isn't close cover. She doesn't need a bodyguard. I believe Aidan and Lucas can handle that. You're here to investigate the threat. Are you sure these two are ready?"

"Ian is absolutely certain. Chase is genius-level smart and Ben has some incredible instincts," Sean replied, nodding toward the guy in the T-shirt.

Ben winked. "I've got great abs, too. Are we sure she doesn't need a bodyguard?"

Sean shook his head. "You're going to need a body bag if you fuck this up, Ben." He turned back to Julian. "Ian's been working with them a lot lately because we're taking on a case in Fort Worth. It's a big one and requires most of the team." He frowned. "I have to play the corporate role. I hate going undercover as a dude who works in sales, but I'm the only one who can do it. Ian's too sarcastic. Liam is a walking sexual harassment suit. Alex is too morose, and Jake and Adam are going in with me. I'm pretty sure our target is straight. That leaves Eve out. I'm the man meat, as Ian would say. So you're left with these guys. Don't worry. We'll be monitoring them for the next couple of weeks."

Dani leaned in and whispered in Lexi's ear. "That's Ben and Chase Dawson. They're private investigators and bodyguards. Ben used to be on Leo's SEAL team, and Chase was on another team. Julian asked McKay-Taggart to train them specifically to be in his in-house security. He's going to put them on retainer because so many of his friends end up with people trying to murder them that it made sense to get a group discount. Part of their deal is that they get access to The Club."

"Thank you for the play-by-play, little one." Julian gestured toward the doors to the elevator. "Could we take this upstairs? I'd like to talk to Aidan and Lucas and fill in Ben and Chase. Finn has already contacted the DA. I assure you they will take this seriously."

Lexi held up her hand. "Uh, hello, victim here. Shouldn't I be in on this conversation?"

Julian's left eyebrow practically reached the ceiling. "Are you going to be reasonable?"

"Nope. I'll be a bitch." She decided it was a night for honesty.

"Then no," Julian replied, utterly nonplussed. "Please go and retrieve Lucas's bag from the suite you vacated without your Dom's permission. Then perhaps you and Danielle can have a drink in the bar."

She frowned. "Yeah, I don't think I'm allowed to do that anymore."

A brilliant smile crossed Julian's face as the elevator dinged open. "Then my evil plan, as my wife so lovingly put it, has worked."

Sean stopped in front of her. "Are you all right? I heard you got shot, but you look okay."

She shrugged. "Physically, I'm cool. It was nothing but a scratch. I guess I'm good at ducking."

"That is a good life skill to have." His lips tugged up in a grin. "How's your mom?"

Sean liked to flirt with her mom. Way more than he'd ever flirted with her. "Still married to two incredibly mean men."

He sighed. "Well, if that ever changes, you tell her to give me a call."

"I don't think she needs more..." What had he called himself? Sometimes she wanted to sit in at the offices of McKay-Taggart and take notes. They were an interesting group. "Man meat."

The man they called Little Tag winked her way. "Every lady needs some man meat, sweetheart. And I tease your mother because she's quite lovely and safe to flirt with because of those men of hers. I like her. Oddly enough, the target of this new investigation reminds me a little of her. She's a single mom, too. Smart. Pretty."

"Sounds like you're already interested." She had to wonder what kind of single mom became the target of a McKay-Taggart investigation.

"She could be a terrorist. I probably shouldn't be, but you know the nights can be long," Sean said.

"Taggart, it's late," Julian said impatiently. "Could you stop flirting?"

"Why is he allowed to flirt and we're not?" one of the gorgeous twins asked.

"Because I'm the boss tonight." But Sean was already turning. "Until Big Brother comes out of his yearly weird funk that we're not supposed to talk about, I'm responsible for you two. Let's get this briefing over with. I've got a flight to Chicago in the morning."

The men piled into the elevator, but she held back. Dani stayed at her side.

"We'll catch the next one," Dani said. "And I'll make sure all of Master A's things are packed and ready to go."

"Thank you, Danielle," Aidan replied with a gentle smile that turned to a slight scowl when he turned his attention to Lexi. "You behave."

"I make no promises." She turned to Dani after the doors closed. "You are too good. I was going to shove everything he owned into a trash bag and toss it in the back of the truck."

Dani held her hand and rushed into the next elevator that opened. "Come on. We need to hurry before Julian figures out what's going on. I thought you might like to meet the competition. Some woman showed up in the lobby asking for Aidan, claiming to be his fiancée. The concierge called Julian, but he was all freaked out because of the shooting thing, so he told me to handle it. Want to help me handle it?"

Aidan's fiancée? Oh, yeah, she wanted to help handle that.

Dani turned to her. "I didn't know. I'm sorry. If I had any idea of what Julian was planning, I would have called you."

And then she would have gotten into serious trouble with her Dom. "Don't worry about it. Lucas is happy. He wants to try the Dom thing for a while. I would rather it wasn't with the man who ripped my heart out of my body, stomped on it, and set it on fire, but I owe Lucas. And I owe Jack. And, quite frankly, I owe Julian."

It was true. She was drifting, and she knew it. She hadn't done a very good job on her own. Maybe it was time to give something else a try. If this could get her out of the funk she'd been in the last several years, it would be worth it.

The doors opened to the lobby. The lobby of The Club was an elegant showcase. Part hotel lobby, part wealthy office space, it was streamlined and modern. As Lexi exited the elevator, she could hear

115

the high-pitched whining coming from the front desk.

"I don't care about what your job is. I want to talk to my fiancé. I know he's here. I'm not going anywhere until I get escorted up to his room." The blonde standing at the front desk actually stomped her foot.

She had big, platinum blonde hair. She wore white jeans and a tight top that showed off boobs that were far too large for her small frame.

"Mrs. Lodge." The concierge was visibly relieved. "Thank you for coming down. I'm having a bit of a problem with this lady. She doesn't seem to understand that we are a private club."

The blonde's scarlet red lips pursed. "And I explained that my fiancé, Aidan O'Malley, is a member here. He's a rancher. He owns one of the largest spreads in Central Texas."

"His dad died?" She hadn't heard that information. She'd met the man a time or two. Aidan hadn't been terribly close to his father. He'd lost his mom at an early age, and Conner O'Malley had been a bit distant, but it had to have hurt Aidan to lose his dad. What else had changed in Aidan's life?

The blonde shifted her focus, and cool blue eyes narrowed. "Do you know Aidan?"

Dani stepped forward. "I would say she does. She was engaged to him once."

Her nose turned up as though it had caught a whiff of something vile. "You're that Lexi person?"

Oh, she was going to be trouble. First, Lexi didn't honestly believe that this woman was engaged to Aidan. Aidan had been a rat bastard, but he'd never lied to her. He wouldn't have come after her and Lucas if he had a fiancée tucked away somewhere. "Yep, that's me."

"What are you doing here?"

Dani stepped up. "Lexi is a member of this club. Her stepfather is the largest independent rancher in the state of Texas. And she's here because Aidan brought her here. Aidan is upstairs with my husband. He should be down in a minute. I'm sure he'll be thrilled to see you."

That overly painted mouth opened and closed like a fish out of water. "Well, he doesn't know I'm here. I thought I would surprise

116

him."

She tapped her foot, and it finally clicked. Karen Wilcox. Aidan's high school girlfriend. Lexi hadn't had the privilege of meeting her. She and Aidan had only gone to Deer Run a few times. From what she could remember, Karen had been married to someone significantly older than she was.

"I think he'll be surprised," Lexi allowed. She was pretty sure he'd be pissed. A kernel of evil joy lit inside her. She pulled out her cell phone. "Why don't we give him a call?"

She dialed Lucas's number. He answered immediately, his voice low, as though he didn't want to disrupt what was going on. "Lexi? Are you all right?"

"I am more than fine, babe. I'm down in the lobby talking to Aidan's fiancée."

"What?" Lucas practically screamed over the phone. "We'll be down there in a minute."

She disconnected the call and felt a smile split her face. "He'll be down in a minute."

Dani turned back to the concierge, shaking her head. "Paul, I think we're going to need someone from the staff to go grab Mr. O'Malley's and Mr. Cameron's bags. Please give them to the valet. I don't think Lexi is going to want to miss this."

"Not for anything."

"He dumped you." Karen's perfectly manicured nails curled around her purse. "He called off your wedding."

"Yep," Lexi agreed. "Which begs the question of why he's dragging my ass back home to Deer Run when he has such a lovely fiancée waiting for him?"

Dani leaned over. "Does she come with a superhot, somewhat submissive, bi guy?"

"What is that? Is that some city talk?" Karen huffed a bit as though that was the worst thing she could think of. "It doesn't matter. I want to know what you're doing with my fiancé."

She went over the mental list before explaining her night to Karen. "Well, let's see, he's spanked me, forced me to undress in front of an audience, shoved a plug up my ass, followed me home, and now he's kidnapping me."

"Drama queen," Dani said with a grin.

Karen actually took a step back. "Aidan would never do that. He's a former soldier. He served his country."

"And soldiers don't like to spank girls?" She wondered how sheltered Karen's life had been. She turned to Dani. "And I had to take that plug out myself. I hope he doesn't expect to see that one again."

The doors to the elevator slid open, and the former soldier they were talking about stalked out, a fierce frown on his face. "What are you doing here, Karen? How did you even find out where I was?"

The blonde's whole demeanor changed. One minute she was the queen bee bitch of the world, and the next, she'd softened and even her voice went little-girl high. "Well, I wanted to be with you. It's been a week since you came and saw me."

Aidan's face bunched up in confusion. "I came out to your place because I was dropping off a check for the charity dinner. I wasn't seeing you."

Karen moved closer to Aidan. Her voice was all breathy and pouty. It made Lexi want to gag. "Well, we can fix that. Dwight let it slip where you were, and I tracked you down. What kind of place is this? Are you okay here? This woman is making all sorts of accusations about you."

His head shook, and Lexi could have sworn he smiled a bit. "Yes, I'm sure she did. Lucas, will you escort Lexi down to the truck? We're done here. Ben and Chase can come out to the ranch if they need anything else. I'll deal with this one."

Lucas seemed perfectly satisfied to take her by the arm and start to lead her away.

She wasn't happy though. "Hey, I was enjoying that."

Lucas slipped his fingers through hers. He leaned over and kissed her firmly on the lips. "Yes, I know. Now stop causing trouble, or we'll both get spanked again."

"Unfair! I'm not the one who hid my identity. And that whole shooting thing was not my fault." She was arguing, but she didn't put any heat behind it. Despite what she said, she did feel safer now that they were leaving town. Someone had shot at her. She was putting on a brave front, but she was scared. And she couldn't go to her mom's place. She wouldn't put her sister and brother in harm's way.

And she could figure out why Aidan had come back. That was the worst reason of all to want to go. That way led to danger.

"And the drinking?"

Lexi shrugged. She had no excuse for that. She leaned into Lucas's strength. As they walked away, it struck her that Karen smelled like she smoked.

Maybe Deer Run wouldn't be so safe. Either way, she was going to find out.

Chapter Nine

Lucas pushed through the double doors of the ranch house with a slightly reinvigorated lease on life. Lexi was sleeping peacefully in the ridiculously oversized bed Aidan had set up in the master bedroom. Lucas had never been to Aidan's Central Texas ranch, and last night's 4:00 a.m. arrival hadn't told him much. However, he seriously doubted that the master bedroom had been in this elegant and oversized condition when Aidan's father had been alive. As far as Lucas knew, the elder O'Malley hadn't been a ladies' man, so he doubted he'd required a custom-made bed with a delicate white quilt and three dressers. That room had been remodeled to fit a ménage.

Aidan was thinking positively.

Aidan would need a dose of positivity after the way his night had ended. The man had been mulishly quiet during the long drive from Dallas to the ranch. He'd apparently had some form of conversation with the woman named Karen that put him in a mood. When Lucas asked about her, Aidan had simply said that she wasn't his fiancée or his girlfriend, and Lucas wasn't to worry about her.

But Karen had that look, that psycho "I'll cut you" look under all the sugary sweetness she'd laid on Aidan. He knew the type all too well. One of those had tried to kill Lexi just a year ago. He wasn't taking any chances. He'd already emailed the Dawson brothers with Karen Wilcox's name and cc'd Taggart on that bit of information. He wanted a full report. It was a long shot. She hadn't seemed to know Lexi was involved with Aidan, but he couldn't leave that stone unturned.

Lucas shook off the thought and started to look around for a coffee mug. His darling was a bit of a nightmare before she had her coffee. He often set the coffee down on the nightstand in front of her, shook her gently awake, and ran before she was in angry-badger mode.

The kitchen looked worn, with old appliances and faded curtains. Now that Lucas really looked around, the whole place had a slightly dilapidated air to it as though he knew it had once been prosperous. Those days were now gone. It surprised him because the bedroom he and Lexi had been taken to last night had been polished to perfection.

"If you're looking for the mugs, they're in the cupboard on the left."

He turned and smiled at the slightly younger man who could only be Aidan's brother, Bo. He was the spitting image of Aidan from four years before. "Thank you. I'm Lucas."

"Yeah, I know who you are. You're my brother's...buddy."

And he knew about Lucas's relationship with Aidan. That one word "buddy" held an edge of distaste. Some of his friendliness was whisked away. He poured Lexi's coffee in the mug. "I was at one point. Thank you for your help."

He turned to go back toward the room he and Lexi had stayed in the night before.

"Wait."

He glanced back at Bo. The young man looked like he was in his early twenties, dressed in jeans and a T-shirt. His hair was still wet, probably from a shower. The sun had come up hours before. Aidan had been out working with the dawn, despite only a few hours of sleep. Lucas knew that because he'd heard him moving around and then glimpsed him on horseback through the window. He waited patiently for Aidan's brother to further castigate him for his sexual proclivities.

"Is Lexi all right?" Bo asked, staring down at his feet.

Lucas sighed. *Well, naturally*. Lexi was stunning, with raven black hair and a figure that harkened back to a fifties pin-up. He knew she was always worried about her weight, but she was utterly perfect in his mind. Soft and sweet and so fuckable he was getting hard just thinking about her. It wasn't a surprise that Aidan's baby brother had a thing for Lexi. He would have been a teen when they'd been engaged. "She's fine, but we all need to watch out for her. Someone took a shot at her. We don't know everything yet, but if you notice anyone odd hanging around, let me or Aidan know."

"Yeah, okay. I was real upset to hear someone tried to hurt her." Bo paused, a flush heating his face. "So you're my brother's boyfriend?"

Lucas answered because the question had been asked with a modicum of civility. "No. I was your brother's failed experiment. Now we're involved in a short-term D/s relationship which means that for the time being, as long as it pleases me, I will do as he says."

Bo's eyes were back up and there was an unmistakable note of confusion in them. Lucas wondered exactly what Aidan had told him about their relationship. "But you slept with Lexi last night. Aidan slept in the guest bedroom."

"He did, indeed. Lexi isn't terribly happy with Aidan right now. We'll see. I have some plans that might bring her around." Now that he'd started down the path that led he and Lexi into a permanent sexual relationship, he was impatient. He'd played a very long game with her. Being with Lexi forever was far more important than immediate gratification, but now that the finish line was in sight, he was anxious. The D/s relationship they were exploring gave him exactly what he needed to move this along. And he knew he was fooling himself. Short-term wasn't what he was interested in with Aidan.

Bo's head shook. "I don't understand a lick of this. If some guy was coming after my girl, I would kick his ass, not try to come up with a way to get her into bed with him."

"Oh, my plan doesn't involve a bed at all, so don't worry about it."

"What's going on in here?" Aidan's big, beautiful form suddenly filled the doorway. He walked in from the back porch into the kitchen. He wore a pair of faded Levi's, cowboy boots, and a T-shirt that was already drenched in sweat and clinging to his chest. A cowboy hat sat on his head, pulled down over his brow. His brown eyes shifted suspiciously from his brother to Lucas and back.

"Not a thing," Lucas said, watching the way Bo suddenly puffed up the minute his brother walked in the room. His demeanor went from slightly unsure to arrogant in a heartbeat.

Bo's face tightened, and his lips became slightly cruel.

"I was talking to your butt buddy here. I think I'll go into town, be around some real men." Bo turned on his boot heels and started toward the front door.

Aidan's face hardened, and he started to go after Bo.

"I would prefer you didn't, Sir." He kept his voice even and quiet, not argumentative. He really was making a request.

Aidan stopped, his hand on the door. "He's being an ass, and I won't allow it. He won't be allowed to insult you or Lexi in my home."

There really was something about another person protecting him that got Lucas's juices flowing. Perhaps it was his crappy childhood, but Lucas was well aware he was a sucker for a protective man or woman. Lexi had made him her slave the day she defended him to some of the nastier people of her mother's hometown. Of course, his crappy childhood had taught him other things, too. "First, it's his home, too. And second, I seriously doubt Bo would ever hurt Lexi. He cares about her. Now, I'm another story."

"He's being a small-minded, homophobic prick, and I won't stand for it."

Sometimes siblings couldn't see the forest for the trees. Lucas's own full siblings saw him as a waste of flesh. Of course, his father had done nothing to help. But Lucas knew what it was like to want an older sibling's attention. "No, Sir, he's being your baby brother. Tell me something, Aidan. Were the two of you close when you were younger?"

Aidan's head came up, turning to Lucas. "Yes. We were really close. That's what makes me crazy. We had to survive our father. Dad was remote and unapproachable and exacting. We were never quite good enough for him. He was particularly hard on Bo. I had to take

123

care of him, especially when Dad got to drinking."

"Yes, and then you left him to go to college, and then the Army, and now you're back and in control of the ranch with not one, but two potential lovers. He doesn't understand where his brother went," Lucas explained. "He misses his brother. You might consider not being so hard on him."

"Lucas, you can't expect me to let that go."

"It was merely an observation." Lucas started back out the door.

"Wait. I'll think about what you said." Aidan stood close. Lucas could feel the heat from his body, but he couldn't give in to it. "Can you come out and help me in the barn? My foreman hasn't come in to work, and obviously Bo isn't going to be helpful. I need an extra set of hands."

Ranch work. Yeah, he knew a bit about that. Some hard physical labor might calm his cock down. Between cuddling with Lexi and being so close to Aidan, he was pretty damn frustrated. He held up the coffee mug. "I can do that. Let me feed the beast and then I'll go with you."

Aidan's lips quirked up as he looked at the mug in Lucas's hands. "Be quick. She's deadly before she has her coffee."

Lucas's heart seized a little. This was what he wanted. He wanted the camaraderie of a threesome. He was self-aware enough to know that he wanted to have his cake and eat it, too. There was a component of getting everything he wanted sexually in there, but it went beyond that. He wanted to not be alone. Even in a traditional relationship, there was a certain amount of loneliness. If he married Lexi, no one else would know what it meant to be her husband. Oh, but if they had Aidan, he would always be there, backing Lucas up and laughing over all of Lexi's adorable quirks. When she confused him, he could lean on Aidan. When she was hurting, they could surround her.

"Lucas?" Aidan's hand came out as though he realized Lucas was getting emotional.

Lucas stepped back. He couldn't. Not yet. Sex was fine, but he wasn't ready for that true, pure intimacy that came with comforting another human being. "I'll be ready in a minute."

He didn't miss the way Aidan's face fell.

* * * *

Aidan wanted to scream. Every time he thought he was getting close to making a breakthrough, Lucas pulled away. As for Lexi, well, she'd made herself plain the night before when he'd shown them to the room he'd renovated with every bit of savings he had. He'd taken the master bedroom and turned it into something comfortable for them.

And Lexi had slammed the door in his face.

"You can make me come out here, but you can't make me sleep with you," she had said.

He hadn't expected to, but it rankled that Lucas was on the other side of that door and he wasn't. Would they have sex now that he'd gotten them together? Aidan was well aware that they hadn't had intercourse up to this point. Would they use the big bed he'd made for the three of them to remedy that problem?

Jealousy had burned through his gut. He wanted to be with them. He had to be patient. Lucas was the smartest man he knew, and Lucas had been patient. It was time to take a cue from him.

Aidan watched Lucas walk away and promised himself he wouldn't fuck up again. He'd lost them once because he'd been an idiot who couldn't handle his own emotions. He'd been a slave to convention and terrified of what his father would have thought. His father, who had never once said he loved him. His father, who had told Aidan that playing the guitar was for wimps and real men ranched or went into the Army.

Patience. He had to believe he could win them back. Bringing them out here was the first step. He wished he had a nicer place to bring them to. Lucas had grown up rich, and Lexi's stepfather was one of the wealthiest men in Texas. The ranch was falling apart around him. The land itself was worth a fortune, and he had a fine herd, but he was putting almost everything he had into changing his practices so he could go organic. He had gone into business with Barnes-Fleetwood, but it wouldn't pay for a couple of years. What could he really offer them?

The back door banged open, and Dwight came in. "Hey, nice to have you back, buddy. I thought you were staying in Dallas for a while."

"My plans changed. I brought Lucas and Lexi back here."

Dwight's eyes widened, and he whistled through his teeth. "I hope Deer Run is ready for that."

"I don't care if they are or not." The town could go to hell for all he cared. This town was one of the reasons he'd walked out on the best thing he'd ever had. It was important to fit in. Small towns thrived on community, and flaunting one's individuality didn't work. He'd been horrified at the thought of bringing Lucas home with him, horrified that someone might find out he wasn't "normal."

Normality could rot. He wanted love.

Dwight put a hand on his back. "Well, I'll stand behind you. You know I got your back."

Dwight had proven a dependable friend. It was strange. They hadn't really been close until that terrible day when Aidan had almost died in the sand, the sound of gunfire and barking dog filling his senses, the thought of Lexi and Lucas the only thing he could cling to. Since that day, Dwight had been by his side. Sometimes he worried it was all survivor guilt that made Dwight follow him back to Deer Run. They were the only two of their squad to survive that terrible day.

"Where did you get off to last night?" Aidan asked, remembering Bo's complaint from the night before. Dwight lived in the foreman's house behind the barn. He was a loner. He didn't have many friends aside from Aidan.

"Oh, I went out for a beer and then, well, you know."

Aidan grinned. "Which lovely young lady caught your eye?"

"One of the new waitresses at the Two Horse Saloon."

"Ah," Aidan said, happy Dwight was getting out a bit. The Two Horse Saloon was a bar on the edge of town. Deer Run was dry, but cowboys always found a way around things like the law when it came to getting a beer after a hard day's work.

"And I am sorry about Karen. Did she find you?" Dwight asked, his mouth turning down. "She caught me in a weak moment. I was talking about you to Darla, the waitress I hooked up with. I was talking about The Club and how nice you said it was. I didn't realize Karen was sitting next to me. That girl is psycho."

Well, at least he understood how Karen had shown up. He'd tried to explain to her that he wasn't interested. He wasn't sure she'd gotten the message. But that wasn't Dwight's fault. "Don't worry about it."

Once Karen saw him around town with Lexi and Lucas, she would get the picture.

There was a scratching at the back door and a little whine. He walked across the kitchen and let in the only good thing he'd found in Iraq.

"Hey, Ike, how you doing, boy?" He got down on one knee, wincing at the pain, but he was used to it. The dog was a mutt, some odd mix of retriever and Great Dane. He was a huge monster, but sweet as the day was long after he'd settled in. He'd been adopted by Aidan's squad. Though the Army banned pets on base, the truth was most officers looked the other way. He'd nearly cried the day his former platoon CO showed up on the ranch leading Ike by a leash.

Ike's nub of a tail wagged, and he licked Aidan's face frantically. It was like this every time he left. Though Ike didn't mind Bo, he preferred Aidan to everyone else. Ike looked up and started to growl.

"Don't," Aidan commanded.

Ike growled at a lot of men. He'd done it in Iraq, growling and barking at everyone. It had taken Aidan a while to get the dog to come to him. He wasn't sure why he'd tried. Maybe he'd seen something in the dog that called to him. Ike had obviously needed affection, but he'd been too scared to take it. Yeah, he and the dog had a lot in common. Eventually Ike had calmed down, but despite the fact that he'd been around Dwight during their time in Iraq, the dog still growled when he got too near. Aidan really hoped Ike and Lucas got along. The last thing he needed was for Ike to hate Lucas.

"Dumb dog," Dwight said as he started out the back door. "I'll be out in the south field. We're going to have to replace that whole section of fence. I'll take Clint with me."

Dwight slammed out the back door, and Ike calmed down.

"Hey, boy," Lucas said in that honey chocolate voice of his. Aidan looked back and he was on one knee with a hand held out.

"He doesn't like a lot of people," Aidan warned him.

"That's okay," Lucas replied. "He doesn't have to do anything he doesn't want to."

127

But Ike was already moving toward the stranger. He sniffed Lucas's hand warily, his nose poking and retreating as though he expected a slap at any moment. Lucas was patient, allowing the dog to become accustomed, to make his own judgment.

"That's right, boy. We can be friends." Lucas patted the dog's head, and Ike's stub started to wag again.

Just like that, Lucas made friends with a dog who took forever to get used to anyone. Aidan watched them with a great deal of pleasure.

"This coffee needs sugar," Lexi groused as she walked into the room. There was a dour look on her pretty face, and her hair was tousled from sleep. She wasn't a morning person, but Aidan had always thought she looked so damn cute when she was grumpy. She frowned at him, but her face lit up when she saw the dog. "Oh, hi, puppy!"

Lexi set the mug down and was on her knees in an instant. Aidan's first thought was to warn her about the dog's bad temper, but apparently they were soul mates. Ike abandoned Lucas and started sniffing Lexi. She ran her hands all over the dog's massive, somewhat stinky body.

"He needs a bath." It was stupid but Ike was important to him. He wanted Lexi to think his dog was nice to be around.

Lexi grinned as the dog licked her face. "He's perfect. You're a pretty boy, aren't you?"

Lucas stood and lent Aidan a hand. "Come on. She's lost to us now. Let's get some work done. Actually, there's a side project I'd like to talk to you about."

He took Lucas's hand and allowed Lucas to help him up. Even with the help, his back seized, and Aidan stumbled. Lucas steadied him, but the weakness had shown itself. Aidan flushed and inwardly cursed the muscles that always let him down now. He pulled away, not wanting to lean on Lucas.

Lucas's arm tightened on his. "Stop it, Sir. Let me help."

He made it to his feet, but he couldn't help the sense of shame that flushed through his system. His legs still didn't work right even after all the work he'd done.

"Doms." Lexi was shaking her head as she petted the dog. Aidan looked at her, ready for the rush of pity he got from a lot of people.

"Such dumbasses."

No pity from his girl.

"I believe what our lovely and infinitely sympathetic female is trying to say is, lean on us," Lucas explained. "The mistake most Doms make is to think that we're burdens or something soft to play with in bed. We're a part of this. If you don't want our help and support, then we're worth nothing to you. I don't intend to submit to a man who needs nothing from me but sexual pleasure."

"What he said," Lexi shot back, but her lips were quirking up.

He leaned into Lucas and allowed himself to steady before he pulled away. He took a long, deep breath to control the deep emotion welling up inside him. What Lucas was talking about wasn't a D/s relationship. He was talking about a family. "Thank you. I promise the next time my back gives out and I'm going to fall to the floor, I'll let you catch me."

"I would appreciate it, Sir. Now, can I go play cowboy?"

He nodded. Lucas was a lawyer, but he'd spent enough time on a cattle ranch that he knew what he was doing. Lucas on a horse was a sight to be seen.

"Great. What am I supposed to do?" Lexi asked, standing up. Ike sat down beside her, his loyalty already obvious. "Since I don't have a job anymore."

He had an answer for her. He pulled the notebook he'd stashed hours earlier from its drawer along with a pen. This was the good part about being the Dom. He was obligated to order her around. "Write. I don't care what it is. You can write Aidan is an asshole four hundred times, as long you write."

She stared at the notebook like it was a snake that might bite her. "It won't do any good. It's not like I haven't wanted to write. I just don't do it anymore."

Aidan shrugged. "Bullshit. It's like anything else. You sit down and do it. I don't care if it's any good. You will drink your coffee, and you will write whatever comes into that perverse, gorgeous brain of yours. You'll meet me and Lucas for lunch at noon. If you don't write something down, there will be punishment."

She took the pen and paper. "Fine. But it's going to be crap."

She turned and flounced out, Ike padding after her.

Lucas picked up her forgotten coffee and added a spoon of sugar. "I like this. I get to be the good cop."

Lucas followed her back down the hall. Aidan could hear Lexi's soft voice thanking him. She went up on her toes to kiss Lucas's lips before she disappeared into the bedroom Aidan had designed with her in mind.

Lucas walked back down the hall with a smile on his face. Yep, the good cop looked ready to work. He watched as Lucas practically jogged out the door. He was comfortable with his role, but he really had to make sure the bad cop got a little love, too.

Chapter Ten

Lexi walked out on the porch and into the midday sun. It was warm but not overly hot, yet the sight in front of her sent her temperature soaring.

Lucas and Aidan were working outside the barn, loading carefully packed hay into the back of a bale rack attached to an oversized truck. Their shirts had been flung off at some point, leaving two gloriously hard male bodies on full display. They wore nothing but low-slung Levi's, boots, and their Stetsons.

She'd gone way too long without sex.

They were so different, much more now than they were before. They seemed more mature. Pain in each of their lives had changed them. Aidan was physically changed, but she could see the mental scars, too. She'd glimpsed the naked pain on his face when he'd had to lean on Lucas for balance.

She could have told him that Lucas was the best balance in the world. Lucas thrived on people needing him. Jack had been the first person to honestly give a damn about Lucas. Lexi had been there that first summer. She'd watched Lucas change from a scared boy to a calm, patient, infinitely strong man.

Why was he willing to let Aidan back in? Did she love Lucas

enough to follow him?

Pain had changed her, too. Had it changed the three of them enough that maybe it could work this time?

Lucas used the bale hooks to hoist the last of the hay onto the rack. His lean muscles rippled in the sunlight. He glanced up and saw her standing there. He took his hat off, his thick, dark hair curling around his ears. A devilish glint came into his eyes. Aidan walked up close to the back of the rack and secured it. He drew the lock on the rack and turned. Lucas was in his space. Lucas said something to Aidan that had Aidan's lips curling up and his dimples flashing.

Lucas's hand came up and trailed down Aidan's chest. It was a soft touch, the sort Lucas was good at. He always treated her so gently. The way he'd fucked her mouth the night before had been different. Lucas had been fully in command. He'd been rough, and she'd loved it. He'd held her head and forced his cock in and out of her mouth. She had loved looking at the dark expression on his face as he used her. It wasn't like she wanted to be abused. She wouldn't allow anyone but Lucas to do that. Lucas loved her. Hell, most of the time Lucas worshipped her. It was safe to submit to Lucas. It was perfectly fine to indulge that part of her sexuality with him.

And suddenly, with Aidan around, Lucas felt safe to indulge his. It was the only explanation. He'd spanked her and performed scenes with her, but the night before was the first time he'd let go. Lucas had trusted Aidan to make sure she didn't get hurt.

She wanted to have sex with Aidan.

Damn it. She'd always known Aidan would be masterful. She'd tried to steer him that way once she'd figured out a bit of what she wanted, but Aidan had been very vanilla.

He didn't look vanilla now.

Aidan leaned forward and whispered something into Lucas's ear, his big hand cupping Lucas's waist. Even from here she could see the way Aidan's cock was pressed against his jeans. And then Lucas turned his head the slightest bit and their mouths met. It was gentle at first, a playful whisper of lips on lips. Then Lucas's tongue came out and traced the line of Aidan's mouth.

Aidan's reaction was instant. He grabbed Lucas's head, fingers tangling in his hair. Aidan pulled Lucas's back and mastered him.

Aidan was only a few inches taller, but in that moment he towered over Lucas. Their mouths ate at each other. Aidan devoured Lucas like a starving man. It didn't seem like simple lust to Lexi. There was infinitely more than that. Aidan needed Lucas, and Lucas needed him.

Lucas suddenly broke the kiss and turned to her.

Son of a bitch. Lucas had known what he was doing, and he'd known she couldn't resist.

"Alexis, in the barn, now. Clothing is not an option." Aidan was the one who barked the order, but Lucas was the one who smiled. It was the long, slow, satisfied smile of a master manipulator who'd gotten his way.

Lucas wanted the three of them together, and he would play dirty to get it.

Lucas strode toward the barn after picking up a towel and wiping off his chest. Even that was calculated to show every inch of his gloriously cut torso. "You better obey, Lexi. He's got the whole barn rigged for play. There's some fun stuff in there. Of course, there's also some stuff to torture a little sub who doesn't mind her Masters. I'd love to use some of it on you. I might submit to our Dom, but don't you dare forget that I top you, too. So get your pretty ass in that barn."

She stared as he disappeared inside the weathered barn. Aidan stood watching her. In that moment, he was more timid than Lucas. Though his jaw was square and his shoulders thrown back, she could still see his anxiety. He was expecting rejection. She could hurt him now. Lucas would follow her. She could force Lucas to make the same decision Aidan had foisted on her.

But all that would be was revenge. She could get some revenge on Aidan, but what did that buy her? Some momentary satisfaction? Aidan had been scared and confused when he'd forced her to choose between him and Lucas. She was scared, too, though for different reasons, but she couldn't hurt Lucas like that. And she didn't want to.

Aidan's face fell as he waited. Lucas came back to the door, not quite as sure as he was before.

It was her choice.

Lexi set the notebook down and walked to the barn, her fingers already undoing the buttons on her shirt. "If you think you're touching me when you're sweaty, you're all kinds of wrong, mister."

Aidan's hand came out as she passed him, and she felt a sharp shot to her ass. "That's Sir, to you."

She shrugged out of her shirt and unhooked her bra, noting Lucas's smile and Aidan's rising interest. "Fine, you should clean up, Sir."

Aidan followed her inside. "Not going to happen. I'd just get dirty again. Lucas and I will have you as sweaty as we are in a few minutes. We washed our hands. That's going to have to do. Get your pants off and assume the position."

For someone who used to be vanilla, he seemed awfully comfortable being bossy now. Maybe this was what she needed. Maybe a few days of submitting to Aidan would prove that she didn't like his way of topping. She'd only had Lucas as a Dom before, and he'd been very indulgent with her. Maybe she wouldn't like real D/s.

She tried not to think about how her skin was already humming. She had gone soft and wet. She wouldn't be able to hide how interested she was. She could be the biggest brat in the world, but the minute one of them shoved a finger up her pussy, they would know it was all an act. So much of what she did on a daily basis was all an act. She moved through life like a walking corpse when Lucas wasn't around to make her smile. But being with both of them was making her feel.

She kicked off her shoes and pushed the jeans over her hips, snagging her panties as she went. The barn was warm, with soft sunlight filtering in. The whole place was gauzy and strangely romantic. It was filled with hay and equipment, but no animals. Though it was large, it felt intimate with only the three of them inside. Aidan closed the door behind him. Lucas was sitting on a bale of hay, leaning back like the centerfold to some uber-hot cowboy calendar. He had a length of rope in his hand. No comfy, fur-lined cuffs for her this time.

"I believe the Master told you to get on your knees, baby."

She'd never heard as much confidence in Lucas's voice before. It had her dropping to her knees and spreading them wide. She placed her hands on her thighs and lowered her head. She relaxed. She wanted this. She needed this.

Dark, worn cowboy boots came in to view. Aidan. He stood for a moment looking down at her, and then his boots disappeared. He pulled the band out of her hair, sending her dark tresses tumbling around her shoulders. "Very nice. Someone who didn't know you might think you were a sweet sub."

"She can be, when she wants to." Lucas's boots were suddenly close to her knees. They were expensive, though he'd broken them in. His hand tangled in her hair, and he gently forced her head up so she looked him in the eyes. "Are you ready for this, baby? Are you ready to serve two Masters?"

Since her heart was pounding like mad, she figured she probably was. Even if she wasn't ready for this emotionally, she didn't think she could stop. "Yes, Sir."

"Lexi, I want to make love to you and Lucas." Aidan's dark brown eyes looked almost black in the soft light. "I want to set the ground rules before we start. I won't make you do anything we don't agree to at the beginning."

He was going to force her to say yes. He couldn't just take her? No, the bastard Dom had to put all the responsibility on her. She would have greatly preferred he ordered her to spread her legs. She could have blamed it all on being in subspace.

Lucas knelt down. His hand stroked her cheek and then traced a line from her neck all the way down her torso to her pussy. She held herself very still, though she wanted to force those long fingers to fuck her hard. It had been so long since she'd really had a partner. Lucas couldn't count because he only gave and, until last night, hadn't taken anything in return. She wanted her pleasure, but she needed to please, too.

A single finger slid through her pussy, parting her labia and wiggling all around. She could feel the arousal coating her pussy. Lucas's finger teased her for a moment and then was gone. She let a whimper escape her lips.

Lucas stood and held his hand up. "Well, she might not be willing to admit it, but her pussy is plain and open about what she wants."

Aidan moved beside him, his eyes staring at Lucas's cream-coated fingers. "It could all be about you. She loves you."

"A fact I am grateful for every day, but I know my girl," Lucas explained. "She's a dirty sexy thing, and I wouldn't have her any other way. She's thinking of two hard cocks right now."

That was the problem. She wasn't merely thinking of two hard cocks. She was thinking of Lucas and Aidan. She was thinking about their hands on her, their tongues lavishing affection, their bodies worshipping hers. She was thinking of them, not some random and faceless lovers.

Lucas licked his fingers, the image sending a shiver of desire through her.

Aidan stared into her eyes. "I need a response, Lexi. Unlike Lucas, I don't have a telepathic link to your pussy."

"I wouldn't mind a little sex," she managed to say. She didn't have to admit anything beyond that. She wasn't going to lie down and beg him to love her. Begging didn't work with Aidan.

"I said I want to make love to you," Aidan replied, emotion plain in his tone. "That's what this is for me. This is coming home. I want to come home, angel."

"All I can promise you is sex. I want to fuck you out of my system." That was as honest as she intended to get. She meant it. She was self-aware enough to know that he still moved her. She wanted to be indifferent to him. She needed to prove that it hadn't been as good as she remembered. And she definitely wanted to banish the idea that the three of them together would have been perfect.

Aidan fell to one knee, his eyes hardening. His hand went around the nape of her neck, pulling her forward. "I have no intention of allowing that to happen. You won't get rid of me. I love you. I love Lucas. I will say it until you believe it. For now, if sex is what you want, then I'll give it to you. But you're going to please your Masters before you get anything for yourself, you bratty sub. Tell me something, did you do your work?"

She'd sat and stared at that notebook for the longest time. It had been strangely peaceful to sit on the front porch, cup of coffee in one hand, pen in the other. The morning had been warm and quiet. Every now and then Ike had thumped his stub of a tail against the porch. And finally, finally she'd written. Only a page and a half. She wasn't sure where it was going, if it was going anywhere at all. It was the beginning of a small-town story. It had felt good to write again, to let her mind roam without limits.

"I did."

Lucas's face lost its masterful look and softened. "Really? That's great, baby."

Aidan looked far too satisfied. "Good, then we can forgo the violet wand."

Lexi felt her eyes widen. "What? You were going to use a fucking violet wand on me?"

Lucas's mouth slid right back to decadence. "The Master is into all kinds of play, baby. Julian taught him well. He has a TENS unit he wants to attach to your pink parts. I would be a very, very good girl if I was you."

"You behave too, Lucas," Aidan interjected. "I can strap that to your cock."

The look on Lucas's face let Lexi know he might misbehave. "I'll take that under consideration, Sir. And she cursed. I didn't think that was allowed."

"It's not. Hands and knees, angel. Count of ten."

A certain sense of trepidation filled her system. It did absolutely nothing to quell her desire. If anything, she was tightening in anticipation. She'd always known what to expect with Lucas. She'd always been able to manipulate him. She got the feeling Aidan wasn't going to play that way.

She moved forward, the hard wood of the barn floor biting into her knees. She let her hands find the floor and tried not to sway.

Aidan's hand found her hair. He stroked her as he spoke. "We're going to explore. You have your safe word, and you can use it if you need to, but I will push your boundaries. I'll push Lucas's, too. Today is about you, though. Today, Lucas and I intend to play with our sexy sub. And Lexi, if you curse again, I will get out the wand. Have you used it before?"

"No." She'd stayed away from it. She'd planned to stay away from violet wands forever, but it looked like she'd get acquainted with them in the future. She doubted she'd be able to be good for long.

"I've tried it. Julian forces all of his Doms to try the toys. He

137

won't allow himself or anyone he trains to use something when they don't know how it feels." Aidan's hand trailed down her back, lighting up her skin everywhere he touched. "The wand is very diverse. It can feel like bubbles on your skin. Imagine that. I could tease it against your pussy and your asshole. You would shiver and beg for some more. I could move the setting up when you're bad. It cracks against your skin, like holding a firecracker in your hand. I won't ever take it too high. It's intense when it's high. It feels like you're being cut, but it doesn't leave a wound. You have to trust me. I'll punish you when you need it, but I won't ever hurt you, Lexi. Never again."

Lucas didn't seem interested in that. "Don't pull that shit with me, Aidan. I want to try it all."

Aidan chuckled. "Yes, you're my masochist, aren't you, Lucas? You'll push me hard."

"Fuck yeah, I will."

Lexi brought her head up, unwilling to let that pass. "Could I point out that Lucas is cussing like a sailor?"

There was a sharp slap to her ass. "And ten more for questioning us. Lucas isn't subbing today. Lucas is topping you. And now he owes you ten."

She felt the floor shudder a little as Lucas fell to his knees. "Thank you, baby. I've been wanting to spank this hot ass for days. I didn't get to last night."

"You don't get to complain about that," Aidan said. "You were too busy shoving your cock in her mouth."

"Oh, and that was heaven. But I did miss this." Lucas brought his hand down on her right cheek.

"And I miss her mouth sucking at me." Aidan's hand slapped her left cheek.

She wanted to scream. They were making her crazy with their hands and their hot words. More than that, she was with them. She didn't have to fight. She could savor the sensations of being with these two men.

They spanked her, alternating turns. All the while, they talked about her. They talked about how beautiful she was and how they couldn't wait to fuck her. They talked about how her ass looked all sweet and pink. They slapped and spanked and discussed all the ways they could torture her when she was bad. Aidan wanted to use a whip, but Lucas preferred the crop.

The pain sank into her skin, lighting her every nerve. The words rolled over her, making her feel lovely and desired. Over and over, the spanks came. She lost count, trusting them to stop when the time was right. Instead, she just felt. The slaps rained down on her backside. They struck her ass and thighs. She heard Aidan say fifteen and then felt his hand on her back.

"Get down, Lexi. I need that ass higher." Aidan's voice had gone deep and lost some of its smoothness.

She leaned forward, folding her hands together and resting on her elbows. Her ass ached, but she wanted whatever they were going to give her.

One of them had a hand on the small of her back.

"That's gorgeous," Lucas said.

"So fucking pink and perfect," Aidan replied.

"I think she likes her spanking," Lucas continued. Now she sighed because a thick finger teased into her pussy. She couldn't help but clench, trying to keep it in, but the playful digit was too fast. "God, I love the way she tastes."

"Hey, you've already had a taste. Give that to me."

She craned her neck to catch the barest glimpse of Lucas's fingers disappearing into Aidan's mouth. His tongue came out, lapping up the cream of her arousal.

"Eyes front, sub." Another slap from Lucas.

She obediently complied. She might not be looking, but she doubted she could get the sight out of her brain. Aidan and Lucas were beautiful together. Aidan was all big, burly alpha male while Lucas was just fucking gorgeous. Lucas was a decadent dream.

"We still owe her five, Sir."

"Yes, we do." There was a moment's pause and then a smack.

"Oh, god." She groaned and shook as they slapped at her pussy. It stung and then warmed her already overheated flesh. She wiggled her ass trying to get them to do it again. In quick succession, they gave her four more slaps, each one sending her closer and closer to the edge. She felt something building inside, but when she thought she would burst, Aidan spoke again.

"Twenty. Now she's really creamy and ready to go. I think we should move on. She's far too free to move around the way she is now. I'd like her tied down. Pick her up and move her to the rack."

Before she could protest, Lucas had his arms around her waist, lifting her up. He swung her into his arms and moved toward a big wooden table she'd thought was a work bench. Now she could see the hooks that had been drilled into it. From each of the four hooks there was a length of rope attached.

"Relax, baby," Lucas said as he placed her on the rack. "The hard part is over. You'll pleasure your Masters, and then we will be happy to please you. Obey, and I promise there isn't a thing we won't do to make you come."

She laid back, content to allow Lucas to move her limbs into position. Her ass still stung, but the ache in her pussy was far worse.

"Leave her legs untied," Aidan ordered.

She looked up, and Aidan was standing over her, watching as Lucas tied the knots. Aidan had shed his jeans. His body was hard all over. Every muscle glistened with sweat, but it didn't bother her now. She was far too busy looking at his cock. It stood out from his core. His hand lazily stroked up and down as he watched Lucas prepare her.

Aidan had been able to fuck forever when they'd been engaged. He would thrust in and out like he didn't have a care in the world. He would fuck her until she'd come so many times she couldn't remember anything else, and only when she told him she was sore would he sigh and pick up the pace and finally let go.

She felt Lucas tighten the rope. Lucas. He could play with her for hours. He was patient and willing to deny his own pleasure.

"I missed you." Aidan was serious as he looked down at her. He stroked a hand through her hair.

"I don't want this. I'll take the sex, but I don't want to talk about this." She couldn't go there with him. Not yet. Maybe never.

He nodded his head, but the light in his eyes had dimmed. "Then I'll show you. I'll show you how much I've missed you both."

Aidan leaned over and took her mouth. There was nothing tender about his kiss. He possessed her. His lips molded hers, forcing them open, and his tongue invaded. He surrounded her with his taste and feel and smell. He was overwhelmingly masculine.

She shivered with desire when she felt a hot mouth on her breast. Lucas. While Aidan's tongue danced against hers, Lucas pulled a nipple into his mouth and began to suckle.

"You're going to give us everything," Aidan said when he came up for air.

She looked up at his face, his handsome, scarred face, and worried that he was right.

* * * *

Lucas pulled that perfect pink nipple between his lips as Aidan spoke. He wasn't so sure that Lexi would give them everything. She was stubborn, his girl, but damn he wanted it all. She felt heavenly under his hand. He stroked her perfectly soft skin as he curled his tongue around her nipple and sucked. He wanted Lexi, and he wanted Aidan. His girl and his guy. Well, his father always told him he had unrealistic expectations.

He banished that thought. He hadn't gotten anywhere listening to his politician father. Now Jack was a different story. Listening to Jack had gotten him a good job and Lexi. Listening to Jack was going to get him Aidan, too.

Lucas had known what he was doing when he'd gotten close to Aidan and pulled their bodies together. He'd seen Lexi walk out, and her eyes had been as wide as saucers as she'd looked at them. It had been a simple thing to lean in and explain to Aidan that they had a peeping Lexi who might like a show.

It had been an excuse. Lucas had wanted that kiss. He'd denied himself for so long that he couldn't go on without it. And it had been wonderful. A kiss from Aidan when he wasn't tipsy or seized with lust.

"Lucas, I want to watch. Take her pussy."

Now Lucas was the one who was seized with lust. He'd avoided fully making love to Lexi because the time wasn't right, because he wasn't sure she would stay, and he couldn't live without her. Since the moment he'd seen her, she'd been the sun in his sky. He'd been orbiting around her. She was tough and kind. She had a heart that was as big as he'd ever seen, and she hid it behind a sarcastic exterior because life had kicked the shit out of her more than once. She was his haven.

It was time to be with her.

His cock hardened painfully.

"Lucas," she whispered his name.

Aidan leaned over the table, his face close to hers. He placed kisses all over her cheek and neck.

Lucas dragged himself off her breast. He stood and looked down at his love. Her bright blue eyes shone up at him. She was beautiful, with porcelain skin and raven dark hair, but beyond that he saw the young woman who had befriended him despite his past. She'd opened her heart when he needed kindness so badly. She'd taught him how to love. He couldn't, wouldn't fail her.

"I love you, baby. I loved you yesterday. I love you today. I'll love you after we're both gone from this earth." It was his first time making love with her. He wouldn't change it into something less. He wouldn't play a game. He turned to Aidan. "We should do this later. I can't play a game the first time."

Aidan kissed her cheek one last time and straightened up. Aidan took Lucas's face in his hand, surrounding Lucas with his rough warmth. "No more games. That first night in Austin I should have let you have her, but I was selfish. I want to give you this, Lucas. I want to be here when the two people I love the most finally get to be together."

"Lucas, please," she said, watching them. There was a watery gleam in her eyes. "I need you. I've always needed you."

Lucas leaned forward, pressing his lips briefly to Aidan's before turning back to his girl. "Do you want me to untie you?"

She frowned. "Don't you dare. This isn't a game, Lucas. I want this. I want this life with you. I want to submit to you. You better take me up on this, babe. I seriously doubt I'll be compliant anywhere but the bedroom, or barn, or wherever you happen to tie me up."

Just one of the reasons he loved her. He kissed her, letting his tongue have its way. He wouldn't have wanted her as badly if she hadn't been difficult. She was smart and funny and creative. She was his.

Lucas kissed his way down her body. He loved her touch, her sweet scent, the taste of her skin. He nipped at her breasts and tongued her navel. By the time he made his way to her plump pussy, she was writhing.

"Lucas, do it now." She didn't sound terribly submissive.

He chuckled against her flesh. Her clit was poking out of its hood, practically begging him. "I like to take my time, baby. You know I never rush things."

Not anymore. He used to rush things, but he'd learned the power of patience.

"You're going to kill me, Lucas."

He breathed in her arousal and took a long, slow swipe. She tasted sweet and savory all at once. She was a treat, and he indulged in her. He licked and sucked, spearing his tongue into her pussy, imitating what his cock was going to do. He pulled her labia gently apart so he didn't miss an inch. He traced a line from right below her clit all the way to that tight asshole he intended to fuck one day. He licked her there, and she squirmed.

"You stop, Lexi," Aidan commanded. "You behave or I'll spank you, and Lucas will have to start all over again."

"Please," she cried. "Please don't stop."

That was where Lucas wanted her. He wanted her begging for his cock, because Lexi begging meant something. She wouldn't beg for a mere orgasm. She had to be involved soul deep to truly submit.

Aidan's voice softened, but only a bit. "Then calm down and let Lucas have his way."

She stilled, though her pussy was weeping and clenching. Lucas looked up, and Aidan was staring as he stroked Lexi's hair. A look of longing crossed his face as he watched Lucas lavish affection on her.

How long was he going to pretend with Aidan? It hadn't even been twenty-four hours since Aidan had walked back into their lives, but Lucas was ready to throw his stupid heart at the man. How long before he gave up? Lucas had been offering his heart since he was a kid, and only Lexi had ever stayed. How many times did he need to get his heart stomped on?

"Come down here, Sir. Help me send her to heaven."

Aidan was beside him in a heartbeat, his head leaning over.

Aidan touched their foreheads together, the contact sweet and gracious.

How many times would he try? He would try until he had what he and Lexi needed. He understood why Aidan ran. He'd been afraid. Accepting oneself was hard and frightening when it meant giving up so much. Aidan had been afraid of losing his family, his community. He was back, and he wasn't afraid anymore. Now Lexi was the one who was afraid.

Lucas bent down and lapped at her pussy, Aidan's head joining him. Their tongues played in the heated pool of her pussy. Every now and then they would slide together, exchanging her taste. Lucas's cock was begging, but he had a point to prove.

Aidan speared his tongue into her, and Lucas finally gave in to her little cries. He sucked her clit between his teeth, and she screamed.

Aidan lapped, his tongue licking up all that cream. Lucas was done being patient. He fished into his jeans and pulled out the condom he'd put in there when he'd dressed. Lucas watched Aidan rubbing his nose in Lexi's pussy as he kicked off his boots and jeans. His cock bobbed up and down. It was so hard it was painful, but relief lay there on that hard rack. She was glorious with her hands tied, her body helpless against their assault. Lucas rolled the condom over his dick and prayed he lasted more than a stroke or two.

"Get up, Aidan."

Aidan's head came up, and Lucas watched the Dom in Aidan threaten to take charge. Aidan's whole body tensed, and an icy glare came over his dark eyes.

He didn't have time for a fight. "Spank me later, Sir. I'm going to fuck her now."

The Dom fled, Aidan's expression softening. He hopped off the table and kissed Lucas gently. "All right. Thank you, Lucas."

Lucas hugged his partner, because he couldn't think of Aidan as anything less. He would have to find a way to convince Lexi to forgive Aidan and leave the past behind. His cock bobbed against Aidan's. Oh, he wanted that, too. He wanted to fuck Lexi while Aidan screwed his ass. He wanted it all.

But now he needed Lexi.

He climbed onto the table and spread her wide.

"Oh, Lucas," she whispered. "I love you, Lucas."

Tears pricked at the back of his eyes because he'd waited so long to hear those words. "Forever, baby."

He lined his cock up and started to thrust.

"God, you're so tight. So fucking tight." Lucas heard himself groan. She clenched around him. She felt insanely good. His balls were already drawing up. He pressed forward.

"I've only had one lover, Lucas. I'll only have two in my life, I swear." Those dark blue eyes were filled with tears.

He'd had so many he couldn't count them, but she'd had Aidan, and now him. It was a gift. He pressed forward, but he was in control now. He had to make it good for her. Lucas leaned down and kissed her, savoring their connection, mind, body, soul. She was a part of him. The best part.

"You'll never regret it," he promised.

He worked his way in. She hadn't had a lover since Aidan. Since then, Lucas had been her intimate connection, and he'd been careful. He'd used a vibe on her, but he was bigger than the one he'd bought for her. He pressed in until he was finally all the way in his love.

He felt a hand on his back. Aidan. He smiled at the joy in his heart. They weren't home yet, but they were together.

Lucas pulled back and plunged in. He thrust into her, over and over. The feel of being inside her was overwhelming. Lucas ground his pelvis against hers as he pushed up. He might have had an enormous amount of meaningless sex with men and women, but it had taught him how to please a lover. It was all worth it if it brought Lexi joy. He pushed his cock deep as he ground against her clit, and Lexi's whole body tensed and shuddered.

"Oh, Lucas!" She shouted his name over and over.

And he was gone. She tensed around his cock, squeezing him tight, and his balls shot off. Pleasure coursed through his veins as he gave up everything he had.

"Fuck." Aidan was beside him. Aidan's cock strained, and his hand stroked helplessly.

Lucas moaned as he continued to thrust, wanting to get out every last drop. But he wanted something more, too. "Shoot it on her breasts. I want to see you come."

"Give it to me, Aidan," she said, her voice a throaty groan. "You know you can get it back up. I want you both. One in my ass. One in my pussy."

"Oh, god." Aidan's hand pumped up and down his huge cock.

Lucas kept up his connection with Lexi, stroking into her as he came down. She shuddered every time he hit her clit. Aidan's cock throbbed in his hands. It was huge and thick. Aidan pumped, cream pulsing from the slit. Lucas remembered what he tasted like. Salty and masculine. He'd loved deep-throating that cock.

Aidan's head fell back, and he poured himself on Lexi's round breasts. Lexi's eyes watched that cock as it gave up. She was coated in Aidan, her nipples covered in pearly fluid.

Lucas felt his cock swell again. Lexi might get her wish.

Aidan pumped his cock for the longest time. His head fell forward, and he panted for breath.

Lucas slipped out of Lexi's pussy. He leaned down, pressing his chest to hers. He loved the fact that Aidan's semen was slick between them. He kissed her, a deep sense of satisfaction and belonging coursing through his system.

"I love you, baby. You won't get me off you now."

She grinned against his lips. "Never."

Lucas turned to smile up at Aidan, but he was staring at the door, his eyes widening.

"What the hell is this?" a feminine voice shouted as the light of day spilled into the playroom.

The blonde from last night stood in the doorway, her mouth open in horror. But that wasn't the worst of it. She'd brought a friend or two. Lucas quickly cupped himself and dove for his pants.

"Is that who I think it is?" Lexi asked, trying to crane her head around.

Lucas looked at Aidan. He couldn't help but laugh a little. His Dom was in some serious trouble.

"Alexis Ann Moore. What the hell do you think you're doing here?" Abigail Barnes asked.

Lexi flushed a pretty red. "Hi, Mom."

Chapter Eleven

Aidan was pretty sure that if looks could kill, he would be dead six ways from Sunday. He had faced down some rough motherfuckers in his life, but he would rather be back in Iraq than standing in front of Abigail Barnes. Unfortunately, she was currently pacing in his living room.

He scrubbed his hair with his hand as he looked into the living room from the kitchen. He knew exactly what Lexi's mom was seeing, a weathered house in need of money and attention, neither of which he had a great deal to spare. His father had damn near run the ranch into the ground with his stubborn refusal to try anything new. Jack Barnes had offered Aidan a way to keep the ranch that had been in his family for four generations, but it wouldn't start to pay for a while. Abby wasn't his biggest fan, and seeing the home he could offer her daughter hadn't helped.

While Abby Barnes paced, Sam Fleetwood sat on Aidan's easy chair with a sleeping toddler on his chest. Jack Barnes stared a hole through his wife from the worn-out couch. It was obvious there was some dissension amongst the Barnes-Fleetwood clan.

At least Aidan was clean now. And dressed. Somehow he figured Abby seeing the other thing he could offer her daughter hadn't helped her opinion of him, either.

"Mrs. Barnes," he began, wishing like hell that Lucas and Lexi had finished cleaning up first. But nope, they had retreated into the master bedroom and hadn't shown up again. He'd been forced to shower in the tiny guest bathroom, shut out once again. "Can I offer you a drink?"

Hazel eyes turned to him, narrowed in irritation. "You can explain to me what sort of game you're playing with my daughter, and don't you even try to give me the 'we're just playing at D/s' explanation. You were engaged to her. You can't waltz back into her life and experiment on her."

"It's not a game, Mrs. Barnes," he replied. "It's serious."

"It can't be too serious since you have a fiancée."

He had to stop himself from putting his fist through a wall. He was going to have to deal with Karen. "I do not have a fiancée. I haven't touched that woman in years, since long before I met Lexi."

Sam perked up. "I told you she had that crazy-stalker-thing going on. I know how it feels, brother. One day I'll tell you all about Melissa Paul."

"This is different, Sam," Abby insisted.

"Really? How?" Jack asked, his mouth a flat line.

Abby turned that look on her husband. "It's different because this is my daughter. You stay out of it, too. You've done enough damage, Jack."

A single eyebrow arched up. "Sam, that's another five."

Sam closed his eyes and patted the toddler's back, rocking in the easy chair. "I gave up writing down her punishments back in Waco. Let's all agree it's going to be a weekend project."

Jack stood. "I'm sorry, Aidan. I sat her down and explained what was going on, but she's being entirely unreasonable. I couldn't stop her from coming out here."

He had always known he would have to jump this hurdle in the end. Of course, he hadn't expected it to happen this damn soon. And certainly not when he was five minutes from heaven. Lexi had agreed to let him make love to her. Oh, she had called it sex, but he would be making love. If Karen hadn't noticed the Barnes-Fleetwood family asking for directions and decided it was a perfect way to see him again, he would be balls deep inside Lexi and one step closer to getting her back.

At least Karen had run off in tears. It had been suitably dramatic. She'd cursed Lexi's name and completely ignored the fact that Lucas was there. Maybe she would finally get the picture.

Jack stared out the window, his eyes widening. "Um, I think I better go save your brother. He offered to show our daughter around. She's trying to ride your dog. I don't see your brother. I hope she hasn't killed him. Or tied him up. We all know you have a lot of rope around here."

Jack took off running, the front door slamming behind him. Sam kept up his rocking, and Abby closed in on Aidan. Apparently Olivia Barnes-Fleetwood wreaking havoc wasn't anything new.

"My husband might think you have good intentions, but I don't care. I was there after you dumped my daughter," Abby said. "I remember how hurt she was. She wouldn't even come home for nearly six months. She was devastated. Did you dump her for that blonde bimbo?"

"No, Momma," Lexi said, walking somberly into the room. Aidan wanted to scream his frustration. While they had been in the barn, she'd been alive again. Now she was shut down. "He didn't leave me for Karen. Karen was his high school girlfriend. He didn't exactly dump me."

"What?" Abby asked.

Now Sam's eyes were open, and he watched the scene in front of him.

Lucas walked into the room looking like he'd never gotten caught with his pants off. Lucas was smooth as silk. It intimidated Aidan sometimes. Lucas always seemed to know what to say, to do, in order to make things run like clockwork. Aidan fumbled so often.

"I'm afraid this is mostly my fault, Abby." Lucas slid an arm around Lexi, giving her his support. "You see, Aidan asked Lexi to choose between him and me."

Sam snorted. "Didn't look like she was choosing a while ago. And Aidan's obviously bi. I believe I mentioned that back when I met him a few years ago. He was looking at Lucas back then, too. What's up with all these guys not realizing they're bisexual? Here's the clue, buddy. When you're around another dude and you get a hard-on, you might be bi."

"Sam!" Abby turned on her husband.

But Aidan actually didn't mind. He laughed a little. So much of dealing with his sexuality had been wrapped in endless drama. It felt good to laugh about it. He did owe Abby an explanation. "I had never, um, loved a man before Lucas. I fought it for a long time. I thought that wanting Lucas made me gay. And I didn't understand how I could want Lucas when I loved Lexi the way I did."

"And being around her family made you believe that wasn't a workable relationship?" There was no mistaking the offended air pouring off of Abby. Aidan knew her story. She'd been surrounded by small town judgment all her life. "I will admit that I wondered if you left Lexi because you disapproved of her mother's lifestyle."

"No." He said it, but it rang untrue. He had worried about it. Damn it, he had to be honest. "Yes, Mrs. Barnes. It's why I never invited you to meet my father or even told him more than the fact that you were married to Jack Barnes. I never mentioned Sam."

Sam shook his head. "The best looking one is always the dirty little secret. Although I'm not little. I'm a big secret, if you know what I mean."

"Sam," Abby scolded him again, but her lips had curled up, and she shook her head with affection. She leaned over and brushed her lips against his. "I would never keep you a secret. I want the whole world to know about us. Jack feels the same way. It's you and me and Jack forever."

"I hope you still feel that way next weekend, baby."

"I'm not afraid of Jack." She stood back up and crossed her arms over her chest, going from adoring lover to pissed off momma in an instant. "So you're telling me that now you're fine with your sexuality—or are you trying to make Lexi choose again? I warn you, she will choose Lucas. Lucas is good for her."

"No, he's not. Not entirely," Aidan said.

Lexi opened her mouth to speak, but Lucas's hand came around, closing neatly over her lips.

"Agreed." Lucas was the only one who seemed completely at ease. "Lexi needs a firmer hand than I like to give. I greatly prefer to be the indulgent one. And I also like a nice discipline session from time to time. I'm a switch, but Lexi has never enjoyed playing the Domme. Though she does like to play the brat. You can lick my hand all you like. It's not going to make me stop."

"Don't you dare bite him," Aidan barked, anticipating her next move.

Lucas pulled his hand back.

Lexi shook her head. "You wouldn't take it from me, babe. I get that we need a Dom."

"Well, it doesn't have to be him." Abby reached out and took her daughter's hand. "Come on, we're going home. Lucas, you can come with us, but I'm not terribly happy with you, either. You let this happen."

Lucas stepped out from behind Lexi, his face going hard. "Be as unhappy with me as you like, Abby, but Lexi and I made this decision together. We decided to come out here, and we're staying out here. And I might be a switch, but I top your daughter, and I expect you to respect that."

"Mom, I'm not going anywhere," Lexi said, holding on to her mother's hand.

Abby didn't give up easily. "We can protect you better at home. Julian has those new guys Ian trained investigating the situation. They're going to work with police and figure out who's after Lexi. I talked to Ian today. We had a long discussion on the way here. They're busy but he can spare Alex McKay, too. Jack can hire extra security if we need to."

"And so can Aidan and I," Lucas replied. He looked over at Aidan, his green eyes clearly expecting something more from him.

"We can," Aidan said, stepping up. He squared his shoulders. Abby Barnes might be his future mother-in-law, but on this he wasn't going to indulge her. He didn't have the money, but he could borrow it. He had things he could sell if he had to. He would go bankrupt if it meant Lexi was safe. "Lucas can look into it this afternoon. We chose to come out here because it's isolated, and everyone notices a stranger. I have a security system, but more importantly, I will die before I allow anything to happen to Lexi, and I know Lucas feels the same."

"Damn straight." Lucas relaxed back a bit, seemingly happy to let him take the lead. "Besides, we don't have to worry about Olivia and Josh out here. At least we didn't until you brought them with you. Out here we only have to worry about Bo and some ranch hands."

"And Karen," Lexi sniped. "She seems to love it out here."

The brat was back. Aidan replied with a sharp edge. This was a conversation for private. "Alexis, I did not invite her."

Lexi shrugged. "Just so you know, if someone takes another shot at me, I'm ducking behind her."

He smiled. He did love the brat. "You do that, baby."

Lucas's phone rang. He answered it as Jack opened the door. A small red-haired girl ran in. Olivia was wearing overalls and bright pink cowboy boots. Ike followed behind her, his tongue lolling out.

"Daddy, Momma! I made a friend. His name is Ike, and he ain't got no tail because they chopped it off, but Aidan didn't chop it off. Tourists chopped it off. But then Aidan went and fought the tourists. I hope we don't get no tourists here. We would have to hide all the dogs."

Abby laughed for a moment, but then got on one knee so she was talking on her daughter's level. "First off, young lady, the dog doesn't have *a* tail, and you hope we don't get *any* tourists here."

Jack put a hand on his daughter's head. "She spends a lot of time with ranch hands."

Abby glowed as she looked at her daughter, the dissension of before vanishing. "And I believe it's 'terrorists,' though I doubt they chopped off that poor dog's tail. I believe it's the culture in some parts of the world. Even here in the States, for some breeds, it's considered common."

"It would terrify me if someone tried to chop off my tail," Sam replied.

Bo was standing in the doorway. His face was red, and he was out of breath. "I'm never having kids. My heart can't take it. She never stops. Never."

Aidan took a long look at his brother. Was Lucas right? Was Bo putting on an act? Why would he tell a little girl that terrorists cut off a dog's tail, but his brother had fought them? Since the day Aidan came back and announced that he was going after Lucas and Lexi, Bo had acted like he had a disease. Maybe he needed time—or some kindness.

Lucas hung up his phone. "I hate to break up this intriguing political discussion, but the Dawson brothers are waiting for us in town. They want to talk to all three of us about the case. They're at some place called Patty Cake's."

Aidan knew it well. "It's a diner. Is there a reason they won't come out here?"

Lucas shook his head. "Apparently they don't believe in places without Wi-Fi."

Patty Cake's was the only place in town for wireless Internet. It looked like they were headed into Deer Run. Aidan hoped Deer Run was ready for them.

* * * *

Lexi perked up as Aidan pulled into the parking lot of Patty Cake's Diner and Pie House. The afternoon was not going the way she'd expected. What had she been thinking? If her mother hadn't interrupted them, she would have let Aidan climb up on that table and fuck her senseless.

But it was only sex, that mocking inner voice said. *You only want the sex.*

She didn't want anything else. She didn't love the way it felt to be squeezed into the cab of Aidan's truck. She didn't adore how small she felt surrounded by Aidan and Lucas. She wasn't even vaguely enamored of the idea of being their girl. Aidan had lost his chance when she'd lost their...

"Lexi?" Aidan looked down at her, concern in his brown eyes. "Are you all right? You don't have to be here. I can handle this, and Lucas can take you home."

Oh, she really didn't like the way he said "home." The thought of a home with Aidan and Lucas did nothing for her. The idea of taking Aidan's ramshackle house and turning it into something they could be happy in—it did nothing for her. *Who are you fooling?* "No, I don't want to go back to the ranch. I want to talk to them."

Lucas opened his door and hopped out, turning to help her down.

153

That was Lucas's way. She had never, ever been allowed to let herself out of a car when Lucas was around. He treated her like she was precious. Lucas held his hand out, but his eyes fell. Lexi turned to see what had him upset. Aidan stood there, his hand out to help her down. He hesitated, pulling back as he obviously believed she would prefer Lucas. She looked back at Lucas, her heart a little torn. Sure Aidan had been an asshole, but she still felt his pain.

Lucas winked at her and walked away. The bastard left her with no choice but to take Aidan's hand or get out on her own and look like a bitch. She could hurt Aidan. She could choose to scoot out and stand on her own two feet, proving she wanted nothing from him. She turned and let her hand find his. In the end, she couldn't hurt him that way. He helped her from the truck and set her on her feet.

"You say the word and I'll take you home, angel."

"I'll be fine." She tried not to think about how nice it was to stand close to him. Lucas, that manipulative weasel, had moved in behind her, reminding her of how amazing it was to be surrounded by them. Lucas's hands were on her hips while Aidan's cupped her shoulders.

"Of course you will be. We'll make sure of it, baby," Lucas murmured in her ear.

"I want waffles, Momma!" Olivia ran by, her booted feet tearing up the sidewalk.

Her mom chased after, and Lexi couldn't help but laugh. Her sister was an adorable ball of chaos. Jack walked by, cradling her baby brother, and she had to look away. Lucas's hands tightened around her.

Aidan forced her face up. She feared he'd seen too much. "Are you all right?"

She could hide behind the whole "someone tried to shoot me" thing. "I'm nervous. Let's go and get this over with."

Aidan took her hand in his while Lucas took her other hand, winding their fingers together. She couldn't take it for anything but a promise. Those hands promised to stay with her, to protect and stand beside her. The only trouble was Aidan had promised that before.

She was so rattled by what had happened in that barn. She'd thought she could hold herself apart and enjoy the sex, but now she knew she'd never been that girl. She'd slept with one man in her whole life before today and that was Aidan. Making love with Lucas in front of him had felt so right. Having him there when Lucas finally took her had made it more emotional than she could have imagined. What the hell was she doing?

Aidan opened the door, and she was assaulted with the amazing smell of fried food. Her stomach grumbled, reminding her that she hadn't had lunch. She'd been far too busy being right and properly fucked by her men. *Damn it.* She couldn't think of them that way.

"I want waffles and chicken strips and French fries and chocolate cake and gummy bears." Olivia was shouting out her order in her usual style. And the waitress was smiling down at her because no one could resist her smile.

"Not happening, baby girl," Sam said with a hand on his daughter's head. "She'll have a kid's waffle and a nice big bowl of fruit."

Jack, Sam, Abby, and the kids had taken a table next to the Dawson brothers, who had made a workstation of their table. A pretty brunette waitress was kneeling down next to Josh's highchair, obviously absorbed with the kids.

One of the Dawson brothers stood and held out a hand. She thought it was Ben. He seemed the friendlier of the two. "Lexi, it's so good to meet you. We weren't allowed to be formally introduced before, but believe me, I noticed how lovely you are."

"Who pays your check?" Aidan asked the question on a low growl.

Ben Dawson's lips turned up, showing off his movie star quality smile. Dark, thick hair and crystal blue eyes made him one hot Dom. And yet he had nothing on her men. "For the time being we get our paycheck through McKay-Taggart, though if this works out we'll work exclusively for Mr. Lodge. I have to admit, we're unbelievably wealthy all on our own. Our father was a bastard and ran through wives like they were water, but he was good at making money. The trust fund is still quite healthy. We do the Scooby-Doo thing because it's fun, and it gets us into The Club. Don't tell Taggart but it's much more luxurious than Sanctum. Someone should blow that place up and start over."

Chase nodded in agreement. "It's far too industrial for my tastes. The Club is better. We love spanking pretty subs. I watched your spanking the other day, Lexi. You took it with such grace."

"Shut that shit down now, Aidan," Jack advised. "Otherwise, you'll deal with it forever. I still have to warn Leo that I intend to kill his ass every time I go into The Club."

Aidan reached out and grabbed Ben's shirt, pulling him close. "She belongs to me and Lucas. If you have a problem with that, we can solve it right now, out in the back. Many an ass has been kicked in the back of this diner."

Lucas leaned over to talk to Chase, who had an amused look on his handsome face. "I won't do anything so forward. My partner is the aggressive one. I'll wait. I'll ruin you financially, and then when you think I've forgotten you, I'll be that dark figure in an alley you see just before you get your throat slit."

"Lucas!" She was shocked at how dark his voice had gone.

Chase rolled his eyes. "God, I hate switches. They know all the tricks."

Jack looked up, a paternally proud expression on his face. "I taught him well."

Ben sat back down and took on a distinctly professional air. "Fine. The girl is off-limits. You can't blame us. She doesn't have a collar."

"Pretend it's there." Aidan held out a chair for her.

"You are both Neanderthals," she groused as she sat down and picked up the menu.

"Get used to it, baby," her mother said, grinning at her from her seat. "You'll find that's the way men get when they're damn serious. It doesn't matter. Dom, switch, sub."

"Well, I'm not a sub when it comes to my woman getting hit on," Sam said, an odd primness to his tone. "My fists work just as well as Jack's."

"Hi." The waitress who had taken her mom's order turned to Lexi. Her eyes widened as she took in Lucas. The pretty, slender brunette flushed. "Hi. Can I get you anything? Anything at all?"

"He's taken, Mandy," Aidan said with a laugh. "I can see I have to deal with a lot of this. Men, women, even my damn dog has taken to my subs."

Lucas winked, and Mandy looked back and forth, her lips going up in a giggle. She took the orders and bounced off.

"She'll gossip, you know," Lucas said with a frown. "This is a small town. It could cause trouble for you."

"It will cause trouble," Lexi corrected. Her mother had grown up in a small town, lived there now. Only her husbands' money granted her any acceptance, and Lexi had heard they still called her "That Woman" behind her back. Maybe Aidan didn't know what he was in for.

"I don't think Aidan cares," a new voice said. Lexi looked up and saw a cowboy with a pleasant smile standing by Aidan. Aidan stood and shook hands with the man.

"Lexi, Lucas, this is Dwight Creely." Aidan introduced the man who stood a few inches shorter than him but was thickly muscled. He had a quiet air about him. He shook Lucas's hand and tipped his hat at her. After all the introductions were made, he sat down.

"I'm Aidan's foreman. He asked me to come to this meeting. I take care of the security for the ranch," Dwight explained.

Ben Dawson sat forward. "You were also in the Army with Aidan, right?"

Dwight stilled, and then the smile was back. "Yes, I was."

"Interesting," Chase added, his hands flying across the keyboard of his computer.

"Not really. That was a long time ago," Aidan said, shifting uncomfortably, his hand going to the small of his back.

Without even thinking about it, she reached out and massaged the spot.

Aidan's whole face softened. "Thank you, angel."

She stroked the tight muscles, telling herself she'd do it for anyone.

Ben and Chase started in on their report. They had found out all of the usual stuff. Her job was boring, and no one would want to kill her over it. Most of her close friends were at The Club. They were almost all submissives, and even their Doms liked Lexi. They couldn't find a single person who she hadn't done something nice for. She was known for having a sarcastic mouth and a ridiculously warm heart. Her neighbor had been so upset about the shooting that she'd cried. She took Mrs. Darren, an elderly widower, to her frequent doctor appointments.

"I can't imagine anyone wanting to kill my daughter," Abby said, leaning across to pat Lexi's shoulder.

She gave Aidan's back one last squeeze. The muscles had stopped seizing. "I don't know, Momma. That jackass last year seemed very determined."

Lucas's face went stark white. "Could this be about me?"

Ben stared for a moment, and Lexi could practically see his brain working. "We've had McKay-Taggart's resident shrink work up some profiles on people close to Ms. Moore and Mr. Cameron. She didn't find anything that worried her. I haven't discarded the idea that this is someone close to one of you yet, but I don't think so. Your legal work revolves around your brother's business and Mr. Lodge's investments. You acquired several companies for Mr. Lodge recently. I'm exploring the possibility that one of the former owners could be upset."

"I also checked into your brother, Aidan," Chase stated bluntly. "Eve disagrees with me, but I don't trust profiles. They can be wrong. And she's working with one hand tied behind her back because she's not allowed to interview her subjects."

"We can't haul all the people in our life in for invasive interviews on the off chance that they might have taken a shot at me." She couldn't stand the thought of her friends and acquaintances being put through an Ian Taggart interrogation. "But why would you be looking into Bo?"

Aidan tensed beside her. "He was here in Deer Run last night. He called me from the house phone."

"At what time?" Chase asked.

"Before the scene at The Club."

Ben and his brother looked at each other. They seemed to have a whole conversation through a series of small facial movements. Finally Ben, who seemed to take the lead most of the time, turned back. "It would be tight, but he could have made it. The two of you fought over the terms of your father's will?"

She couldn't imagine it was Bo. He'd been a sweet kid when

she'd known him. Even today, he'd treated her sister with kindness.

Aidan's hands folded together, and he seemed to be squeezing them tight. "He was unhappy when he realized Dad had left the ranch to me. Bo felt like he deserved it. I never wanted to ranch when I was younger. I wanted to be a musician. Then I went into the Army and lost a couple of fingers in a firefight. My hands don't work the way they used to."

Ben leaned forward. "Why did your father leave you the ranch?"

Dwight snorted. "Because he had a brain in his head. Bo couldn't find his ass with a GPS locator."

"Don't. He's just a kid," Aidan protested.

"He's twenty-four, Aidan," Dwight shot back. "He needs to grow up. He needs to get a job."

"He has a job," Aidan insisted.

"I'd like to talk about what happened to your squad. It's the one thing Eve and I agree on. There's something off about the reports." Chase Dawson said the words smoothly, but they dropped with a thud as both Aidan and Dwight paled.

"I don't see how it has anything to do with this," Dwight said, sitting back in his chair. "It happened a long time ago. No need to bring up bad memories."

Chase shrugged as though it didn't matter. "I have a nose for these things."

"I thought you were investigating the shooting." Aidan put a hand to his head. Lexi could see how his eyes tightened as though he was in pain.

"We are, but before that Big Tag worked up a report on you and he included records of your military service," Chase replied. "He still has deep ties with the military and several intelligence agencies. He was very thorough."

Aidan frowned. "I knew he'd looked into my background, but are you saying Taggart had someone profile me? Like a serial killer?"

"Absolutely he did. She interviewed you. Remember Eve St. James? She cleared you," Ben replied. "Unequivocally stated you're not a serial killer. But yes, she worked up a profile on you at Mr. Lodge's request. If it helps, Eve liked you very much. She believes that now that you've made the decision to embrace this lifestyle, you won't go back. You'll remain faithful."

"Yeah, Eve likes all the yucky emotional stuff," Chase said. "I'm more interested in that firefight. I go where the information leads me, and sometimes I simply follow my own instincts."

"Chase is a brilliant investigator," Ben explained. "He's the brains. I'm the beauty."

Well, that said a lot since they were identical twins. But she could already tell the difference. Ben was charming, while Chase was dark and broody. If she was going to write them, she'd give Chase a single scar on his face to utterly differentiate them. Chase was the one who would get into trouble. He was the one who could hurt someone. Ben would balance his brother. He would be funny and open. She could write them into a romantic suspense novel. They were perfect for it.

"Lexi?" Lucas leaned in. "Are you with us or on another planet?"

Her mom was looking at her, too. "That's her working face. She's had it since she was a kid. When she was thinking up a story, she would get that far-off look, and I would know to let her alone for a while."

"She wrote a bit today," Lucas offered. "She's probably thinking about that."

Her mother looked misty, and she suddenly seemed to see Aidan differently. "Are you getting a headache?"

Aidan turned to Abby. "A little one, yes. I get migraines from time to time."

"Well, given the extent of your injuries in the line of duty, I would say migraines are the least of your problems. Jack mentioned how badly you were hurt. How long did it take for you to walk again?" Abby asked.

Aidan flushed. "The better part of a year."

"Spinal cord injury?" Her mother's tone had taken on that nurse practicality. She'd worked in some of the busiest trauma centers in the Dallas-Fort Worth area. "How many surgeries?"

"Eight," Aidan replied.

She felt her stomach turn. He'd had eight surgeries? She'd seen the scars, but he seemed so healthy. With the exception of the weak knee and his back spasms, she hadn't seen him have a single problem. How much was he compensating to look strong?

"Do you remember the incident that led to your injury?" Chase's blue eyes were laser-focused on Aidan. Ben sat back, obviously ceding the floor to his brother. "I've read the Army's official report, and I have some questions. Mr. Creely was the only one who survived? He got out of the incident relatively unscathed."

"He took a knife to the gut. I hardly call that unscathed." Aidan massaged a place right between his eyes. "I wouldn't have survived without Dwight."

Chase looked at his computer screen. "Really? According to the leader of the team that found you, it was the dog barking that led them to you."

"I stayed," Dwight said. "I stayed with him. I kept the Iraqi soldiers off us until the G Squad could get to us. And how did you get that report? It's supposed to be classified."

Chase leaned forward with a silky smile. He cracked his fingers the way a virtuoso piano player might. "There's not a lot of security that these fingers can't get through. I told you. I follow my nose, and I don't like that report. Maybe it has nothing to do with this. Maybe it does. But all of that is superfluous. The report states clearly that Sergeant Aidan O'Malley remembered nothing of the attack that decimated his squad."

"I dream about it at night." Aidan's voice was low and gravelly. She reached out and placed her hand on his back again. Lucas sat forward.

"Those dreams don't mean anything. He's talked to me about them, and they don't make a lick of sense." Dwight's hands were threaded together, red from tightness. "He didn't dream when he was taking the sleeping pills the doctors prescribed."

"I told you why I stopped. They make me drowsy even during the day. I can't live my life like that." Aidan's eyes closed.

Dwight pushed back from the table. "Yeah, well, you should have told me when you decided to stop taking them. I would have helped you. Damn it, Aidan. You know I've told you everything that happened. Why do you have to push this? You're going to kill yourself over this, you know it."

Dwight stalked out of the room.

Aidan watched him go. "Forgive him. He remembers. Sometimes

I think he wishes he didn't. Does anyone have an aspirin?"

"Could we get a glass of water, here?" Her mother stood and gestured for Lucas to stand as well. "Lucas, rub his scalp. Aidan, close your eyes and don't think about it. I would bet the migraines come when you try to think too hard about that day. I've seen this in PTSD patients with memory loss. Let the memory go, and you might be able to avoid the migraine."

Aidan closed his eyes but laughed a bit. "That whole 'don't think about it' thing never works. Now I can't help but think about it."

Lucas massaged his scalp, eliciting a groan from Aidan. Lucas leaned forward, his voice low, but Lexi could hear. "Think of something nicer. Remember how hot our sub looked tied to the rack? She was so tight, Sir. She practically cut off the circulation in my dick, but I wasn't about to stop fucking her."

Lexi felt her eyes go wide, but her mother merely shook her head.

"I did not need to hear that, Lucas." Abby moved back to her table, where Jack was laughing, and Sam was trying to figure out what Lucas had said.

"Hey," Jack said. "He's not thinking about what happened to him in Iraq anymore."

"No," Aidan said sullenly. "I'm thinking about what didn't happen to me in the barn."

"Who had the waffles?" Mandy asked, returning with a tray of food.

"I did!" Olivia screamed. "I had waffles." She sank back down. "But Aidan can have them if he needs them. He's not supposed to remember stuff, so he might not have remembered that he wants waffles. I think he's doing a good job at not remembering, cuz I heard that he forgot to marry my sister."

Everyone stopped and stared at Olivia who seemed mighty comfortable with all the attention on her.

Aidan laughed, his head falling forward. He looked up, and for a second, she saw the old Aidan in his eyes, the Aidan who laughed and sang and played the guitar, the Aidan who had loved her so long and so well that she'd never been able to forget him.

"I won't forget this time, Olivia," Aidan said with a broad smile. "I promise."

"You better not," her mother said with a tight nod.

Lexi's chest felt tight. She wasn't sure what was going to win, heartache at what had happened between them, or hope that it might be different this time. She wished they weren't having this discussion in front of her mother.

"Are you going to marry my Uncle Lucas, too?" Olivia asked.

"Absolutely," Aidan replied without hesitation.

Mandy's tray clattered to the floor, food spilling everywhere.

Lucas merely chuckled and went back to his massage.

Ben and Chase exchanged a glance.

"Gotta love a small town," Ben said with a grin.

Chapter Twelve

Aidan felt much better as he pulled the truck into the driveway. Ben and Chase Dawson were checking into the only motel in town, as was the whole Barnes-Fleetwood clan. He might have been happier if his future mother-in-law had gone home for the time being, but Olivia had spotted a Ferris wheel. Aidan had completely forgotten that this weekend was the end-of-summer fair. They all now had a date to attend the fair later that night.

Lexi had been quiet all through lunch. She'd seemed contemplative rather than irritated with him. He had to be grateful for that.

"How could you tell my parents that you were going to marry me?" Lexi asked quietly, her hands folded over her lap.

His senses went on high alert. She might be moving out of her contemplative state.

He didn't miss Lucas's sharp sigh. It was his way of telling Aidan that he better not fuck this up. They were starting to have their own language. "Because I mean it. Because I love you. I'm going to marry you and Lucas."

"So, you get to drop back in and take over?" Yep, the irritation was creeping into her tone.

Oh, he'd figured out long ago how to handle this discussion. "I am the Dom, angel. I'm in charge, but Lucas and I will figure this out. We'll all three of us hold a rational discussion about how to handle the legalities, but I want us together. If you want to legally marry Lucas, then that's what we'll do. I love you."

Lucas quietly got out of the car, but Lexi charged after him. She didn't wait for Aidan to hand her down as she had before. She stomped off, every muscle in her body tense and ready for a fight. Before he could get out of the cab, Lexi had slammed into the house.

Lucas stood at the door, his face a solemn mask. "She won't go down easy. She's been through a lot. You have to know that if I didn't think you were good for her, I wouldn't be here."

His stomach did a weird flip-flop. "I don't want you to be here only for her. God, I know you don't believe me, but I'll prove it to you. I love you. I'm in this for life now. I won't ever leave."

Maybe he should track down that profile the shrink had done on him and force them both to read it.

A secret smile crinkled Lucas's perfect face. "Next time you leave, I'll hunt you down, Sir. I might allow you to top me, but never think I'm not your equal."

That was the furthest thing from his mind. "Oh, Lucas, I know how good you are. And I've never suspected I was your better. I left because I couldn't handle how the world would view me, but there was another reason I left. I was jealous of you."

Lucas's brow furrowed. "What? That's the stupidest thing I ever heard. I was the guy the tabloids proclaimed was killing his own father with embarrassment."

He'd seen the articles that described Lucas Cameron's misspent youth. Lucas had pulled a lot of stunts to get his politician father's attention. It had landed him on the cover of several tabloids. It had always been hard for Aidan to reconcile that sad boy with the put-together man he'd met. "I didn't know you then. All I knew was that you had it together. You knew what you wanted and how to get it."

Lucas snorted. "I wanted Lexi."

"Yes, and you manipulated both of us into a position where you got what you wanted. What you didn't count on was the fact that I had issues with my father and brother."

Lucas's eyes shuttered. "I don't like to think of it as manipulation."

"But you worked to get what you wanted. You wanted Lexi, and you got her."

"No, I wanted the three of us," Lucas admitted. "Even when you walked out, I truly expected you to come back. I thought you would go blow off some steam, maybe write some angry songs where you brutally murder me, but I thought you would be back."

Aidan flexed his ruined hand. He couldn't get it to open all the way, and the muscles ached from even the small movement he'd performed. "Showed you, didn't I? What you don't know is that I had a big career setback the day after I left. I had a shot at a recording deal that fell through. My dad heard and gave me a lecture on how I should be doing 'man's work.' I enlisted the next day."

Lucas's hand came out, cupping his shoulder. "We all do stupid things. You paid for yours. I paid for mine. We need to move on."

Lucas was right. He needed to move this forward. "I intend to walk into that house and get her underneath me."

He was done waiting. If he let her put distance between them again, she would use it to rebuild her walls, and he had no intention of allowing that to happen. He couldn't keep her here forever. Once the mystery of who had tried to take her out was solved, she would be back in Dallas.

Lucas's eyes slid away. "I understand. I'll find your brother and see if I can find something to do."

Aidan reached out to him. "No. I want you with me. Hold her while I fuck her. Let her know how this is going to be. You and me, a united front against all of her fears. You and me. Partners in her need, her pleasure."

That mischievous smile he loved lit Lucas's face. "She does enjoy being held down, Sir."

Lucas joined him as he walked through the door. Lexi was standing there, as though she'd been trying to listen, but she turned quickly when she saw them enter. Her heart-shaped ass swayed as she walked down the hall.

"Lexi!" Aidan barked.

She stopped but didn't turn around.

"We're in private. I didn't give you leave to walk away."

That hot ass of hers wiggled as she started up again. The only gesture she gave that let him know she'd heard him at all was to shove her happy middle finger in the air.

He felt his blood start to boil.

"She wants it bad, Sir." Lucas's eyes had gone dark and predatory. He might be a switch, but when the Dom came out, Lucas was a force to be reckoned with. He wondered if Lucas knew how hard it got him when Lucas decided to top their girl with ferocity.

"Then we should give it to her." He stalked down the hall after her, well aware of how his blood was pounding in anticipation.

He'd meant to make the first time back with Lexi gentle and loving, but that was gone now. It wouldn't be vanilla. He'd meant everything he'd said to her mother. He would marry her and Lucas. Now it was time to let Lexi know he was damn serious.

Lucas moved ahead, clearing the way. He tossed open the door immediately after Lexi had slammed it, the sound a volley in the little war she'd started. There would be a conqueror and a conquest. It was only a battle. Aidan knew Lexi had already won the war. He was her slave. He'd do anything for her, except let her go.

"Alexis!" Aidan shouted her name.

She turned finally, her face closed and shut off. She wore a T-shirt and jeans that hugged her every curve. "What do you want, Aidan? You can tell my family whatever you like, but I don't have to believe you. I'll do what you tell me to because that's the only way I can get my access to The Club back, but as soon as Leo and Julian clear me, I won't see you again. Lucas and I will find another Dom."

"Will we?" Lucas asked. "You're assuming a lot."

Aidan hated the way her shoulders slumped, and tears filled her eyes.

"Really?" Lexi asked. "You said this was only temporary. You're going to choose him over me after everything we've been through?"

Lucas shook his head. "No, I'll always choose you. I'm yours. If you decide you can't forgive him, I'll go with you, but you should know that I want to try. I want you to give this an honest shot."

"I told you I'm staying." Lexi couldn't quite meet anyone's eyes. She stared at the floor.

Aidan took over. "That's not the same thing as trying, but you can give it a shot, angel. I know you. I know you won't be able to hold back."

"Maybe I've changed."

He wouldn't, couldn't believe that. "Lexi Moore doesn't change. Now get your clothes off and get on your knees. I want what you promised me in that barn."

She took a quick step back. "That was a mistake."

"No. That was truth. Everything else is you pretending."

Lucas moved behind her. His hands slid under her shirt. "Play with us. Your Masters want to play with their pretty sub. Do you know how much we adore you?"

Aidan had to hand it to Lucas. He knew how to handle Lexi. He was the smooth operator to Aidan's alpha male. Her hands drifted above her head, and Lucas slipped the shirt off.

"Show the Master your breasts, baby." Lucas's voice was a seductive tease. "Take off that bra and show him what you have to offer. Those breasts belong to us. We want to see them."

Her fingers found the clasp of her bra. She paused, her eyes coming up. "It's still just sex, Aidan."

He wasn't going to win this one. He might not be able to convince that brain of hers, but he could work on her body. "I'll take what I can get. But you should know I'm making love to you. Now Lucas is right. Those breasts belong to us. Show me."

She released the clasp on her bra and let it open. Her breasts were round and perfect, tipped with pink, tight nipples. She loved to have them sucked on. When they had lived together, Aidan had spent long periods of time just playing with her breasts.

Lucas's hands ran up her torso, cupping each mound. His big, tanned hands played over her porcelain skin, making a lovely contrast. Her eyes were open, glazed with desire, but she watched Aidan. He held her gaze.

"Lucas, I need some help with my own clothes," he said.

Lexi's eyes flared as Lucas kissed her hair and walked toward him. Lucas moved behind him. He felt Lucas's hand at his waist. Those callused hands teased into the waistband of his jeans and his cock twitched in anticipation. He looked at Lexi, who seemed mesmerized by the scene in front of her. He remembered how much she'd liked watching him and Lucas together that night. It had gotten her hot beyond his imagination. Lucas tugged Aidan's shirt up. His fingers trailed up Aidan's torso, lighting up his skin.

Lexi stared him down. "You said my breasts belonged to you."

He thought he knew what was coming. "Yes, angel. Your breasts are mine and Lucas's. Your pussy and your ass are ours. You signed a contract."

"So did you, Sir. So I have to ask—what belongs to me?"

"Everything," he replied.

"Should I show her, Sir?" Lucas asked, getting to his knees in front of him.

He nodded, not trusting himself to speak. He might sound like a pubescent boy. Lucas on his knees was a gorgeous sight. He started to work on the fly of Aidan's jeans, slowly, carefully revealing his taut flesh.

Lucas pulled Aidan's cock out. It was long and painfully hard. It felt like it throbbed in Lucas's hands. "I believe this belongs to us, Lexi."

"Always," he replied, gritting his teeth.

"What else?" Lexi asked.

Lucas's hands found his ass. Aidan groaned as Lucas cupped his cheeks. "I don't know about this. It depends on how adventurous the Master is."

"It's yours." He'd made that decision long ago. If he was in, he was in. No holding back. He wanted everything.

Lucas's head came up, shock plain on his face. "Are you serious?"

Even Lexi suddenly looked discomfited. "You're the Dom."

"Yes." He was the Dom. So why did he constantly have to explain himself? His dick was dying and they wanted an explanation? "If I want my ass fucked, then one of you better fuck it."

"But Julian doesn't—" Lexi began.

"But Jack doesn't—" Lucas started.

He tugged on Lucas's hair so he got the point. "I am not Jack, and I am not Julian. What they chose to give or withhold from their lovers is up to them. Neither one of them has a switch. Sam and Finn

are extremely submissive when it comes to sex. You are not. I want to
share everything with you. I want you to be my first. Unless Lexi
wants to put on a strap-on."

Lexi's whole face lit up.

"Ain't happening." Lucas quickly shut that down. His hand came
back, and he gently started to stroke Aidan's cock, as though he knew
it needed attention. He ran his hand from the tip to the base and back.
"Aidan got your virginity, and I think he'll want your ass first. I get
his."

Aidan's balls drew up at the thought. He knew other Doms didn't
catch for their subs, but Lucas was different. Lucas needed this to feel
whole and complete. Aidan would never deny it to him. Though he
was a bit apprehensive, he would go into it with an open mind. He'd
intended to get inside Lexi, but all he wanted was to be between them.
He wanted to be surrounded by them.

"And what do I get?" Lexi's earlier irritation seemed to have
dissolved, replaced with an open curiosity.

"Multiple orgasms," Lucas shot back.

"I can live with that."

"Excellent. Get your pants off." Lucas tossed the order over his
shoulder.

Aidan realized he was rapidly losing control. He hardened his
voice. "Don't you forget who's the Dom here."

Lucas's eyes softened. "I am sorry, Sir. What would you like for
me to do?"

He let his hands find the silk of Lucas's hair. "Get me hard so I
can fuck our girl while you take my ass."

"Oh, yes, Sir." Lucas's mouth came open, and he devoured
Aidan's cock.

It felt like being thrust into heaven. Lucas didn't take his time. He
swallowed him down. There was such a difference between the way
Lucas sucked him and how Lexi did it. It was a fight with Lexi. She
struggled to take him all the way. There was something infinitely
sweet about the way she worked to get him inside her mouth. Lucas
had no such trouble. He simply sucked until his chin hit Aidan's balls,
and then he sucked some more.

"Please, Aidan." Lexi's voice cut through his pleasure.

Aidan forced himself to open his eyes. Lexi was standing there naked, her jeans and panties tossed off. Her face was open and honest for once. He cocked an eyebrow, willing her to explain.

"I want to watch."

He held out a hand, and Lexi hurried across the room. She didn't protest as he slid an arm around her, drawing her in. She looked down, watching Lucas drag his mouth up and down Aidan's cock. He watched, enjoying the sight. His cock disappeared, enveloped by Lucas's sensual lips. The feel of Lucas's strong tongue whirling all over his dick made him groan.

"Does it feel good?" Lexi asked breathlessly.

He let his hand roam across her back, down to the plump cheeks of her ass. His heart was racing. Lucas's tongue slid around his cock, making him pant. "It feels great. He gives great head."

She smiled, a light airiness replacing her gloom. "I know, Sir. He's taken care of me many times."

Aidan was glad. He was glad they'd had each other while he'd been gone. He knew he should be jealous, and there was a bit of that in his heart, but mostly he was happy for them. The only thing he'd thought of while he'd lain there, the blood seeping from his body, was them. It had given him such comfort to think of them happy together.

Her face was tilted up, and he took advantage. He pressed his lips to hers, tracing the seam of her mouth with his tongue, demanding entry. She softened underneath his onslaught, allowing him inside. Aidan let his tongue glide against hers, overwhelmed by the feel of being inside both of them. He kissed her for a moment and then came up for air.

"Aidan, you're crying." Her fingers traced his cheeks.

He hadn't realized it. It didn't matter. He wouldn't hide anymore. He was done pretending he was something he wasn't. He was a man who loved two people. He loved a man and a woman. They were his heart and soul, and he wouldn't deny them to anyone. If Lexi couldn't forgive him, it wouldn't matter. She would still be his love. He'd go to his damn grave loving these two human beings, and he was better for it.

"I love you." He stroked Lucas's hair. "I love you both."

Every step he took for the rest of his life, he owed to them. He'd said Dwight had saved him, but it was a lie. Lexi had saved him. Lucas had saved him. When he was dying, he'd had a single thought. It was the only part of the whole experience he remembered. *Get back to them. Never, ever leave them.*

"Stop." He couldn't take another second. He was going to come, and he didn't want to do it in Lucas's mouth.

Lucas pulled off. He gazed up, so fucking beautiful with his mouth red and swollen from sucking cock.

"Go gentle on me," Aidan said with a nervous laugh. Why, oh why, had he ever denied himself this? He hadn't wanted the label. He hadn't wanted to acknowledge that he was gay or bi. But this was love. It didn't need any other label.

"Always, Sir," Lucas said with a smile.

Aidan nodded toward the big bed. "On the bed, Alexis."

She practically jumped onto the bed he'd ordered with both of them in mind. She was a vision against the white quilt, her raven black hair stark and lush.

"You two know how to make a girl feel wanted," she said, her lips curling into a seductive smile.

Aidan realized Lucas was standing beside him. They were both watching their girl, their dicks straining.

"You have no idea how much I want you," Aidan said. "Get the condoms, Lucas. I put some in the nightstand."

Aidan got to his knees and reached out for Lexi's ankles. He pulled her down the bed, arranging her silky legs over his shoulders. Lexi had praised Lucas's skill, but it was time for him to remind her that he loved her taste, too.

He breathed her in. Her pussy was gleaming with moisture. Aidan leaned over and took a swipe. He loved the way she tasted. Creamy and sweet, with a nice tang.

She squirmed. Aidan tightened his hands on her thighs. "Be still. I want to enjoy my treat."

Lexi stilled beneath him. He pressed her legs apart further, opening her for his delectation. Her clit was poking out from behind its hood, begging for the swipe of his tongue. Well, Lucas had promised her multiple orgasms. Aidan let his fingers find her cunt, and he started to stretch her while he licked her, teasing that clit, getting close, but never quite touching.

"Please. Please. You're killing me."

"What do you call me, Lexi Moore?" He was playing dirty, but it didn't matter. He wanted to hear her acknowledge his place in her life.

"Sir," she tried.

He backed off. "Not good enough. Any Dom is Sir. I don't want to be a Sir."

There was a pause. He worked his fingers in and out, but it was a slow tease that would take forever to get her off. Lexi's face bunched up in apparent frustration.

"Give it to him, Lexi." Lucas stood behind them with a tube of lube and a couple of condoms in his hands. Aidan groaned at the thought of what Lucas was going to do with that lube. "You know you want to. And deep down you know he deserves it. We wouldn't be here without him."

"I don't know about that, but you did sign a contract, and I go with you." That was his Lexi. She wouldn't give an inch without qualifying it. "Fine. Please, Master."

He had to be content with that. He leaned down and sucked her clit into his mouth.

Lexi went off like a firecracker. She pushed against his hands, and he felt her cream start to coat them. She was so wet, and he tasted every ounce of it. He felt Lucas's hand on his back, caressing.

It was time.

Aidan got to his feet, licking the cream from his lips. He took the condom from Lucas's hand and forced it over his cock. He looked down at Lexi, the world narrowing to her. There had been women before her, but he hadn't loved before he met Lexi. She'd been his first love. Lucas had come later, but she'd been the first time he'd felt his world open. His heart had filled with her, and he'd become a different human being. If only he'd followed that man—the one loving Lexi had created—they would never have separated. He would never have hurt her.

"I love you, Lexi." He pressed his cock against her pussy and pushed in. He didn't wait for her to reply. She wouldn't. Her mouth would remain stubbornly closed because he hadn't earned it yet, but he would. He believed he would win her back.

Her eyes drifted close, and she sighed. It was a breathy sound that told him he'd pleased her. She pleased him, too. More than she could imagine. Her pussy was tight and hot around him. She squeezed him, making him groan.

"Lucas, hurry." He wasn't sure how long he would last. "She feels too good."

"I know she does, Master." Lucas didn't seem to have Lexi's problems with using his proper title, but then he'd always known Lucas would be the easy one to get to. Lucas understood what it meant to fuck up and need a second chance.

He groaned as he felt Lucas spread his cheeks and dribble lube onto his asshole.

"Cold, huh?" Lexi was grinning, a devilish smile.

"Don't tease me," Aidan begged. He was nervous suddenly. Everything he wanted was right here. What if he wasn't good enough? What if he failed them again?

"Hey." She pulled at his neck, dragging him down so they were face to face, inches away. "It's going to be all right. It's only uncomfortable. At least that's what Lucas says. From what I understand, Lucas has lots of experience. Seriously, we could take a poll in several states, and they'll tell you Lucas Cameron knows how to fuck an ass."

"Thanks," Lucas said, sarcasm dripping.

But it had the effect Aidan thought she'd intended. He laughed, the nervousness slipping away. One of the things he loved about her was that she always made him laugh.

Lucas's hand smoothed over his lower back, as though trying to soothe the scars he found there. "Aidan, we don't have to do this. This position could be uncomfortable."

Never knowing what it felt like would be more uncomfortable. "Do it, Lucas. Don't make me tell you again, and don't you dare hold back."

He immediately felt something pressing against his lubed anus. The pressure wasn't pain exactly, but it wasn't pleasure. He tried to relax as Lucas rimmed his asshole. Lexi's hands found his hair.

"Kiss me," she said.

He wasn't going to deny her that. He kissed her with everything he had. His dick pulsed inside her, but he held still. His tongue plunged in a naked imitation of what he wanted to do to her pussy. Over and over he slid his tongue against hers as Lucas pressed his fingers into his ass. He'd taken a plug there before. He wouldn't ask anything of his subs he hadn't tried himself, but warm flesh was different. Warm flesh moved and made him ache in a way no bit of plastic could.

"There it is," Lucas said, his voice breathy with wonder.

Aidan gasped as something utterly amazing happened deep in his rectum. Lucas rubbed a magic spot that had him ready to lose control.

"Prostate. I think he found your prostate," Lexi explained with a wink. Her face quickly turned to a sweet grimace. Her hips pumped up. "God, Lucas, get this bus moving."

"Your wish. My command." Lucas moved between his legs.

Aidan felt something far larger than a couple of fingers at his anus. He heard Lucas groan as he started to breach Aidan's hole. Firm hands gripped his hips as Lucas's cock began to move forward. It was a monster, that cock of his. It was thick and long, with a plum-shaped head. Aidan had stroked him before, but he'd never tasted him. That would have to come later because Lucas was pressing ruthlessly inside. It stung and burned, but there was an intimacy to it that called to him. He was giving to someone he loved. It lit a fire inside him.

"Just a minute more, angel," Aidan promised.

Lexi was biting her lip, obviously desperate to start.

"You feel so good, Master, so fucking good." Lucas drove into him. "I'm all the way in. Fuck, I'm balls deep."

Aidan was so full. He was full of Lucas, and Lexi looked up at him like he was her anchor in the world. It was utterly perfect. He pressed forward, trying to make sure he hit her clit.

"Oh, yes." Lexi's voice was filled with relief as he started to fuck.

He almost lost it when Lucas dragged his cock out. He pulled that dick right over Aidan's prostate, lighting up every nerve in his ass.

"Fuck," he managed to moan. It was low and from deep in his body as he utterly lost control. He plunged into Lexi, driving forward with single-minded intent.

Lucas took his lead. He found a pounding rhythm. Aidan was caught between them. Every time Lucas fucked into his ass, he plundered Lexi's pussy. It wasn't long before she was calling out his name. Over and over, he heard his name being called like a litany as she came around his cock. It sent him over the edge. Between the endless pleasure being forced on his prostate and the clench of Lexi's tight pussy on his cock, he couldn't hold back. He came in pulsing jets.

Lucas shouted behind him, surging in and holding Aidan's hips as he came. He pumped into Aidan's ass again and again.

Aidan dragged in air as he fell forward, his head finding the soft grace of Lexi's breasts. Lucas pulled out of his ass.

"Are you all right, Aidan?" Somehow now that the sex was over and the world seemed softer than before, Aidan was happy Lucas had dropped the Master.

"My back may never be the same." His back was in a vicious spasm, but he wouldn't change it for the world.

Strong hands suddenly rubbed his muscles, easing the soreness.

"It'll be all right," Lexi promised. Her eyes had drifted closed. She didn't seem to mind his weight pressing on her.

And that was how he fell asleep, caught between his loves, utterly safe.

Chapter Thirteen

Soft afternoon light filtered in through the thin, worn kitchen curtains as Lucas walked in from the yard. Sweat poured off his body, but the work was done. He'd left Aidan and Lexi sleeping, wrapped in each other's arms. Lucas had never been a napper, but he did believe in getting the job done. They had left the day's work unfinished, and that didn't sit well with him.

"Damn, I need a shower," Bo said as he trailed behind him.

"Yeah, that's ranch work for you." He'd found Bo on the east range, fixing part of the fence. It had surprised him since Dwight, the foreman, had gone on and on about how useless the young man was. Dwight and the rest of the hands were busy moving the herd from the south field north. Lucas had stopped the truck and given Bo a hand. After that, Bo had been like a puppy following him everywhere.

Somewhere along the way, Bo had dropped his tough-guy act and started to behave like a real human being. He'd asked about Lexi and been open to talking about his childhood on the ranch. It was exactly as he'd suspected. Bo missed his brother and was sick of being thought of as a fuckup.

"Damn, Lucas. I'm sorry," a wry voice cut through the quiet.

Dwight walked in from the office, a thick stack of papers in his hand. "If I had known he was going to bug you all day, I would have sent him into town or something."

Lucas felt his eyes narrow. Something about Dwight didn't sit right. Maybe Bo deserved Dwight's scorn. Lucas had watched the younger O'Malley act like an ass when other people were around, but it didn't fit with how he'd behaved this afternoon. "He was very helpful. He taught this city slicker a thing or two."

Bo snorted. "Hell, you know a lot about ranching."

"His brother is our new boss," Dwight pointed out. "You know, the one you curse on a regular basis?"

Bo flushed, but Lucas had to laugh. "Hell, I curse Jack regularly, too. I worked for the bastard for a year, and every summer while I was in law school. I cursed him a couple of hours ago, too. You should know he's in town."

Bo's eyes were on his boots. "I didn't want to change. My dad did things a different way."

"I understand," he replied. "Change isn't easy. Your brother is proof of that. He wasted years of all our time because he wasn't ready to change."

A loud shout slammed through the room with the power of a fist hitting flesh. It was a masculine scream for help, and then Lexi's voice cut through the wail.

"Lucas!"

Lucas took off running. He burst through the bedroom door. Lexi had Aidan in her arms, trying to shake him awake. He was caught, seemingly in a fever, his body shaking, pulsing as though it was being hit over and over.

"Oh, god, he's dreaming about it again." Bo turned on his heels and left.

Lucas didn't have time to worry about Bo, though it pissed him off that he would leave when his brother was in distress.

"He needs to take his damn pills." Dwight stared down at Aidan with a frown on his face.

Lexi had tossed on Aidan's shirt, but Aidan was tangled in the sheets. Aidan was talking, but Lucas couldn't make out what he was saying. He was pleading with someone to stop.

"Stand down!" Aidan said it over and over.

Lucas tried to shake him awake, hating both the way his Master was vulnerable and the desperate look in Lexi's eyes. "Aidan, wake up. Wake up!"

"If only he took his pills. You're his—whatever the two of you are," Dwight started, sounding disgusted with the whole thing. "Make him take his pills."

"Maybe what he needs is to remember what happened to him," Lucas said resolutely. He couldn't go on like this. Aidan was fighting invisible monsters. He needed to push past his mental block and figure this out.

There was a loud bark and then that enormous dog, Ike, was bounding into the room, Bo following after him. He jumped onto the bed. Lucas started to pull him off.

"Don't," Bo said. "Ike is the only one who can calm him down."

The dog whined and licked his master's face. Aidan's eyes almost immediately came open. He blinked, his hand coming up to pet the dog. He looked around as though trying to remember where he was.

"I was dreaming again." Aidan's voice sounded gravely, as though the shouting had done damage.

"Yes," Lucas said, his heart calming down.

Despite Lexi's stubborn claims that everything between her and Aidan was sex, she was clutching him to her breast, talking to him in soothing tones. Aidan wasn't trying to be macho. He let Lexi hold him.

"You're a good boy," Lexi said, patting the dog.

"The dog was with you in Iraq?" He'd heard stories of soldiers bringing back the dogs they found.

"Yes." Aidan held on to Lexi like a lifeline. "He was the squad's mascot. We all loved him."

Dwight stood at the back of the room, looking out of place.

"Have you told him absolutely everything you can remember about that day?" Lucas asked, his eyes narrowing on Dwight.

Dwight's brows came together in consternation. "Of course. What would I hold back? Our whole squad got cut down by insurgents. We only survived because I dragged him to cover. I thought he was dead, to tell you the truth. I was surprised when the medic said he'd survived."

"I had something to live for," Aidan murmured.

"Will you let me call Leo?" Lucas's mind whirled with possibilities. Aidan obviously had some form of post-traumatic stress. "He would know something about this. Julian says Leo is an excellent therapist, and he served in Afghanistan. He might be able to help."

"I've been seeing Leo for a while," Aidan admitted. "Julian wouldn't let me in The Club without Leo's okay. Leo wants to me to go under hypnosis. I didn't think it was a great idea, but I seem to be getting worse. And I hate those pills. They make me groggy all day, Dwight. Don't mention them again."

"I was trying to help. I can see you don't need me now. I'll get back to work." Dwight slid out of the room, his boots quiet on the floor.

"Come on, Ike," Bo said, slapping his hands together. The dog was reluctant, but Bo pulled out a stick of beef jerky. "You know you want it."

Ike gave up his precious master in favor of flavored, dehydrated beef. A wisp of a smile traced over Bo's face.

"I'm glad you're feeling better, brother." Bo's smile turned distinctly wolfish. "And it was nice to see you again, Lexi. All of you. I mean, you are looking fine, darling. My brother is not good enough for you."

Lucas glanced down and snorted a little when he realized what Bo was talking about. "Baby, you should pull that shirt down. You don't have any underwear on."

"Oh, my god!" Lexi pulled the covers up and tossed a pillow at Bo's fleeing body. His laughter rang through the room as he opened the door to allow both him and the dog out.

He turned back one last time. "I am younger than him, you know. And way prettier."

"You're going to be way deader if you don't stop looking at my girl." Aidan shouted the warning, but there was a lightness to it. He was playing with his brother, and from the look on his face, Lucas could tell it made him happy.

"Everyone got a glimpse of my cootchie today," Lexi grumbled.

"Naw." Aidan pulled her back down and snuggled against her. "Just me and Lucas, and your mom, and Karen, and Sam and Dwight and Bo. That's all. Jack was taking care of the kids. So not everyone. Oh, and yesterday it was everyone at The Club."

She slapped at him playfully. "I'm going to be fully dressed from now on."

Lucas wasn't going to allow that to happen. He tossed his sweaty body right in the middle of the bed, covering both Lexi and Aidan.

"Lucas, you smell so bad!" Lexi tried to get away, but he and Aidan held her down.

"He smells like a working man, angel. Get used to it." Aidan seemed to be on the same wavelength.

"Besides, we have a few hours before we meet your mom and stepdads." Lucas leaned in for a kiss. "We can all take a shower."

"After," Aidan said, his hand pulling Lexi's shirt off.

"After," Lucas agreed.

* * * *

Lexi walked across the fairgrounds, the neon lights playing through the night. Blues and pinks and greens twinkled all around her. The smell of funnel cakes frying tickled her nose. Lucas and Aidan had wandered off to grab hot dogs. Olivia shouted her joy about everything. She loved the games and the food and the rides.

Lexi followed her family, feeling strangely out of place. She was intensely aware of everything moving around her. The world was flowing and changing, but she felt stuck in place. She'd spent the entire afternoon in Aidan's arms. While she was there, she hadn't thought about it. She'd simply let herself be. But now she was back to reality.

He'd left her. He'd walked out on her, blaming her for things that hadn't been her fault. Aidan had been gone long enough that he'd changed in almost unfathomable ways. And when he came back, he'd done it under false pretenses. How was she supposed to forgive that?

And how would she ever tell him what had happened to her while he'd been off figuring himself out?

"Alexis?" Her mother slowed down to walk beside her. "Are you all right?"

She nodded and made her best attempt at a bright smile. "I'm great."

"I want to ride the Ferris wheel!" Olivia motored by, making a beeline for the rides.

"I want to ride the bumper cars!" Sam yelled, winking at his wife as he ran after their daughter. Jack was more leisurely, walking with Josh on his hip. Lexi looked away from the sight of her baby brother.

Her mother's mouth was tight as she crossed her arms over her chest. "Are you going to be able to forgive Jack?"

She sighed. That wasn't the biggest question of the day, but she knew how much her mother was worried about it. "I can forgive him, Mom. I don't want to cause trouble between the two of you."

"He did that all by himself," Abby said. "He's not perfect, you know. His instinct is to protect."

"By tricking me into getting involved with a man who ripped my heart out?"

Abby stopped, and she stared at the ground for a moment. "I've been thinking a lot about this, baby. You've been lost since Aidan left. My first instinct was to get mad at Jack for bringing him back into your life. You've been with Lucas and that was enough. But I've been fooling myself. I think I've seen what I wanted to see. I told myself that you and Lucas were happy."

"We are happy."

"Oh, baby, you're not functional." Her mother's hazel eyes held a sheen of tears that threatened to rip Lexi's heart out. "You and Lucas don't work without someone like Aidan. I know the rest of the world doesn't get how this works, but some people have two soul mates. Could Jack and I have been happy without Sam? Maybe, but we wouldn't have been complete. Sam and I would have been lost without Jack. I only know that I was lucky enough to find both of them. You and Lucas have been fumbling. I know you weren't making love, and that's so important. You are now, and I think Aidan had something to do with it."

An uncomfortable feeling took a hold of Lexi's gut. "We would have gotten there."

"I know what Jack did was manipulative, but he did it because he loves you. He did it because he was scared. He spent a long time getting to know Aidan. He brought Aidan into the business. His herd is now affiliated with Barnes-Fleetwood."

She felt her mouth fall open. That was a pretty permanent connection. "He did what?"

"He's made Aidan a partner in Barnes-Fleetwood. Junior, but a partner. Jack believes in him. I know that man. I know his heart. He would never have done that if he thought Aidan wasn't the best thing in the world for you and Lucas. I was mad at first, but I saw you today. You were more alive than you've been in years. God, Lexi, I want my daughter back. I spent the afternoon realizing I would have done much worse than Jack to get you back."

Lexi looked at her and thought of all the ways her mom and her stepdads had tried to engage her in the last couple of years. Jack and Sam had moved her from Austin to Dallas. They were wealthy enough to have simply paid for the move, but they had shown up and carried out her furniture and boxes and loaded them into her rented truck. They'd driven her the whole way and hauled it all out again when they'd made it to her apartment. Jack had offered job advice. Her mother had tried to get her to come out to the ranch on weekends, and when she wouldn't, had shown up on her doorstep claiming she needed to shop. They'd tried in a thousand different ways, and then Jack had brought the sledgehammer down because he wasn't a man to give up.

And she'd felt more in the last two days than she had in two years.

It wasn't that she didn't love Lucas. God, she loved him, and he loved her. But they needed Aidan. Aidan pushed them.

She could forgive Jack, but she still wasn't sure how to handle Aidan.

"I think you need to give this time, baby girl," her mother said.

"I have a lot of that now. Aidan quit my job for me."

Her mother smiled. The light joy on her face made her seem years younger. "He's a Dom all right. Such pushy men, but there's nothing like a good one. Ask yourself something. Did you love that job?"

"No, but it was mine. What am I supposed to do now?" She knew she was being stubborn. She'd been thinking about quitting the job anyway. She had money in the bank. She could always find another crap job.

"What do you want to do? Because it occurs to me that Aidan is offering you a chance. Between Aidan and Lucas, you don't have to work if you don't want to. I know that sounds unliberated of me, but given the fact that your stepfathers are multimillionaires, it's not like you'll be on the streets if something happens to Aidan or Lucas. You're in a unique position, one a lot of women would kill to be in. You can follow your dream. You don't have to work eight hours a day and then try to get some words on a page. Don't you see? By making you quit a job you didn't even like, Aidan is trying to give you what you need."

"Shouldn't that be my choice?" Again, she knew she was stupidly stubborn, but damn it, she wasn't ready to concede yet.

"It is," her mom said with a sad sigh. "It's always your choice. Once the Dawson brothers figure out what's going on with the attempt on your life, you can go back to Dallas and take up your old life. Lucas will follow you. Lucas will do whatever you decide. Jack can get you your old job back, or you can find a new one. I've heard McKay-Taggart is looking for a receptionist. You can spend your days annoying Big Tag. You don't have to see Aidan again."

Yes, she could always say no. She could have said no this afternoon when he'd driven his cock inside her, and she'd felt that connection she'd been missing since the day he walked out. Something had fallen into place this afternoon, some sweet sense of peace in a world that had been chaotic for too long.

God, she didn't want to tell him what she'd done. Was that the real reason she was holding back? When she stopped thinking about the accident, she was happy with them. Lucas was thrilled. He was happier than she could remember him ever being. Was she willing to give it all up so she could pretend it never happened?

"Good lord, here comes trouble." Her mom's lips were pursed in a frown, and her auburn hair shook as she looked at something coming across the fair grounds.

"Hey, Lexi," Bo said, coming up behind her. He had two bags of cotton candy. He opened his mouth, Lexi assumed to say something flirty and smart, but his eyes caught on the same thing her mother was worried about. "Damn. Come on. I can find us cover."

Karen Wilcox led a small group of young women. They were all small-town princesses in tight jeans and tops that looked like someone had taken a Bedazzler to them. There wasn't a natural hair color among them, but damn they knew how to tease that hair. Lexi had to smile because she was sure one of those women had added almost a half a foot to her height with her hair.

"That is so awesome," Lexi breathed.

They slunk toward her like a bejeweled pack of hyenas. This was the way she used to view the world. Each and every incident was a wild thing, something she could use down the line. The world used to be a surreal carnival. There had been sadness, yes, but even that had lit something inside her. She'd felt with her every breath. Now she could see how shut down she'd been.

"I'm going to go get Aidan," Bo said, backing off a little.

"Don't you dare," her mother said with a laugh. "My girl can handle this. There are only three of them. I got your back."

"Mother, we are not starting a fight. Jack told you to stop that." Her mom was famous for taking down younger women in bar fights. There had only been the one, but it was legendary. And Lexi had no intention of fighting with Karen. She greatly preferred the pen to the sword.

There was Karen. She was Blonde Number One. Lexi quickly named them in her head. Blonde Number Two was short with enormous boobs. She named the third Talon because she had the longest, reddest fingernails Lexi had ever seen.

"Well, well, lookie here. These are the women I told you about. These city slickers have come to grace our town." Karen stopped in front of her. She smiled maliciously down at Lexi. She was wearing four-inch heels to a carnival.

Her mother opened her mouth to say something, but Lexi put out a hand, silencing her. "Don't correct her, Momma. Willow Fork has three whole stop lights. Deer Run makes Willow Fork look positively cosmopolitan."

"Is she insulting us?" Talon cocked a hip as she looked Lexi over. "She shouldn't be. I have no idea what Aidan sees in her."

Bo took a step forward. "This is Aidan's fiancée. You need to treat her with some respect."

"Technically, he hasn't asked me to marry him again," Lexi pointed out. She opened the bag of cotton candy. This looked to be an interesting argument. She might need the sugar.

"See, I told you he wouldn't marry her." Karen smirked as she slapped Blonde Number Two's shoulder. "He's trying to make me jealous. He's making me pay for marrying someone else."

Lexi gave her a thumbs-up. "Damn, you figured it out. I told him you were smarter than he thought you were."

"When did you get to be so mean, baby girl?" But there was a smile on her mother's face.

Lexi chose to avoid confrontations when she simply didn't give a shit about the person confronting her. Oh, she would rail and fight Lucas and Aidan all day. They would find her very stubborn indeed, but if Karen needed this to feel decent about herself, then she didn't care. If these girls wanted to think she'd been used to make Karen jealous, she was okay with it. The night was nice. She had a bag of cotton candy. Her body still hummed because the boys had been serious about those multiple orgasms. It was all good.

"Come along," Lexi said. "We should go join the rest of them. Maybe a ride on the Ferris wheel will fix my broken heart."

Actually, it did sound like fun. And so did those bumper cars. She bet Olivia would be a hell of a driver.

They all turned to go, even Bo, who seemed to feel a need to defend her but gave up when she smiled at him.

"You're nothing but a big-city whore," Karen taunted. "Aidan was never going to marry you. You're willing to do all kinds of things a lady wouldn't do."

Lexi stopped and turned. That was utterly unforgivable.

"Lexi," Bo said calmly, as though trying to figure out how to handle a dangerous animal.

"It's all right," she replied. "I need to make a few things clear to Karen."

"Are we going to fight now?" her mother asked.

She almost snorted. "No, Momma. Relax."

"You got something else to say?" Karen seemed ready to throw down. She probably watched way too much reality TV.

"I do. I am entirely insulted."

Talon's lips curled up. "I think that was the point. Karen told us all about what you were letting those men do to you in that barn. What a whore."

They did not understand her. "I'm not insulted that you question my ability to attract two unbelievably hot men. I'm really not, but I won't allow you to call me a whore. A whore accepts money in exchange for her favors. I only accept orgasms. I'm a slut. Seriously, get your lingo down."

Karen finally looked confused. "What?"

"And while we're at it, whore is overused. So is slut. If you're going to insult your sisters, please expand your vocabulary."

She was well aware that she was gathering a crowd. Several families stood watching, covering their little one's ears, but obviously unwilling to miss the showdown between the queen bee and the city girl. She noticed Aidan and Lucas looking in. Aidan started to step forward, but Lucas stopped him, a bemused smile on his face. She took it as permission to go all out.

"Let me give you some examples. First, whore isn't exactly modern. Ho-bag, hookerbop, boom-boom girl, DPF—that stands for dirty penis face—chlamyidiot, hozo, slank…I like that one because it's a great combo of slut and skank. You could go with dumpster if you're really dirty. Now, that last one is a more urbane way of saying cum dumpster, but if you're trying to be insulting, it really works."

There was silence from the crowd and then snickers. One very properly dressed white-haired lady in a green polyester suit actually clapped.

"Nicely done, dear. I used to be an English teacher. That girl always needed a thesaurus."

"You're a crazy bitch," Karen said, her face flushed. She looked around as though realizing how stupid she looked.

The crowd moved fast, hauling their children away as Lexi opened her mouth to give Karen a stern lecture on how common the word bitch was.

"You're good, baby," Lucas said, covering her mouth with his hand.

She was quiet long enough that he took it away. "You do that a lot."

Aidan answered for him. "Well, angel, you have quite a mouth on you." He leaned in and kissed her cheek. "Not that I don't love it."

"Aidan, you can't mean to do this," Karen protested. "I'm done being put through hoops. I'm sorry I picked Carl over you, but he's dead now, and we can be together. All you're doing by running around with this…woman is causing a scandal. Can't you see that?"

An unholy gleam lit Aidan's eyes. "You think I'm causing a scandal now? How about this one?"

He reached out and dragged Lucas toward him, planting his lips on Lucas's and kissing him for all he was worth. Lexi watched as everyone stopped and stared. Well, Aidan had certainly declared his intentions. For better or worse, he was out in the open.

"Well, at least the church ladies will stop talking about my beer drinking now." Bo's face was red, but he held his ground.

Her mother shook her head and put her arm around Bo. "Yes, I think Aidan has given them plenty to pray about."

Aidan came up for air. "I'm not apologizing for loving someone. Not ever again."

Karen huffed and hurried away as fast as her heels would carry her. Karen's pack turned and trailed after her.

"Well, you could have warned me I was coming out," Lucas said with a frown. "I would have thrown a party."

The retired English teacher made her way to the front. "I am so glad about this, boys. I have been waiting for years. This town is so dreary. We need your kind to spice it up. I loved *Will & Grace*. I was not as happy about *Queer as Folk*, but that *Will & Grace* was so funny. Could the two of you do something about town hall? It's so dingy. I've been trying for years to find a good designer."

"I will get right on that, ma'am." Lucas stifled a laugh.

Jack walked up to the group carrying Olivia under her arms and as far from his body as possible. Lexi stared at her little sister, who seemed to be wet from head to toe."

"She fell into the trough at the petting zoo," Jack explained.

"That's not giving her enough credit." Sam jogged behind them toting a giggling Josh. "She dove in."

"I went swimming, Momma."

Her mother's face fell, and she took her youngest daughter. "Let's get her back to the motel." She shook her head as she looked at Lexi. "I hope your first baby is as easy on you as you were on me. The second is hell on wheels."

Lexi knew her mother meant well, but the whole night dimmed. She'd already had her first baby. And she'd lost him.

And now she had to tell his father that she'd failed.

* * * *

Dwight tried to put on a calm face, but his stomach had been in knots since this afternoon. He'd thought when he'd managed to get Aidan home that he would be in control again. He was Aidan's best friend, after all. He was the one who had stood beside Aidan in the hospital. Now he was the one Aidan ignored in favor of a couple of people he fucked.

Dwight stood by the popcorn stand and wondered what the hell he was going to do now. He'd thought if Aidan came back, he would get into his routine, which included taking his sleeping pills. It was only when he dreamed that he started to remember that day—the worst day of Dwight's life. If Aidan remembered, Dwight's whole life would be over.

He should have smothered that dumb cowboy while he was in his hospital bed. Better yet, he should have made damn sure the bastard was dead that day in Fallujah.

Dwight had lived with the guilt long enough that it had turned into a strange form of entitlement. He'd made a mistake. Everyone made mistakes. It wasn't his fault. It was the goddamn US Army's fault for putting him in the position. He'd had a few weeks training and then he'd been shoved into combat. Was it his fault he'd panicked?

The gun had gone off on its own. It was a piece-of-shit gun anyway.

What the hell was he going to do?

Karen Wilcox stomped through the fairgrounds, making a beeline for the parking lot, her face screwed up in a mask of rage. What had put that look on her face? Karen caught sight of him and turned on her heels. Dwight had the sudden urge to flee but held his ground.

"How could you? You told me he wanted me."

Ah, so Aidan had finally had it out with the bitch. He'd been a pussy about it. It had been easy for Dwight to convince her that Aidan was just mad that she'd chosen someone else. Karen was thirty and there weren't a lot of prospects in a town as small as this. Dwight had fucked her a couple of times, but she wouldn't consider him for anything long term. Though Aidan might not have a ton of cash, he had land and that made him wealthy to these people. Aidan was the catch.

"Well, who wouldn't want you, darlin'?" Dwight had found that she was very susceptible to flattery. All he had to do was tell her she was hot, and she suddenly was willing to listen to anything he said.

Karen's face was bright red with rage. "And you didn't mention that he'd gone queer. It was one thing when he was fucking that whore to get back at me, but I can't sleep with him now. He's kissed another man. I can't believe it. He humiliated me in front of the whole town. Everyone's going to say I made him gay."

Dwight's mind raced with the possibilities. And if everyone had seen that drama play out, then maybe he could use it to his advantage.

"He's insane. You could make a gay man straight with that body. Come on, darlin', you deserve a drink. Let's take your car."

He walked with her, nodding at the people they passed. Everyone they walked by looked at the blonde with sympathy. They talked about her behind their hands. Dwight could tell she was getting more and more worked up with every pitying glance. Her shoulders got tight and her fists clenched. By the time he got her to her SUV, she was practically vibrating with rage.

He opened her door. He had a plan in mind, and it might work. Dwight had talked to Aidan moments before Karen had found him. He'd intended to gently introduce the idea of taking his sleeping pills, but Aidan hadn't had time to talk. He'd told Dwight not to wait up. He, Lucas, and Lexi planned to stay for a while. That was fine with Dwight. It gave him a little time to do what he needed to do.

"Why don't we get you a drink, darlin'?"

Karen nodded. "Yes, I think I could use one."

Or five. Once he had her drunk, she would talk and then everyone would know how angry she was. She was the perfect scapegoat.

Dwight pulled out of the parking lot and aimed toward the bar. If he had a bit of luck, maybe his problems would all go away.

Chapter Fourteen

Two hours later, Aidan opened the door of his truck and handed Lexi up, wishing he could go back to that moment when she'd been triumphantly happy. After the smackdown with Karen, she'd practically glowed. She'd been Lexi, sweet and incredibly sarcastic. Something had happened to shut her down again, and for the life of him he couldn't figure out what. Had it been him kissing Lucas in public? He doubted it. Lexi had never been afraid of what other people thought.

The cab was quiet as Lucas got in and shut the door. Aidan shuffled around, putting off that moment when he had to sit beside her, when her hand didn't find his thigh the way it used to.

With a heavy heart, he got in and started the truck. He didn't miss the way Lucas's hand slid over hers, their fingers entangling. They were so close. They were a unit, and he might never be one of them. He might be able to worm his way in, but they would always have had those years together without him. They had bonded because they'd survived his desertion.

Did he have the right to even try?

Maybe he should try to find them a new Dom. It was obvious they were happier with one. Lexi had been responding. He pulled the truck out of the parking lot and decided to try to understand what had gone wrong.

"What happened back there, Lexi?" He kept his voice quiet. He was as non-threatening as possible. He would never order her to tell him. There would be no punishment if she chose not to trust him, just an aching sadness in his heart. "One minute you were giving Karen hell and the next you shut down."

He pulled onto the one-lane highway. At this time of night, it was full dark once they left the neon lights of the fair grounds. The moon was new, so the only lights in the night came from his headlights. It felt like they were the only three people in the whole world, and yet he was alone.

He thought she might ignore the question. For a few minutes, the only sound was the soft thudding whirl of the tires on the pavement.

"I'm fine," she finally said in a small voice that lent not one ounce of credence to her words.

Aidan felt his whole soul sag. She was shutting him out.

"Lexi." Aidan could hear the warning in Lucas's tone.

Aidan glanced over, and Lexi's face had hardened into a stubborn mask. "I'm fine. Maybe I don't like small-town carnivals. Maybe I don't like having to deal with Aidan's old high school girlfriend calling me a whore."

"Well, I don't think she'll do that again," Lucas replied. "She'll come with a printout from Urban Dictionary before she insults you again. And that wasn't what got you upset. You enjoyed that. We both know what upset you. I heard what your mom said to you. Don't you think it's time we all talked about this?"

Aidan put his eyes back on the road. There weren't usually a lot of people driving at night through this part of the county. The road led out to his ranch and a couple of homes, but there were deer and small animals that could jump out. He wouldn't be the first driver to total a car on this stretch of asphalt. His eyes were on the blacktop in front of him, but his ears were focused on the conversation. What had Abby said? Had she and Lexi argued about him?

"There's nothing to talk about. I want to go home and rest. It's been a trying couple of days." Her eyes were down, studying the dash.

"You know you're going to have to talk about it eventually,"

Lucas insisted.

Talk about what? All of his instincts were telling him this was an important conversation. Everyone had talked about Lexi hiding something that had happened to her. What the hell was it? He wanted to stop the car and force her to talk, but that would break trust with her. Lexi was like an animal he was trying to feed by hand. He couldn't force her, or she'd run as fast as she could.

But Lucas seemed determined to do exactly that. "Don't you think it's been long enough?"

She turned on Lucas. "Drop it, Lucas, or I swear I'll call my mom, and she'll pick me up. I won't give a damn about the contract or getting back into The Club."

Aidan heard what sounded like the whine of an engine revving, but he didn't see another car. He looked in the rearview mirror. Nothing. He turned his eyes back to the road, but his mind was on the woman beside him. "Lexi, you don't have to talk if you don't want to. We can go home and go to bed. It will be better in the morning."

He was unaccountably nervous about this conversation. Now that it was here, he wasn't sure he wanted to have it. Indecision clawed at his insides. It might be best for her if he let her go, but he couldn't do it.

"No, it won't be better in the morning," Lucas insisted. "It won't go away, Aidan. She's been trying to make this go away since it happened. Don't you think he deserves to know? Don't you owe it to Brandon?"

Who the hell was Brandon? He'd been told that Lexi had only dated Lucas since they broke up. Now there was someone named Brandon? His first instinct was to shout and try to figure out how to call the bastard out. But he'd left her. He'd walked away. If she'd slept with a hundred men, he couldn't say a damn thing about it.

"Don't you dare say his name, Lucas Cameron." Lexi practically vibrated with rage.

Lucas pointed a finger at her. Even in the darkness of the cab, Aidan could see that Lucas's face was red, flushed with emotion. "I'm not going to do it anymore. I won't pretend he didn't exist. I won't pretend it didn't happen. You can tell him or I will."

Aidan was ready to insert himself into the conversation. He was going to tell both of them to stay calm and wait until they got home. He needed time to figure out how to handle them. They were both on edge. Lucas was never this aggressive. Lexi never yelled at Lucas. He needed to separate them and find out what was going on.

He opened his mouth to take control of the situation, but the truck suddenly lurched forward. The truck jerked from the force of something hitting the back end. He had to tighten his hands on the wheel to stay in control.

"What the hell was that?" Lucas asked, craning his neck to see behind them. "I can't see anything. Is that a car?"

It had sure felt like one.

"A drunk driver?" Lexi clutched his leg as though she needed something to hold on to.

"Could be." He kept his voice measured and even.

Lexi had been through this. She'd had an accident that put her in the hospital. He needed to stay calm for her sake.

He wasn't sure he wanted to stop and sort it out with the other driver while she was in the car. It was too dark and too isolated to risk her. He sped up. He'd pay for his own damage. There wasn't anywhere to pull over. The road dropped off on either side right here. On the right there was the reservoir that fed the county, and the left sloped on to what eventually became his own land. He wasn't far from home. He hit the accelerator.

The truck lurched again, this time harder.

"He's trying to hit us." Lucas's voice was tight with anxiety.

"Don't you take off that seat belt, Lucas," Aidan ordered when he saw his hands moving.

"I'm trying to get a good look at him," Lucas replied.

"Call the cops, now." Aidan didn't care in that instant who was behind the wheel of the other car. Rage could come later. Now he was panicked for the people he had inside his truck. Lexi and Lucas being safe was the only thing that mattered.

Aidan forced himself to stay calm. His vision had started to recede. It was what happened when he had an episode. The world got fuzzy around the edges, and he would be able to feel the heat of Iraq on his skin. The noises around him became the never-ending sound of gunfire. He couldn't let that happen. He couldn't let them down.

He focused on Lucas's voice, calmly requesting assistance from the 911 operator. He concentrated on Lexi's hand on his leg.

He looked for anywhere to go. The truck pitched, jerking forward in a chaotic movement. There were only two lanes here, but a half a mile ahead, the ground to the left became flat. He could pull off the road and see if the man followed.

He watched the road ahead of him, waiting for that moment when the ground leveled. Then he could make his move.

The air around them cracked with the sound of an engine roaring. The sound seemed to get closer with each second.

"He's passing us," Lexi said with an irritated sigh. "What an asshole."

Aidan tried to slow down to allow the car to pass. He got a quick glimpse of an SUV, and then it slammed into the side of the truck.

"Fuck." Aidan tried to regain control. He felt the wheels grasping for purchase. The world was tilting on its side.

"Hold on," he heard Lucas say.

There was one final crash, and the truck began to tumble. Over and over. It rolled three or four times before it hit the water with a slapping splash. His head snapped forward. The seat belt bit into his chest. He had to force his eyes open. The world seemed out of place.

Upside down. He felt gravity working against him. He hung in his seat against the belt. The car had flipped. Everything was dark, so stinking dark. They were sinking to the bottom of the reservoir. Only the headlights showed anything at all and that was a watery universe. Ghostly light filtered in.

Aidan clawed at his belt, finally managing to get it off. He fell forward, his chest hitting the steering wheel. He had to get them all out of here. The reservoir was large, serving the entire county. It wasn't a recreational lake. It had been dug thirty feet deep in the middle, and it hadn't been a dry spring. The reservoir had overflowed at times. He tried to think. Here at the edge it couldn't be more than ten, maybe fifteen feet down, but it didn't matter if they couldn't get out of the vehicle.

He tried the door. It didn't budge.

"Aidan?" Lucas finally came to, and Aidan could hear him trying to release the belt.

"Don't panic. You're upside down. Prepare to fall when you get out of the belt." He tried the power window. His side had taken the hit. He could already feel every muscle in his body screaming, but he wouldn't give in.

There was a muffled groan as Lucas made it out of his belt.

Aidan's window wouldn't move. There was no hope for it. There was so little room to move. He couldn't get his boot up to break the window. The truck thudded as it hit the bottom. Aidan moved to pull Lexi out of her belt, cushioning her fall with his body. She dropped into his arms. Water dripped on her face.

"She's breathing." He had to thank god for small miracles.

"Aidan?" Lexi's voice sounded tiny, but his heart leapt at the sound.

"Hush, angel. We're in trouble, but Lucas and I are going to get you out of here. Hold on to me and don't let go. Lucas, try your window. It's the only way out. I can't fit through the back. If the window doesn't work, we'll smash through the back and shove Lexi out of here."

Her arms tightened around his neck. "I'm not going anywhere without the two of you."

Sweet words, but he couldn't allow it. Now he would play the Dom. "You will mind me. If we have to, you'll get the hell out of this truck, and you won't look back."

"No need, I got it." Water began to pour in as Lucas spoke.

"What if he's waiting?" Lexi had to shout the question. The sound of the water rushing in pounded at the silence.

It wouldn't be long before the water invaded the cab, and they would be forced to get to the surface or die.

He'd already thought about the possibility that someone would be waiting for them. It hadn't been an accident. It hadn't been some drunk. That car had a purpose, and it was to take out everyone in his truck. He'd caught a glimpse of it. A dark SUV. Karen drove a dark SUV. He'd never imagined she would go so far. But her husband had owned many guns. If she was waiting to finish the job…

He felt so fucking helpless sitting in the dark, waiting for the cab to fill up. His heart raced because even though he knew he had to wait, his primal brain was screaming that he was going to drown, and

Lexi and Lucas would drown, and it would all be over. It couldn't be over.

The water reached his chin. He tried to push Lexi up, putting off the inevitable time when she would be submerged.

"Lucas goes first. He'll get out and pull you through. He'll get you to the surface and swim for the other side. I'll deal with whoever is waiting for us. Lucas, you understand? You take her and run. You don't look back."

"Yes."

Aidan heard Lucas take a deep breath, and he went under. There was nowhere left to go. Lexi took a breath and then she went under, too. It was the hardest thing he'd ever done, but he let go of her hand. It would be all right. Lucas was here. Lucas would take care of her.

That was the comfort of this arrangement. He always had a partner. He'd cheapened it by calling Lucas his partner in Lexi's pleasure. Lucas was his partner in her joy, her love, her needs, and her comfort. Now he was Aidan's partner in saving her life. Lucas would be there. He would do what needed to be done. Aidan wouldn't be alone because Lucas was here.

As he felt his way to the window, he caught a shadowy glimpse of them swimming, their hands tangled together. Lucas pulled her along, doing everything he'd promised. Aidan would be able to do what he needed to do—take out the person who was trying to kill his woman.

His whole body tensed for battle as he reached the surface, but he was assaulted by lights. A bright one shined right on his face.

"That you, O'Malley?" Aidan recognized Sheriff Lou Mark's voice.

The bright light disoriented him for a moment. He shielded his eyes. Now he could see the red and blue lights of the squad car flashing their signal of safety. He took a deep, cleansing breath. The air had never seemed so clean, so pure.

"Yeah, it's me. My truck's at the bottom of the damn lake," Aidan shouted.

Lucas was treading water next to him. Lexi was beside him. They seemed strong and secure. They were alive and whole, and Aidan felt an overpowering sense of relief threaten to take him under again. His eyes watered at the sight of them. In the distance, he heard an ambulance.

He nodded at Lucas and all three began to swim for the shore.

* * * *

Lexi hated hospitals. She loathed them with every fiber of her being. They were too bright and always cold. The clinic in Deer Run was no different. It was small, with only two exam rooms, but it had all of the applicable machinery. And it had an efficient nurse and a doctor. Luckily, she'd managed to convince Lucas not to call her mother. She had enough to deal with. Lexi was fine without dragging her family into yet another attempt on her life.

She sat on the narrow hospital bed and wondered how long they were going to keep her here.

"It won't be long now, angel." Aidan seemed to be reading her mind tonight.

He stood there looking surprisingly masculine in the green scrubs they had given both he and Lucas to wear. She was in a damn hospital gown because she'd hit her head at some point in time during the accident, and Lucas and Aidan were demanding the doctor run every possible test.

"I feel fine." She had a bit of a headache, but overall she felt physically well given the fact that she'd been in an accident. It was worse than the other accident even though…

She lay back on the hospital bed. Not going there. She didn't have to go there no matter how hard Lucas tried to make her. Some things were best left in the past.

"After they get the test results back in, I have no doubt they'll let us head home," Aidan explained. "The truck is being towed in as evidence. I already called Bo. He's on his way up here."

Lucas smiled a little. "I'm glad you called him. He loves you. He's just a little lost. When he makes a comment that upsets you, knock him on his ass. He'd prefer that to you ignoring him. You'll see. He'll get used to us."

Lucas was talking like they were going to be here awhile. Lucas was getting invested in this whole threesome thing, and she wasn't sure what to do about it. What the hell did she want? When she was in the water, she'd clung to Aidan. She'd been utterly terrified that she could lose him after she'd gotten him back. She'd known how much she loved him, that she'd never stopped loving him. Lucas had pulled her out of that car, and she'd looked behind to make sure Aidan followed. All that had mattered in those moments was the fact that they were together. Her anger and pain had fallen away, and all she'd been left with was love.

And then she'd been forced to come to the hospital. The easy love had been pushed aside as grief bombarded her again.

Lucas and Aidan were talking quietly.

"I'm willing to try if he is," Aidan was saying. "He seems so mad. It's been that way ever since I got back. The only person he doesn't spit bile at is his best friend, Beth Hobbes."

"He missed you," Lucas insisted. "He missed his brother, and he doesn't know how to say it."

She listened to the two of them talk and couldn't help but wonder. Was that what was wrong with her? Lucas seemed so willing to forgive. She remembered back to the day Aidan had left. She'd cried, and Lucas had told her that he would be back.

It might not be tomorrow, but he'll come back. He loves you. Deep down I think he loves me, too. When Aidan gets used to the idea, he'll come back, and we need to be ready to forgive him.

He'd held that line until the accident. After that, Lucas had stopped talking about when Aidan would come back. He'd shut down and focused on her. He'd subjugated his own needs.

What if the accident had never happened? Would she be as willing to forgive Aidan as Lucas was?

Who was she scared of forgiving? Aidan or herself?

"I'm going to go and talk to the cops." Aidan leaned over, and his lips brushed the top of her head. "I won't be long."

He strode out of the room.

"He knows something." Lucas watched the door as it closed. His hair was rumpled, and an air of weariness hung over him. He'd avoided meeting her eyes since they had made it to the hospital. "Did you get a look at the car that hit us?"

"No." It had been too dark. Everything had seemed like someone had hit the fast-forward button until the roll. That had taken forever. Still, she had her suspicions. "Does anyone know what Karen drives?"

Lucas walked to the window. He pulled the curtain back and stared into the night. "You think Karen did this?"

"Well, I think she hates me. She was in Dallas on the day I got shot. I think she smokes. You found cigarette butts where you think the shooter stood, right?" It made sense. She couldn't think of anyone else who might want her dead. She was obnoxious, but most people didn't want to kill her over it.

"I don't know. She seems like a woman who wouldn't ruin her manicure, much less her car. I wasn't surprised she tried to queen bee you, but actual murder? I don't know. And I don't know how much we can count on the cigarettes leading us to a suspect. Lots of people smoke. Hell, most of Aidan's ranch hands smoke. I already put in a call to Ben and Chase. They're going to start working with the police here."

"Well, I'm sure the Wonder Twins will figure it out eventually." She sighed. "I guess I won't be let off the ranch for a while."

"No," Lucas replied. "But I have to go back to Dallas for a few days. I have loose ends to tie up. If I'm going to be in Deer Run, then I have to find a way to do my work from there."

The room fell silent. Though it was quiet, there was nothing peaceful about it. It was awkward and heavy. Lucas let his head rest against the window pane.

The argument in the truck played back in her brain. The words assaulted her, but more than that she was starting to listen to what was underneath those words. Her head hurt, but her heart was aching.

"Do you honestly think I pretend he didn't exist?"

Now he was looking at her. His green eyes bore through her. "You never talk about him. He's always there between us, but you never mention his name. I can see that it's killing you, but you shut down the minute I try to talk. I was there, Lexi. I held him, too. I ache from that night, but I'm not allowed to talk about it. Not even with you."

She wanted to shrink into herself. She'd avoided this for so long.

201

How could she have not seen that it affected Lucas, too? She'd selfishly believed she was the only one who hurt, and she'd shut him out of her grief. She'd made him her accomplice in forgetting, in refusing to move on.

"I thought if I didn't talk about him, I would forget."

Lucas nodded. "I know. But you won't and you shouldn't. You shouldn't forget him. Can't you see that?"

"It hurts too much. I don't want to tell Aidan." Her eyes were heavy with tears. She looked down at her hands, but Lucas was suddenly there, his palms sliding over hers.

"He deserves to know."

The ache had opened again, as fresh as it had been that night. "The hard part is, I can't figure out why I don't want to tell him. Am I trying to spare him the pain? Am I punishing him? Am I terrified that he won't ever forgive me?"

"All of the above." Lucas forced her chin up so she had to look at him. His eyes were glossy with unshed tears. "And every single reason is valid, baby. But it's time to move past that now. It's time to step up and tell the truth."

"Did you love him?" Aidan stood in the doorway, a cup of coffee in his hand. His face was blank, his skin a stark white.

How much had he guessed? Since the moment he'd walked back into her life, she was always going to have to make a choice. She could choose to tell him what she should have before or she could keep stubbornly silent. It was so clear to her now that two paths lay before her. She could refuse to tell him her secret and walk away—or she could be brave and share the pain that had always been theirs to share.

"It's all right if you did," Aidan said. "I understand if you met someone else."

"Brandon wasn't a boyfriend, Aidan. He was our son."

Chapter Fifteen

The cup of coffee fell to the floor, splattering across his pants. Aidan felt the burning heat, but it didn't register.

"What did you say?" he asked because his mind couldn't quite make the connection.

Lucas got to his feet. There was a somber air surrounding him. He walked over and picked up the cup. "I'm going to go and get us all some coffee. I think the two of you need to talk."

The door closed behind Lucas, and he was left alone with Lexi.

She sat for a moment, the tension palpable in the air between them. Aidan wanted to be closer to her, but he could feel the wall there. "I said Brandon was our son."

"You were pregnant? How were you pregnant?" Even as he said the words, he knew how stupid they were, but his brain wasn't functioning. All he could see was Lexi sitting there telling him he had a son.

How could he have a son?

"The normal way. See when a girl and her undercover bisexual boyfriend love each other very much…" The words that came out of her mouth dripped with sarcasm, but her face was flat, with none of her normal animation, like she was a doll and someone had pulled her string.

"Don't you dare joke about this."

That blank face moved a bit, her mouth turning down slightly. "I'm sorry. I hide behind it. I know I do."

He had a son. She was telling him he had a son. Lucas had known. She'd told Lucas, but not him.

"Stop. Just stop. Just tell me." He needed the story, and he didn't want to have to wade through Lexi's bullshit.

She stuttered and grasped at the edges of her gown. She looked so young sitting there. How young had she been when she'd had their baby? Where was their baby? His mind was a chaotic mess of questions, but that one screamed through his brain. If Lexi had their baby, where was he? Was he being raised by someone else? How was he going to get his kid back? Because if he had a kid out there in the world, Aidan wanted him. Had she been so mad at him she couldn't handle the thought of raising his child? It didn't compute. Lexi had always wanted children. They had talked about it the night they got engaged. And Lucas would have gladly stepped in. Hell, Lucas would have married her and put his own name on the birth certificate if she'd wanted it. A sick feeling opened in the pit of Aidan's stomach.

Lexi would never have given up her baby no matter how mad she was at his father.

"I didn't know I was pregnant when you left. I had no idea. I actually think it might have happened that night. The timing was right." Her voice took on a monotone, devoid of all emotion.

She stared at her hands as though it was too painful to look anywhere else. He wanted to go and grasp her hands, to force her to look at him and fucking tell him what had happened to his son.

He stopped and was still. He knew this woman. Though there was a part of him that wanted to rage at her for keeping this secret, he knew the only reason she had was the pain he'd caused her.

"When did you find out, angel?" It was easier to shove down the anger when he realized how much this was costing her.

"Uhm, about a month after you left. Lucas came down for the weekend. I was moving out of our apartment, and I passed out. Lucas freaked and made me see a doctor who told us that I was pregnant."

He'd been in Basic by then. He'd been getting the shit kicked out of him. He'd thought after that first day of training that he'd be so tired he'd be able to sleep without thinking of them, but he'd been wrong. He'd closed his eyes and they were there, holding their arms out and taunting him with everything he couldn't accept. While he was pushing them away, Lexi had been pregnant with his baby.

Lexi continued. "You have to understand, Aidan. You were gone. I was in a state of shock. I made the doctor do the test again. I went out and bought five boxes of tests. I couldn't be pregnant. I said a lot of things back then. I told Lucas I didn't want the baby. I told him I was going to fix the situation."

The words cut at his heart, but damn, he understood them. Lexi railed and fought against anything she viewed as unfair. She said things she didn't mean when she was mad. It would have been worse than just mad. She would have been afraid.

"I didn't. I mean, I didn't really ever plan to."

He put a hand on her back, needing the connection to her. "It's all right. Tell me what happened."

He knew. He could feel the tears slipping from his eyes. His child was dead. Julian had mentioned an accident. It didn't take much to put two and two together. His child had been gone for a long time, but Lexi was here. Lexi was still in pain.

"I pretended it wasn't happening. Lucas tried to get me to tell my mom, but I wouldn't. I made him promise not to tell. It was easy because after that one fainting episode, I didn't even notice I was pregnant. I told myself I would decide what to do later. I told myself I could make an appointment the next day, but I never did, and one day it was too late."

She'd put it off because she hadn't really wanted to make an appointment. She wouldn't have been able to go through with it. But she hadn't been ready to admit she wanted the baby. Aidan had lived with her long enough to know what had happened. And now he could see what was wrong between them. He just wasn't sure he could fix her.

"I never bought anything, you know," she said quietly. "I didn't buy a baby name book. I didn't buy tiny socks. I didn't even buy maternity clothes. I didn't run around telling my girlfriends about it. I only told Lucas."

He felt a sob threatening. God, he wanted to cry. He wanted to scream and pound into something until his fists bled. He swallowed it all down and sat down beside her. "How did Brandon die?"

Brandon. His son. Their son.

Her head was down, but he could see the tears falling like raindrops against her clenched hands. "I was driving to Dallas. It was late, really late. I shouldn't have been on the road, but I couldn't stand being alone. I had to see Lucas. I didn't even call and tell him because he would have insisted on driving down to pick me up. I didn't want to wait five hours. The car came out of nowhere. One minute I was driving and the next some paramedic was pulling me out of my car. I was in and out for a while. I had a concussion, but otherwise I was fine. I was five months along, but you could barely tell I was pregnant. It was hours before they did a sonogram. There was no heartbeat. No movement. A couple of days later they induced labor, and he was stillborn."

He sat back, his whole body numb. If he'd been with her, she wouldn't have been on the road that night. He would have treated her like fragile glass.

"He was so tiny, and I never told him I loved him. I know babies don't understand, but I never said it. I didn't even feel it until he was gone. Do you think he knew I didn't want him at first?"

"No." Aidan forced the words out of his mouth. "No, angel. He knew what was in your heart. This wasn't your fault."

It was his. He'd walked out. He'd never even considered that she could be pregnant. He'd simply left because she wouldn't conform to his vision of how life should be. Because she wouldn't leave behind a man she loved for another man who couldn't accept that he loved them both. He'd walked out with only a suitcase of his clothes and his guitar. He'd left everything else behind, a mess for her to clean up. He'd left behind the couch they'd bought at a garage sale. He'd left the books she'd bought for him. He'd left the table where he'd made love to her that first night they moved in, when everything had seemed possible. He'd left it behind like it was trash when it had been their lives.

"Lucas had to name him. They made a death certificate. Lucas had to name him and make the arrangements."

Yes, Lucas had been the one to do all the things Aidan should have done. Lucas had stepped up. Lucas had tried his damnedest to hold everything together. Lucas had needed him, too.

"The man who hit me accepted a plea. I was grateful for that. I couldn't have handled a trial. It also kept me off my stepdad's radar. Jack was happy with him going to jail. He was even happier when the dude broke his parole and ended up back there. As far as he knew, I was okay after all. I moved to Dallas to be close to Lucas, and I tried to forget."

But she hadn't. Aidan could see that plainly. She'd been drowning in grief, and he'd been gone. Now he'd walked back in demanding that she give him a second chance. He'd gotten her fired and tricked her into seeing him again.

Guilt weighed on him.

"I'm sorry, Aidan."

She was weeping openly, her body curving in on itself as though she could block out the pain. Or maybe, he thought as he watched her, because she didn't believe she deserved comfort.

Aidan gathered her in his arms, praying she wouldn't reject him. He hadn't been there when she'd needed him, but he was here now. Her arms wrapped around him as she sobbed out her grief.

"It wasn't your fault. None of it was your fault." Her grand crime had been loving two men. Her crime had been refusing to settle for a life that would have made all three of them miserable. "You have to know that you would have made a hell of a mother. You would have loved him because you don't know how to do anything else. You can't hold this in anymore. This is a poison that's killing you. You have to grieve."

He understood death. He'd lost his mother and his father. He'd lost his career. He'd lost her and Lucas. Grief could break a person, but if it was shared, if the burden was spread among loved ones, grief could be freeing. When his mother had died, he'd held on to his brother. When he'd lost his father and his ability to play the guitar, all that had kept him afloat was the thought of getting back his loves. He might not deserve her forgiveness, but he was going to ask for it. He would do whatever it took to never fail her again.

It washed over him like a river. He'd lost so much, but he had a chance to fix things if he didn't give in to his guilt. Guilt wouldn't bring back his child. Guilt wouldn't fix Lexi. Love, really loving her, and dedicating his life to her and Lucas was the only thing that might fix it. His first instinct had been to slink away because he didn't deserve her, but that was cowardly, too.

Instead, he let go of her and sank to his knees. He didn't try to stop his tears. He let his grief flow. He knelt in front of her like a penitent. "Please forgive me, Lexi."

This was what he should have done in the first place. The knowledge swept through him as her hand came out to stroke his hair. He should have walked in and dropped to his not fully functional knees and begged. He'd thought he needed to prove he had changed, but he owed her his pleas. She'd tossed her pride aside by begging him not to leave that night. He could do the same. Pride had no place if it kept them apart.

"You didn't do this. I kept it from you. I should have told you. I should have called you when I knew." Something inside her seemed to have eased. Her face was puffy and red. She'd never cried prettily. When Lexi cried, it was with passion. She cried like a woman, and he still thought she was beautiful.

"I walked out. I walked away from the best thing that ever happened to me." He kept talking because she was listening, finally listening, and he wasn't about to waste this chance. "I love you. You're a part of me. You're the best part of me. I don't care if you hate me for the rest of your life, I'll follow you. I'll make sure you're safe, because that's what I was born to do."

"I understand that you feel guilty, but it could have happened even if you had been here. I still could have lost him."

"But I would have been here to grieve with you, angel. I would have mourned and taken care of you. I would have buried our boy, and I would have clung to you like a goddamn life raft, because that's what people in love do."

"I thought you would hate me." She was calmer, though the tears continued. "I thought you would blame me for not telling you."

"I would have come back. Hell, by that time I was looking for excuses, but in the end, I walked out. I should have stayed and fought, but I was weak. I won't do it again. Kick me out and I'll sleep on the porch, but I won't walk. I'm here for life."

She pulled her hand away, her eyes narrowing as she started to weep again. "I feel like I'm in a corner, and I don't know how to get out. I've been here for so long, I don't know how."

Lucas's slow and steady voice came from the doorway. "Just step out, baby. We're here for you. I know you feel like you painted yourself into that corner, but no one wants you there."

"I'll have to tell my mom," she said, her voice anguished. "She's going to be so upset."

"I think she'll understand. She asked me the other day why you never played with Josh. It bothers her that you love Olivia, but you don't even look at Josh. No one is going to be mad at you." Lucas's face was solemn. It was obvious to Aidan that he wanted to join them, but he held himself apart. "I'm a different story. I didn't call you either, Aidan. I knew I should, but I didn't, because I didn't want to lose her. It was selfish, and it cost her. If I had, she might not have gotten here."

Lexi quickly stepped in. "Don't blame Lucas. He made me see a therapist, but I knew what to say. I knew how to smile and act through all the steps she wanted me to go through. I didn't want to give up my grief because it was the only thing I had left of you. I'm sorry."

Aidan stood and hauled her into his arms. "Never say you're sorry. Don't ever apologize for loving someone. We've all made mistakes. We can't let that hold us back. We've wasted too much time."

He held Lexi in one arm and held his hand out for Lucas.

Lucas shook his head. "This is for you and Lexi. I only came back to make sure you're okay. I'll give you two some time alone."

Aidan hardened his voice. "You will not, Lucas. You will come here, and you will stand by your family. This only works if we share everything."

"Please, Lucas," Lexi pled. "We all lost him."

Lucas broke, his handsome face contorting in sadness as he staggered toward them. He practically fell against them. Their arms wrapped around each other as they cried and comforted. They were a circle against anything outside. For that moment, this was the whole world.

They were together finally, and it was enough for Aidan.

* * * *

Deep in the night, Dwight watched as Aidan stepped through the hospital doors and out into the parking lot. He looked cautiously one way and then the next, as though he sensed he was prey.

Fucker wouldn't die. Why wouldn't he die?

Dwight pulled the binoculars from his eyes as Bo's car stopped in the hospital parking lot. He ground out his last cigarette in the dirt beneath his feet. There were too many of them to try anything else now. Besides, Karen was utterly passed out in her wrecked SUV up the road.

He started to hike back through the woods across from the clinic. It had been a brilliant plan. Things had gone exactly as he'd expected. Karen had made an ass of herself at the fair, and then he'd made sure she got rip-roaring drunk at the road house on the edge of town. After two margaritas, he'd talked her into a few shots of tequila. That was when she'd started talking about taking out the bitch who took her man.

She was incredibly easy to manipulate. Dwight picked up the pace after shoving the binoculars in his pack. His car was parked at the fairgrounds, not far from Karen's house. It would be a simple thing to tell the cops he'd dropped Karen off and then gone back to get his car. If anyone asked, he would say he'd met up with some tourist in the parking lot and spent a little time with her. Everyone knew he was a ladies' man.

No one would question him. After all, he was an American hero.

Karen, on the other hand, was a drunken former beauty queen who everyone knew had a bad temper and even worse judgment. No one would be terribly surprised that she'd gotten behind the wheel and tried to kill her ex-boyfriend. All anyone at that fair had been talking about was the fact that Aidan O'Malley had kissed another man and how they pitied poor Karen who hadn't been able to see that Aidan was gay.

Dwight broke into a jog. He'd hated the Army, but they had known how to whip a man into shape. He'd kept up his physical training. He could easily cross the two and a half miles between the clinic and the fairgrounds in fifteen minutes. He would take the back roads home. He lived in the foreman's house set off a bit from the main house. If he turned the lights off, no one would notice him driving in late.

It was all going bad. Aidan was close to making a breakthrough. He'd seen it earlier in the day. Aidan was remembering more and more. That stupid dog didn't help. The dog had stood over Aidan's body that terrible day, barking and growling any time Dwight had gotten close. If he'd been able to get past the fucking dog, maybe he could have taken care of the problem, but by then the firefight was over and he could hear the other squad coming in. They might have questioned a burst of gunfire, and he couldn't get close enough to slit the dumb animal's throat.

Now the dog was a symbol of all Dwight stood to lose. The animal was a touchstone, constantly calling Aidan back to that day. If Aidan remembered, the case would be reopened, and Dwight would be reviled and possibly sent to jail if they could figure out that he'd purposefully shot two of the men so they couldn't tell what he'd done.

He didn't regret it. He wasn't about to give up his life for a simple mistake anyone could have made. The gun had a loose trigger. The US Army spent shit supplying their soldiers. If a soldier wanted top-of-the-line body armor, his family had to pay for it. Dwight didn't have a fucking family. He didn't have anything. That was why he'd gone into the Army in the first place.

He made it to his car. He'd parked at the edge of the lot, and the whole place was dark and empty. He slipped into his car and started it, leaving the lights off.

His cell phone was blinking, indicating a message. He checked the number. Karen.

"Dwight? Dwight? What happened? I woke up in my car. I think I'm in a ditch. Where are you? I feel terrible, and I can't remember anything."

There was the distinct sound of sirens in the background as Karen talked. He felt a smile spread across his face.

"Dwight, the cops are here. Oh, where are you? Please come help me."

A sense of relief rushed through him as he shut off his phone. At least something had gone right tonight. They would find her there, disoriented, in a car that was obviously damaged by side and front impact. The cops here would put two and two together and never think about it again. Everyone would talk about the beauty queen's fall. He was safe.

But it didn't fix his problem. Aidan was still alive.

That had to change and soon. It was time to take out the problem once and for all. After tomorrow, Aidan would be gone, and Dwight would be free.

Chapter Sixteen

Lexi came awake as Bo's car came to a stop. She was slumped against Lucas's chest, her hand nestled in Aidan's. They were all scrunched together in the backseat because no one wanted to sit apart. Bo had grumbled about being a chauffeur, but he'd driven so carefully, as though he had precious cargo.

How had she fallen asleep? She should have been nervous, terrified of getting back on the same road she'd almost been killed on, but she was between Lucas and Aidan. Their big bodies sheltered and protected her. There was nothing between them now. Not her sadness. Not Lucas's insecurity. Not Aidan's guilt. There wasn't room for any of that.

"We're here, angel." Aidan's hand squeezed hers.

"Safe and sound." Bo turned his head and grinned at her. "I'm a way better driver than he is, too. You might want to reconsider."

Aidan sat forward. He ruffled his baby brother's hair affectionately. "I'll give you the driver part, brother. Thank you for coming to get us."

Bo sighed. "You're welcome. I guess you couldn't get a hold of Dwight. It doesn't matter. I was happy to do it. I'm just glad you all were okay."

"I didn't call Dwight," Aidan admitted. "I called my brother because I was in trouble. I know we've had our problems since Dad died, but we're going to work it out."

A brilliant smile broke over Bo's face. "We will. And the whole bisexual thing is all right with me. Lucas is a nice guy. If I had wanted to screw some dude's butt, it would be his."

Lucas snorted and then coughed, as though trying to cover it up. "That's a great compliment."

Bo gave him a thumbs-up and hopped out of the car.

Lexi giggled. She couldn't help it. She felt light. She had cried, finally and truly cried, while they had held each other in the hospital. Aidan had been right. Sharing the pain lessened it. It opened her to love. What had Leo said? Something about sanity and accepting the love offered us. She'd been insane for far too long. She was ready to accept everything these two men had to offer.

The car door opened, and Lucas slipped out. He reached back in and helped her out. Aidan jogged around the other side. Before she could really find her balance, Aidan hauled her up into his arms, lifting her against his chest.

"No walking for you," he said.

She didn't mind. It was sweet to be carried around. She felt light and delicate in his arms. But she didn't want him to think she was too fragile. She needed more than his tender care this evening. Much more. "The doctor cleared me."

"That doesn't mean you have to walk." Aidan's voice had taken on a thick, dark quality. It seemed to change the air around them, making it charged with tension. "You never have to walk when one of your men can carry you."

"I think I'm going to sleep out at the bunkhouse tonight," Bo said with a knowing grin. "If you need anything, you call me."

The world seemed perfect as she nestled in Aidan's arms with Lucas standing beside them. She nuzzled his chest, loving the way he smelled. He was still wearing his scrubs, but they had all been able to take a shower to wash away the reservoir water. She hadn't been able to dry her hair, though. It had done that all on its own in the Texas heat. She must look a mess, but it didn't matter. These men loved her. These men always thought she was beautiful. "So we're going to be all alone in that big house? What are we going to do?"

She had ideas. It was far past time for her to be in the middle.

"We're going to have a talk, sub." Aidan stared down at her, and even in the low light coming from the porch, she could tell his eyes had gone dark and slightly hard. "I need to make a few things clear."

Lucas reached out and touched her cheek, a soft caress that belied his words. "The Master and I feel we should set ground rules for how this is going to work. Since the doctor cleared you and you feel fine, I suggested we have this discussion of ours tonight rather than tomorrow. Please understand, this is not punishment, but we would like to play."

"If you're not up to it, angel, we understand," Aidan said. "But if you want us, you should understand everything is in play tonight. We will push some boundaries."

She shivered at the thought. It was everything she wanted. They would take her together. They would be deep inside of her at the same time. "I want it."

"God, I was hoping you would say that." Aidan swept her up the stairs and onto the porch as Lucas got the door open. Lexi held on as Aidan walked through the front hall and toward the living room. Lexi watched Lucas following behind, a decadent smile on his face as he pulled the scrubs over his head and tossed it aside. Lucas Cameron without his shirt was a sight to behold. From his broad shoulders to his tight abs, he was simply gorgeous.

Aidan kicked open the door to the master bedroom, and she found herself on the bed looking up as both of her men tossed their clothes off. They weren't elegant about it. They were in a hurry. Her heart rate sped up as all that sun-kissed flesh was revealed. She reveled in their differences.

Lucas was lean and elegant. He was dark and broodingly gorgeous. He could have been on the cover of a fashion magazine.

Aidan was thick, with bulky muscles and an angular face. No one would call him beautiful, but even with all his scars, he was all sexy male.

And both of her men had erections that made her mouth water. They turned to her, cocks jutting out from the Vs of their thighs.

"Take off your clothes, angel," Aidan said. There was nothing

215

polite in him now. He was all Dom, and he'd given a command.

She got off the bed. Her muscles were a bit sore, but she needed her men. She needed to feel them all around her. She pulled off the green scrubs the nurse had loaned her. The shirt was tight across her breasts, and she struggled a little. The men made no move to help her. They stared as she dragged it over her head and started to push the pants over her hips. When she was naked, she found her position, dropping to her knees with her legs spread and her head down. She took a calming breath and waited.

Bare feet came into view. "Look up, angel."

She brought her head up and sighed as Aidan's thick cock came into view. It was a thing of beauty, jutting from his neatly trimmed nest of dark blonde hair. His balls were large and heavy. The cock had taken on a purplish cast, and she could see the thick vein that ran along the side was pulsing with blood.

"Lick me."

Oh, she could do that. She leaned forward and ran her tongue along that vein. She was satisfied with Aidan's deep groan as she licked his cock from the base to the bulbous, plum-shaped head. She lapped at his dick, teasing with quick strokes. When she found the slit weeping with pre-cum, she burrowed the tip of her tongue just inside and enjoyed his salty taste.

There was suddenly a hand on her hair, pulling her gently away from her task. "Don't forget me, baby."

Lucas and Aidan stood close together, their cocks touching and brushing against each other. Lucas was longer than Aidan, but not quite as thick. She gave Lucas the same treatment she had with Aidan, drawing the dewy arousal from his slit with gentle suction.

She licked one, and then the other, never favoring one. She had two Masters, and they deserved equal treatment. She reached up and gently pressed the heads together so she could suck both into her mouth. They were far too big to do it, but she could manage to get the heads inside so she could whirl her tongue around. She made a circle around Aidan and then moved her tongue to Lucas, constantly encouraged by the way they groaned. Each man had a hand on her head. Aidan tugged where Lucas stroked. So different, but all hers.

She'd wasted too much time, but she wasn't about to feel bad about it now. Now she was ready to make up for everything they had missed. She sucked at them and reached up to cup their balls. Her body was primed and ready for what was to come. Her pussy was getting soft and wet, every nerve tingling in anticipation.

"Take care of the Master. I need to prep you." With a regretful sigh, Lucas pulled away.

Aidan took advantage. "You're all mine for now, angel. Suck me."

She took his cock in her mouth and tongued him. Aidan set both hands in her hair and thrust himself deeper. Aidan took charge. Aidan liked to fuck her mouth. She relaxed and let Aidan work his cock into her mouth inch by inch.

"You feel so fucking good." Aidan's voice had gone guttural. "Do you have any idea what that hot mouth of yours is doing to my dick?"

If she hadn't had several inches of cock in her mouth, she would have smiled. She could definitely tell she was having an effect on the man. His cock was swollen and pulsing, his breath ragged. He pumped into her mouth, working his way in until his balls bumped her chin with every thrust.

"Master, if I'm going to do this, I need her ass in the air." Lucas's calm, patient voice broke through the frenzy.

Aidan cursed, but pulled out of her mouth. "It's all right. She was about to make me come. I'd rather do that buried deep in her pretty asshole."

Her pussy clenched at the thought.

Lucas's hand pressed on her lower back. "Cheek to the floor, baby. I want your ass high in the air."

She leaned forward, placing her face to the soft, plush carpet. She watched Aidan's feet move around her and heard them talking as Lucas settled behind her. He separated the cheeks of her ass with his hands.

"That is a lovely sight." Aidan spoke in reverent tones.

She had to bite off a laugh since they were talking about her asshole. She'd never once thought of it as a lovely sight, though the thought of Aidan being inside her ass made her rethink it. She relaxed as she remembered how Lucas had taken Aidan. That had been beautiful. Big, strong Aidan letting Lucas in like that had softened her heart so much she'd thought it would break. Never had she imagined Aidan could get to that point. They had all changed and grown. Now they would grow together. It would be Lexi and her two men. They would cherish and protect her, and she would do the same for them. Karen Wilcox better hope she went to prison because the next time Karen came after Lexi's men, she would get way more than a lecture on the proper use of the word whore.

She shuddered as she felt something wet dribble onto her ass. She bit her lip as she felt Lucas's finger press into her asshole.

"She's so fucking tight. She's going to grip your dick like a vise."

Aidan huffed. "Like you're doing now with your hand?"

Lucas laughed. "You know I like to keep a hand on both of you. You two are my whole fucking world. Do you want to know what I'm doing to our Master, baby?"

She had a hunch, but she loved it when he talked dirty. And Lucas was right. They were her world. Her asshole stretched as Lucas added another finger. She breathed deeply as Lucas opened her anus with his fingers. "Tell me."

"Well, lover, I have two fingers deep inside your rectum, getting you ready for the moment when the Master takes this pretty anal cherry and makes it his own. I'm fine with that because I had his yesterday, and it was sweet as pie. He gripped my dick like nothing on earth except your pussy, baby. So, one hand is in your ass and the other is wrapped around his dick. He is so fucking hard. He's going to split you wide and fuck your ass. My own cock feels like it's going to explode because I can only guess what this is going to feel like. My cock sliding against his, deep inside your body."

"We'll fill you up, angel." Aidan's voice sounded slightly strangled. She could guess what was making him sound so deep. "We'll make you scream because you're so full of your men. And we'll slide against each other, only that thin piece of you between us. Oh god, Lucas. You're going to make me come."

She whimpered as Lucas pressed deep. She wasn't sure about the sensation. It wasn't pleasure, but it also wasn't pain. It was a jagged fullness that made her a little jittery. She wanted to look at them. She wanted to watch as Lucas pumped Aidan's hard cock in his hand and the cum began to flow. It would hit her backside and coat her in his pearly essence. She turned her head and tried to look.

A short, heavy slap lit up her backside. It was so much more sharp a sensation for the fingers in her anus. She groaned as the pain radiated into heat that coated her pussy in cream.

"You keep your eyes to the front, Lexi. You take what we give you." Aidan's command was a harsh wave to her ears. He softened his next words. "We love you. Please trust us."

She turned back but smiled as she spoke. "I wasn't worried, babe. I wanted to see Lucas giving you a hand job."

There was a long deep laugh that radiated from both men. Aidan spoke. "You are a righteous pervert, my love."

"And that's the way we like our girl," Lucas added. "He's ready for you. His dick is dripping cream. I'm not going to make him come. He's going to come deep inside this asshole."

Lucas stretched her, making her groan. She wasn't sure she could take Aidan's thick monster. She could barely handle a small plug or two of Lucas's fingers. He was going to ream her ass, but she wanted to try. She wanted to know what it felt like to be between them.

"Is she ready?" Aidan asked on a harsh rasp. Aidan definitely sounded ready.

"Not quite." Lucas seemed to be taking the lead.

It was another reason to love Aidan. He wasn't such a control freak that he couldn't let Lucas have his fun. It was why they worked. She knew from talking to her mom that Sam wouldn't want to take the lead. Dani and Finn didn't want the reins, so Julian was always in charge. Lucas needed to lead at times, and Aidan recognized that. He was willing to put aside his own instincts to give his lover what he needed. He was a Dom. She felt tears prick her eyes. *Fuck that. He was a husband. Her husband.* It didn't matter that they hadn't made vows. They were connected, she and Lucas and Aidan. They were married in her heart because she would never love anyone the way she loved these two men. It was easy to submit, because she knew deep down that she belonged to them.

"On the bed, and spread those legs, sub. Your Masters want a taste of you."

She sprang up at Aidan's command. She practically ran back to the bed. She'd managed to take both those cocks in her mouth. It was only fair that they pay her back. She settled on the feather soft quilt and spread her legs with no inhibitions whatsoever. Inhibitions were for women who were unsure of their men. She could look in the mirror and see all the flaws of her body, but she chose to see herself through Aidan's eyes and Lucas's eyes. They looked down at her, one set dark and deep, one emerald and shining.

"Have I told you that your pussy is a work of art?" Lucas asked with a decadent grin.

Aidan reached down and ran a single finger through her labia. "So soft and ripe. And who is all this cream for?"

"My Masters," she replied honestly. She'd only ever made love with these two men, and they were all she wanted for the rest of her life. They were more than enough. They were everything.

"That's right, angel." He pulled on her ankles, drawing her to the edge of the bed where he got down on his knees. "This is all for us."

Lucas knelt beside Aidan, their shoulders touching. He leaned over and breathed in her scent. "I love the way you smell. You smell like sex and love and home to me."

She was going to say something back, but his tongue came out and took a long, leisurely stroll all along her pussy. He licked almost to her clit, stopping just short. Lexi moaned at the tease.

"I think she wants something more, Lucas."

"I'm sure she does, Master. How about this?" Lucas dipped back down. This time he spread her wide and licked at her clit. He licked downward, lavishing affection with his tongue and teeth. He bit playfully at both petals of her labia before burying his tongue inside her cunt.

It wasn't enough. It felt like heaven, but she needed more. Much more.

"I don't think she's happy yet, Lucas." Aidan had a wide smile on his face. "I think our lovely sub requires more."

"She has always been hard to handle, Master."

"I can believe that. No one man could ever handle Lexi Moore. But two, I think two might be able to take her down." Aidan leaned over and kissed her clit, sending a firestorm across her skin.

Lucas, not one to be left behind, went back to his previous

occupation of fucking her with his tongue. He drove his tongue deep up inside, eating her pussy like he was a starving man. He twisted and turned that tongue, finding a place that made her scream.

And Aidan sucked her clit into his mouth. The nub went off like a rocket. She moaned as the orgasm took her. She let herself float down as they continued to eat away. Every lick and kiss and thrust of tongue made her shiver and shake. She felt boneless as they lapped up her cream.

Aidan brought his head up. She could see the evidence of her arousal coating his chin. "Lucas, I taste like our sweet girl."

Lucas pulled himself away. His lips were slick with her cream. His eyes were lit with mischief. "I don't believe you, Master."

"Come see for yourself." Aidan put a hand around the back of Lucas's neck and pulled him close.

She watched as the two men she loved more than life itself kissed. There was nothing soft and sweet about it. They devoured each other, licking her pussy juice off each other's mouths. Their tongues played, each fighting for dominance. They were beautiful together. She couldn't take her eyes off them. Every muscle in her body was replete with satisfaction. She would be content to lay here and watch them fuck, but they had other plans in mind.

They broke off their kiss and turned back to her.

"Lucas, get under her. Take that pussy." Aidan's cock bobbed, hitting his rock hard abs as he ordered Lucas to get into place.

Lucas wasted not a moment. He sheathed his dick in a condom and took her by the hips, flipping her over. Suddenly she was straddling his hips, her breasts tickling against his chest. He dragged her into place. His cock brushed her clit. She hadn't thought she could get interested again quite so fast, but that dick rubbing against her pussy had her panting for more. Lucas reached down between them and guided his cock to her slit. He soaked himself in her juice and started to press home.

She leaned against his chest as he pushed that cock inside, fighting to gain each inch of territory.

"Fuck, you're so tight. I have no idea how Aidan's going to fit." He pushed down on her hips to force his way inside. She felt him slide in and groan as he seated himself fully.

Immediately there was a hand on her lower back. "I'll fight my way in if I have to. This asshole belongs to me."

He parted her cheeks, and she felt him move between her legs. Lucas held them both still, though she wanted to move. She wanted to fuck the cock she was currently impaled on, but another cock pushed insistently at her backside. Aidan spread her cheeks wide and fit his cockhead to her asshole.

She looked into Lucas's emerald eyes as she felt Aidan start to breach her.

"It's all right, baby. Give it time. Relax." Lucas's words soothed her.

But not much. This wasn't exactly comfortable. "It's hard to relax when someone is shoving a two-by-four up my ass."

Both men chuckled. She could feel that laughter deep inside.

"It's not quite a two-by-four, but I'll take that as a compliment." Aidan stroked in and out in small increments, gaining ground with each careful thrust.

She laid her head on Lucas's chest. There was nothing to do. She wanted them both, and she had to get through this first time. It would get better or people wouldn't do this so often. Lucas had done this. Aidan had done this. She could do it. The sound of Lucas's strong heart beating like a jackhammer inside his chest eased her ache. He wanted this. Aidan wanted it. She would never deny her men. Not ever again.

Slowly Aidan took her until she could feel his balls brush her backside. She wondered if Lucas could feel him, too.

"I'm in. You were right. This is the tightest asshole I've ever been in," Aidan said with a groan.

"Well, Master, you've only been in two," Lucas replied, a light smile on his face as though he deeply enjoyed being in that exclusive club. "You really don't have much room to compare. We'll have to go another round. I have more experience than you."

Lexi could hear the indignation in Aidan's huff. "Your previous experience is over. No more playing around for you. You get two lovers the rest of your life."

Lucas's face tightened, and his eyes took on a glossy sheen. One hand held on to her hip, but the other moved off. She suspected it now caressed Aidan's hip. "I don't want anyone else. Not ever again. This is my home."

Lexi felt something inside ease. *Home.* Home wasn't a place. It was a feeling. It was this amazing sense of comfort and peace. It was a place where she could go and always be accepted and loved for the fucked-up person she was. She never had to apologize for being who she was. She was beloved, and that was all that mattered. *Home.* It was right here, nestled between the two best men she'd ever met. "I love you. I love you both so much."

Aidan flexed inside her. "I think I speak for both of us, angel, when I say we love you, too. Always. Marry us."

There wasn't a hint of hesitation. Not this time. The first time he'd asked, a vision of Lucas had clouded her brain, but they had just been friends then. Now they were together, and it was perfect. "Yes."

She would marry them and be the center of a family. It didn't scare her anymore. It wasn't an insult to the child she had carried, but a way to honor him. He'd been loved and lost, but she wouldn't bury that part of her that wanted to be his mother. She would have their babies and watch them grow strong under their fathers' love.

Lucas pressed up, and Aidan began to pull out. His cock dragged along her every nerve. It was a revelation. Jangled, jittery pleasure flooded her ass while Lucas pressed his cock over her G-spot. She couldn't stop her wail of pleasure.

And then they were off. Lucas fucked into her pussy while Aidan took her ass. Lexi rode the wave. She was tossed back and forth between the men. Every way she went, she was touched and loved and drenched in pleasure. Her orgasm built higher and higher as they rode her body. Aidan ground into her from behind.

"I can't hold back. God, I can't wait." Aidan reached around, his fingers searching. He stroked her clit and then the time for playing was done. She groaned as the orgasm swept through her system. Hot pleasure invaded her veins, starting from deep in her cunt and her ass and radiating outward. She could hear Lucas and Aidan moaning, but it was a distant thing. What was close was the feel of them filling her. Hot, wet. She was full of them.

Aidan collapsed, pushing her onto Lucas who kissed her forehead lovingly.

"I love you, baby," Lucas said.

Aidan's arms surrounded her. His weight pressed against her.

She was whole and safe. Aidan moved to the side but spooned her while Lucas nuzzled against her breast.

"Get some sleep while you can, angel," Aidan murmured. "Our honeymoon is starting early."

If Lexi had any say, it would never end.

Chapter Seventeen

Aidan stretched, his limbs much more eager to move after thirty minutes of yoga. He'd had a hot shower and a cup of coffee and was ready to start the day. He stepped off the porch and started to head toward the barn. The early morning sky was a swirl of oranges and purples. It was quiet at this time of the morning. He knew he should be tired, but he'd woken before dawn with a joyful energy that had him ignoring the soreness of his muscles.

Everything was falling blissfully into place. Lexi was here, finally here. He couldn't help but think about the child they had lost, but he had to be happy about the future. She'd agreed to marry him and Lucas. He was getting married.

Aidan felt a ridiculous grin cross his face. It didn't matter who legally married Lexi. He actually had a thought about how to fix that polyamorous tangle. Lucas didn't have any real loyalty to his family. The last Aidan had heard, Senator Cameron was asking his constituents to help pray the gay out of his son. Lucas had one time mentioned changing his name to Barnes because he felt more loyalty to Jack. But Aidan thought Lucas O'Malley had a certain ring. They were a family. They should share a name.

"'Morning, boss." One of his ranch hands, a middle-aged cowboy named Ron, was leading a big beautiful bay out of the horse barn.

He nodded and tried not to look like a lovesick goofball because all he could think of were the two people he'd left peacefully sleeping in his bed. Lucas and Lexi were tucked in together, their limbs tangled. He hadn't had the heart to wake them. "'Morning, Ron. You seen my brother around?"

The cowboy put a boot in the stirrup and hauled himself easily into the saddle. "He was asleep when I got up. I know he was out late, so I didn't figure it would hurt to let him sleep in. Dwight rides that boy hard, you know. Bo ain't a bad kid. He tries."

That was good to hear. Aidan had only really talked to Dwight for so long, and Dwight couldn't stand Bo. It was good to hear someone say something nice about Bo. He was willing to forgive and forget. Bo had a hard time when their father died. It was time to move past it. "I know he tries. I think I'll wake him up and have him work some with me this morning."

Ron smiled down, adjusting his hat. "That sounds fine. I think that would be a good thing. He and Dwight are like oil and water. Best to keep them apart. I'll see you later, boss. I'm going to join Al and Barney in the east pasture. Oh, and there's something wrong with the walkies, so if you need us, you'll have to ride out."

Dwight had everyone working the east pasture? It wasn't what Aidan had planned for the day. The east pasture was the farthest away from the house. He would have to ride twenty minutes to call the men back in. What was wrong with his walkies? The cell service could be spotty that far out, but he made sure every ranch hand kept a radio on his person. He'd checked the system the day before.

He needed to find Dwight.

In the distance, he could hear Ike barking. Ike barked a lot. He barked at squirrels and passing cars, and anyone he didn't immediately recognize. He sometimes barked at falling leaves. He wasn't the smartest dog in the world, but he was loyal.

Ike kept barking as Aidan rounded the corner of the barn. He squinted, trying to see what had Ike's attention. There was a mist coming off the pond where he watered his horses. It coated the world in a hazy, surreal glow. Ike barked, his stubbed tail down. The dog's whole body looked on edge, every muscle ready to attack.

A terrible pain bit into the back of Aidan's head as his peripheral vision started to fade. Ike was barking at something in front of the bunkhouse. Over and over, the mangy dog was ceaseless in his warning. Just like…

Suddenly the mist wasn't a mist anymore. It was a mixture of sand and dirt, whipping through the city. It had been so windy that day. They were on the outskirts of the city, the whole squad patrolling because the brass was sending in some major players and no one wanted a fuckup.

Aidan could hear it. The sound of spattered gunfire. It was background noise in Fallujah. The world receded, and he was back in hell.

* * * *

The heat was so much worse than anything Aidan had felt back in Texas. Of course, back in Texas he hadn't had to carry fifty pounds of gear and wear ceramic-plated body armor. His feet bit into what passed for a road in this torn up, mottled part of the world. God, he wished he was home.

"Keep up, you green piece of shit." The sarge was staring at the soldier behind Aidan.

Aidan moved past the sarge, who was spewing some serious venom at the new guy. PFC Creely had been with the squad for a month, but he was still the new guy, and the sarge had taken an instant dislike to the soldier from Wyoming. It wasn't surprising. He'd been damn sure the sarge hated his guts in the beginning, too. After a while, sarge had let up and Aidan had been a member of the team, but those first few weeks had been hell.

"You're nothing but bullet bait," Sarge yelled as PFC Creely jogged by. "Do you know that?"

For once Dwight seemed to know to keep his mouth shut. On more than one occasion, Dwight Creely had popped back at the CO and gotten his ass handed to him. If he didn't watch out, he'd get thrown in the brig again. Dwight was rapidly becoming a certified brig rat.

"Take up your positions."

227

The four snipers took off, jogging toward the burned-out building that always served as their perches, but the rest of the squad stayed together.

They had made it to the farthest point of their patrol—a wall that used to surround some sort of business. The building it guarded was in rubble, but the wall could be useful. He took up his position on the west-facing end of the wall. He would watch their backs while the senior team members guarded the road. He set his M16 up and checked for anything out of the ordinary. There wasn't a ton of cover here. Behind him, he could hear the rest of the squad setting up for the few hours they would be here.

Tanner, Mills, and Link were set up on the other side of the wall. Thompson stood at the back with the CO. It was only guard duty, but they had all had to hump it five clicks to get here. His feet hurt, and he missed home. Hell, he didn't give a shit about home. He missed them. Lexi and Lucas. It was getting easier and easier to admit that he missed Lucas, too.

"FTA." Dwight was grumbling as he got into position beside Aidan. He had a lot in common with the Wyoming boy. Dwight came from a ranching family, but there was something about him that made Aidan hold back. He was friendly enough with the man, but Dwight was always getting in trouble.

"Keep it down, soldier," Aidan said under his breath. "You do not want sarge hearing you say that."

Fuck the Army. He thought it, too, sometimes. Hell, there wasn't a soldier alive who didn't think it when the going got really rough and the CO was on your ass, but the Army was also a family. And when a soldier was in the middle of a mission, it wasn't good luck.

"Maybe I don't give a shit anymore," Dwight muttered.

But Aidan could see he did. Dwight's hands were shaking, and his face had flushed. He hadn't seen a moment of combat, and Aidan got the feeling Dwight was really dreading it. Aidan had seen some light combat, but nothing like what others had been through.

"It's going to be okay," Aidan said in an even voice. "Just stay calm and do the job. We don't even know anyone's going to try anything today. It'll probably be smooth as glass. The bigwigs drive through, and then they're someone else's problem."

Dwight's eyes kept moving around. "I heard El Cid came in and talked to the Lieutenant."

Aidan laughed. Dwight thought the CIA was behind this little mission? They were like the boogeyman. Everyone was afraid of the spooks because generally when the CIA got involved, it turned into a clusterfuck, and the lower pay grades were nothing but cannon fodder. The clerks at base loved to scare the shit out of newbies. "Don't listen to the clerks. They love to gossip. This is totally routine. The general is making an appearance is all. Thompson, tell Creely here that we've done this duty a bunch of times, and no one's died yet."

PFC Thompson snorted. "Nope. We're all alive, but you never know. Today could be our lucky day. Don't you worry none, Creely. We'll be back at base in time for whatever crap they're serving tonight. God, I want to be home eating a cheesesteak."

Aidan wanted to be home waiting on Lexi. She couldn't cook to save her life, but she tried. Now Lucas, on the other hand, he was practically a freaking gourmet. The last weekend they had spent together, Lucas had put together a lasagna that he could still taste on his tongue.

He had to keep his mind on the mission. He winked at Dwight, hoping it made him feel better. "This is a relatively safe part of the city. It's constantly patrolled. We cleaned it out a long time ago. Seriously, who wants to be here? There's not a goddamn thing out here."

"Eyes front, soldiers." Sarge walked behind them. He was a big, rough man, but he sighed as he stood behind Dwight. "O'Malley is right. It's safe. We've done this several times. It's a pain in the ass, but it's fine. In twenty minutes, the convoy will move through, and we'll hike it back."

Aidan noticed how the CO shook his head as he walked away as though he knew Dwight shouldn't be here at all. Aidan agreed. Dwight was a nice enough guy, but far too touchy for combat.

Aidan settled in. He would be in this position for a while. He let his eyes roam across the area they were protecting. Another squad was parked a mile down the road, further into the city. They had the more dangerous job. There were only two positions at this point.

Guerilla Squad had a much more difficult position with buildings all around them, a hundred places for insurgents to hide.

He had another year. A whole year here before he had to go back and figure out what to do with his fucking life. He was a good musician, but maybe not good enough. He'd played a bunch of gigs, but his guitar play was better than his vocals. He wondered what he would have done if that recording deal hadn't fallen through the day after Armageddon. It was how he'd started referring to the night he'd spent fucking another man. It wasn't another man. It was Lucas, his best friend. And they hadn't been alone. Lexi had been there. She hadn't been shocked by it. Hell, she'd encouraged it. Her own mother was in the same kind of relationship.

They had made it work, Lexi's mom and her two husbands. Jack Barnes was about as tough as a son of a bitch could get. He was a seriously scary motherfucker and he was bisexual. Jack managed to have both Abby and Sam, and no one bothered him. What would it matter if someone did? Why should he live his life and deny his own feelings because it bugged someone else? Why did he have to live by someone else's rules when what he did would never harm anyone? How did loving someone make him less of a human being?

"Goddamn it, O'Malley." The sarge's irritated huff brought him out of his thoughts. "Your mutt's here. I thought you tied him up."

He turned. Sure enough, Ike, the mutt he'd found starving on the roadside two days after he got to Fallujah, was trotting along as though out for a leisurely walk. His big tongue lolled out of his head, and he walked up, obviously waiting for a pat. He leaned down and held out his hand. "What are you doing here, boy?"

There was the sound of distant gunfire. It came from the east, from the three-story building in front of him. No mistaking the sound. Suddenly sarge's radio cracked to life, the sound splitting the air around them.

"Insurgents! At least five."

He recognized the voice. It was Mike Garza, a corporal. He had led the snipers. The radio erupted with the rapid-fire explosions of a close-in firefight. His heart clenched. His teammates, his friends, were fighting for their lives.

Suddenly the air around him exploded.

230

Bullets hit the dirt around him like lightning striking the ground.

"Fuck!" Dwight shouted beside him.

Someone started firing.

Aidan heard the sarge yelling into the radio for help. Guerilla Squad was up the road, and they were on their way. He hoped they had a medic with them, because Tanner was already down.

He watched in horror as sarge fell, a hole in his forehead. He'd shifted his helmet back, wiping sweat off his brow, and now he was gone. For a moment, Aidan couldn't breathe. It seemed impossible. That building had been swept before by another squad who had proclaimed it safe and clean.

The world had slowed down, and Aidan felt locked in position.

Something struck his chest, sending him flying back, and he came out of his stupor. His heart raced. He had to do something.

Aidan brought the M16 up and pulled the trigger, spattering the building with bullets. A body fell out of the window.

Chaos reigned. The ground around him exploded.

A stinging pain lashed at his face as a bullet whizzed by his head. He could feel the cuts and scrapes on his face begin to open. Blood began seeping from his cheeks, mingling with the sweat.

Aidan tried to focus. He dove for cover at the opposite wall. He sprang back up, trying to get a good line of sight.

His shoulder flew back as he took a bullet. Agony swept through him, but he remained on his feet.

The radio screamed out.

"Two men down. They're dead—" There was a crack and then silence.

He saw the glint of a gun from a broken-out window. He aimed and fired. The gun, a freaking M16—they were getting shot with their own weapons—fell to the ground below.

A sudden, shocking silence fell over the yard.

He was pretty sure he could hear his heart beat. His hands shook. He ducked back down behind the wall, very aware now of a pain in his shoulder. *Fuck.* He'd been shot. He looked down at his body armor. The fucker had gotten him where he wasn't protected, and now the armor was brushing against the wound. It was agonizing.

"You okay?" Specialist Charlie Link knelt down beside Aidan.

They were covered by the wall, but an eerie silence had taken over.

"No." Every word hurt. "I gotta get this armor off."

"That's a bad idea, O'Malley."

"Please, it's killing me. Guerilla Squad should be here any minute." He pulled at the fastenings of the body armor. It had saved his life, but now he couldn't breathe in it. God, he couldn't breathe.

Link quickly got the armor off, even as he protested the whole idea. Ike whined as he lay down beside Aidan. Aidan ran a hand over his body, checking for injuries. It looked like the dog had come out all right.

The minute the armor came off his body, he felt an immediate relief. His shoulder ached like a motherfucker, but he could breathe. Aidan took stock. The sarge was dead. Aidan could barely comprehend it. Sarge was dead. Garza was almost certainly dead.

"Thompson?" Aidan asked.

Link shook his head.

"Tanner and Mills?"

Again, that tiny negative that indicated a wretched outcome.

"How?" Aidan had to ask. He knew the answer, but it seemed so ridiculous. How were they gone? Moments before, they were alive and joking. How could they be gone? It was supposed to be routine.

"Fucking Creely panicked." Link's voice was a mere whisper.

"What?" Aidan glanced over, and Dwight Creely was sitting with his back to the wall, his face a pasty white. He appeared to have vomited all over his armor.

Link's mouth was tight as he whispered. "Keep quiet. I don't think he's in his right head. I tried to get his gun, and he damn near shot me. All I know is Tanner was beside me, and he was shot from behind. He took one in the neck. Creely didn't jump for cover the way you and Thompson did. He just started shooting. He was behind us, so we were in his line of fire. That fucker is going to get court-martialed for sure."

There was a loud crack, and Link's body jerked. Link's dark eyes stared down and Aidan watched in horror as the life drained from them. Ike got to his feet and started barking.

Link slipped to the ground, and Aidan's eyes narrowed to Dwight Creely standing over him. His big body was a shadow, blocking the sun until all Aidan could see was the man and his gun.

"Stand down, soldier." Aidan put a harsh bite to his voice, praying Creely would respond.

"I didn't mean to." Creely sounded like a petulant child. "It wasn't my fault."

A sick feeling took hold in Aidan's gut. His body armor was out of reach. Why the hell had he taken it off? He needed to keep this fucker talking until Guerilla Squad got here. "I understand that you panicked. But killing Link was murder, pure and simple."

Dwight shook his head, his lips firming to a mulish pout. "I won't go down for this. I am not going to fucking prison."

Aidan's M16 was close, but he would have to reach for it. His shoulder ached, but he could do it. The radio squawked, announcing that Guerilla Squadron was five minutes away. It was too far.

"Sorry, O'Malley. You were the only one I would have called my friend. I have to make this look good or my life is over."

Aidan grabbed for his gun, but Dwight was faster. Dwight shot, and Aidan felt his hand explode with pain. His fingers. *Fuck*. Dwight had shot his hand, and now he couldn't feel his fingers. Dwight shot again, and Aidan pulled his ruined hand in. Blood seemed to be coming from everywhere.

"I'm sorry." But there was nothing but a brutal will on Dwight Creely's face as he raised the M16.

He felt a horrible burning sensation in his stomach as the bullet entered. He clutched his gut and rolled, trying to get away. Then there was another blast, and his whole body went numb. His back. He'd been shot in the back. There was another shot, but all Aidan got was a glimpse of Ike running as that fucker tried to shoot at him.

Aidan went still. It was easy since the lower half of his body no longer seemed to function. Through slitted eyes he watched as Dwight jogged across the road and disappeared into the building where the trouble had started. Aidan had a sense of him returning, but he shut his eyes and kept his breathing as shallow as possible.

Lexi was somewhere out there. He wondered if she was with Lucas. He wondered if anyone would bother to tell her that he had died. The sand beneath his face reminded him he wasn't home. He wanted to be home. He didn't want to die in this country.

"I'm here! Please help. They killed my whole squad. I'm the only one left, and I need a medic." Dwight was yelling.

Ike was barking, but it seemed so far away.

Aidan started to float. He didn't want to die. He wanted to be home with them. He should never have left. Never.

It didn't matter. The world went dark, and he dreamed of the love he'd shoved away.

* * * *

Aidan's whole body shook as he came out of the memory. Ike was still barking, the way he had that day. It had been so real. He'd been there again.

Dwight. Fucking Dwight had shot him. Dwight had killed two people that day, one on purpose, and he had nearly taken Aidan's life. The betrayal of it all made his head spin.

Dwight might not have been cool under fire, but damn he'd been the epitome of grace under pressure after the fact. He'd read the reports. Insurgents had taken out the squad in close combat fighting. Several had been taken out by snipers, but one of the insurgents had made it behind the wall. It was all a lie, made up by Dwight to cover his tracks, but no one had been able to refute him.

Dwight had been fast. He must have dragged a body across the street. He'd been quick on his feet. Some of the injuries couldn't have come from a distance. Dwight had set up a scenario with close-quarter fighting. The squad that saved them had moved quickly, because Aidan had still been alive. Coincidence had helped Dwight out as the team sent to investigate had been attacked, too. The area had been declared hot, and they hadn't been able to get back in to investigate.

And the only person who could have turned the bastard in had forgotten the whole incident. Dwight had stayed close to make sure Aidan never told what had happened. That was why he'd been so insistent on making sure Aidan took his sleeping pills. He dreamed about that day when he wasn't on the drugs.

Damn it. It all made sense now. No one had really been after Lexi. She was merely the bait to get Aidan to come home. He remembered the phone call right before Lexi had been shot. Dwight had wanted to know when he would be home. Dwight didn't like it when Aidan left the ranch, because he couldn't watch him. Dwight had shot at Lexi knowing he would bring her back to the ranch to protect her. He'd walked right into Dwight's trap.

"You remember, you son of a bitch."

Aidan turned at the sound of Dwight's voice, but it was too late. Dwight's hand came down, and the butt of a rifle met Aidan's skull.

The world went dark once again.

Chapter Eighteen

"**I**'m going to kill the dog." Lucas murmured the words as he tried to cover his head with a pillow. He fully intended to call in that Dog Whisperer guy because Ike needed to learn how to tone it down. The dog was nice and all, but he needed his sleep.

"You can't kill the puppy." Lexi turned over and cuddled close to him, her breasts nuzzling against his chest.

His cock leapt to life. How did that happen? He'd come so many times the day before he would have sworn he needed more than one night's rest to recover, but that cock of his was ready to slide inside her again.

Lexi shifted and turned her back to him. He wrapped his arms around her, cuddling her close. This was the way to wake up.

He raised his head and looked over Lexi's shoulder. Aidan was gone. He had her all to himself. Sharing was nice, but Lucas wouldn't complain. The day before, Lucas had been the one to get up and get the work done. Aidan could take his turn. And Lucas would take his turn with their gorgeous bride-to-be. He pressed his swollen cock up against her backside and let his lips find her neck. He kissed her briefly.

"Ain't happening, buddy. Do you have any idea how sore I am?"

Lexi grumbled the question. "The only thing getting close to my backside today is a bag of frozen peas. Seriously, after taking both of you there last night, you can't believe that's happening again this morning. Do you know how big the two of you are?"

He had to laugh. She probably was pretty sore, but he could dream. He let his hand slide around to run over her pussy.

"Sore there, too," Lexi said, rubbing her head against the pillow. "No sex for a couple of years and then days of decadent nonstop sex with two men has taken its toll on all my girl parts."

Well, there was always her mouth.

"And don't even think I'm giving you a blow job, babe. My jaw is sore, too."

She knew how his mind worked. Lucas propped himself up on an elbow and looked down at her. "So, this is how marriage is going to be? I should have known all the sex would dry up the minute you agreed to let me make an honest woman of you."

She was so pretty lying there, her eyes soft and sleepy. "I'm honestly sore. The good thing about a threesome, though, is that you can go and pester Aidan for sex."

That was a good idea. He rolled out of bed. The day was definitely looking up. He reached for his jeans.

She shifted toward him, a bemused smile lighting her face. "That was quick."

He shrugged and decided to try to be discreet. He wasn't quite sure how this whole thing worked yet. "I'm just going to go help him out."

"Of his pants, maybe." She laughed, a deep, sexy sound. "Tell the Master I love him, too, when you tackle him."

God, he'd hit the jackpot with her. He slipped a T-shirt over his head and sat back down on the bed, stroking her arm. Her skin was silky soft. So different from Aidan's, and yet he needed both. He'd managed to find the two people in the world who could handle him. Lucas swore to himself that he wouldn't let them down. "I love you. Do you have any idea how much I love you?"

Her smile softened, and she reached out to him. "I think I do. I think you're a man who'll do anything for the people he loves. You've put up with my shit for a long time."

He leaned over, touching his forehead to her. "It was never shit. And there's no such thing as putting up with you. I am honored to be in your life. I wouldn't be anywhere else."

"I love you, too. I wouldn't be half of who I am today without you."

He didn't believe that for an instant, but he would take it. "Are you going to be okay living here? It's a tiny town, and we're going to be the outsiders. We've lived in cities all our lives."

Lexi had been raised in Fort Worth. He'd been all over the world. Deer Run was going to take some getting used to, but Aidan needed to be here. Lexi could write anywhere. Lucas could pare his workload down and do almost everything via computer. He was a corporate lawyer. There would always be some travel, but his two biggest clients were also his brother and Julian Lodge. They were understanding. Aidan couldn't move his cattle ranch.

She lay back with a throaty sigh. "I think I can take it. And we're not merely outsiders. We're crazy, immoral outsiders. The good news is Austin isn't that far away. The ranch hands won't care. Cowboys, I've discovered, are surprisingly tolerant. As long as you can ride and shoot and get your share of the work done, they don't care what your sex life is like. And I think I'm going to try to write that book I've always talked about."

His heart leapt at the thought. "I am glad to hear that."

"Don't be. It might suck."

He didn't care if it sucked. It could be the worst book in the world, and he would love it because she'd written it. "It will be awesome, baby."

"And don't tell Julian or Jack what I'm doing. Tell them I'm being a pampered princess. One of those two will decide to buy a publishing company and they'll send Big Tag out to scare people into buying my book. I'd like to make it on my own." She pulled the covers up.

Lucas frowned. He'd almost caught a glimpse of her nipples. Later. He'd make sure she wasn't sore later. He'd talk to Aidan and they would force her to soak in a hot bath. He had plans to renovate the master bath, but for now it was big enough for Lexi to soak. He and Aidan would treat her like a princess all day, and she'd be ready to take them tonight. Yeah, he liked that idea.

"Get some more sleep, baby. Coffee will be ready for you when you get up." He kissed her forehead and closed the door behind him as he entered the hall.

He was sore himself, but that wouldn't stop him from suggesting that he and Aidan play around. He entered the kitchen and checked the coffeepot. There was enough for him. He poured a cup and then made another pot for Lexi. He sniffed at the brand. It wasn't her favorite. He'd make a trip into town later and stock up. This was going to be their home. It was up to him to make it perfect for her. He would have to relearn all of Aidan's habits.

When had he started getting so much pleasure from making other people happy? Maybe because his own childhood had been utterly devoid of anyone caring about what he needed. Meeting his half brother had been a turning point in his life. Jack Barnes had taught him what it meant to be a man. Being a real man meant being able to love and take care of the people he loved. It was a responsibility he took a deep joy in. He had people who depended on him and who he could depend upon. One day, maybe, he would even have children.

That was a scary prospect. He remembered how hard it had been on Lexi to lose Brandon. But he wanted to try. He wanted it all.

He sipped his coffee as he looked out of the kitchen window over the yard. The barn door looked like it was open. It hadn't swung wide, but he could tell that it wasn't locked. The lock was sitting on the outside of the hinge. It was a windy day. It wouldn't do for the door to swing open. And Ike was obviously running around. He could get stuck in there.

He sighed and left his coffee behind. He let the screen door slam behind him. The sound was a loud shot in an otherwise perfectly quiet morning. Ike seemed to have given up his attempt to communicate. It was almost eerily quiet.

And he smelled something odd. Was that gasoline? Had Aidan been gassing up some of the equipment? It smelled like he'd spilled it—a lot of it.

He pulled the lock off and was just about to secure the barn when he heard something shuffle inside. "Aidan?"

He opened the door and felt his stomach drop. Aidan was lying

239

on the rack, tied down, the same way they had tied up Lexi the day before. Without another thought, Lucas rushed in.

"What the hell?"

Aidan's eyes flew open. They were wide with terror. He pulled at his restraints and seemed to be trying to talk, but there was a rag in his mouth. Lucas raced to him and pulled the rag out.

"Run, Lucas!"

But it was too late. Something moved behind Lucas, and he felt the right side of his head light up before the world went dark.

* * * *

Aidan felt sick as Lucas fell to the ground. Dwight had perfected the art of slamming the butt of a rifle into a person's head. He might not be the best foreman in the world, but he was damn good at knocking people out. And he was an accomplished killer. Aidan's vision was still hazy, and he smelled gasoline. Was that a hallucination? How much of this was real? He prayed Lucas was an illusion, but he didn't hold out hope.

"Don't hurt him. He doesn't know anything." Aidan was pretty sure it wouldn't work, but he was willing to try anything at this point. He couldn't stand the thought of Dwight shooting Lucas in front of him. He prayed Lexi was somewhere safe. How long had he been out? Obviously long enough to get dragged to the barn and tied down with his own damn rope. "Please don't shoot him. I'll do whatever you want."

Dwight stared down at the body at his feet. "When you first told me about those two, I thought you were insane. Now I'm just disgusted. I might be a killer, but at least I'm not a damn queer."

Aidan's head was pounding, but the gag was gone. He didn't scream, because that was a surefire way to get that nasty rag shoved down his throat again. Besides, Bo was too far away to hear him. Only Lexi had a possibility of hearing him, and he couldn't risk her running in here and getting herself killed.

"I've been listening to you talk for a year, and it always made me sick." Dwight reached down and grabbed Lucas's wrists and pulled him, dragging him across the wood floor of the barn. "Do you have any idea what it took to sit there and listen to you whine about your sex life? But it gives me a couple of outs. You see, you might think that you're being brave, but what you did last night was stupid. Everyone saw you kiss Lucas. The police here aren't going to care that you got yourself killed. They'll say that's what happens to gays."

Dwight might have a point about the sheriff. He hadn't been terribly friendly last night, but he'd done his job. It might have been different if Karen hadn't been gift wrapped and served up on a silver platter. That was obviously Dwight's doing, but he let that go for now. Dwight needed to understand this wouldn't be as easy as he thought. "Bo won't let it go. And I assure you Jack Barnes won't take kindly to his brother being murdered."

For the first time, Dwight looked like he was sweating a bit. He dropped Lucas and stepped away. "I can't worry about that now. I can't let you live. I should have smothered your ass while I had the chance, but you didn't remember. The doctors said they thought you would never remember, so I let it go. I didn't want to kill Tanner and Link."

A sudden flash of Link going down spun across Aidan's brain. He'd been so fucking young. Tanner had been an accident. Aidan could almost forgive what happened to him. A firefight was scary and chaotic, but Link died in the quiet aftermath. Link had been murdered in cold blood. "But you did it anyway."

"I had to. I wouldn't survive in prison. Do you have any idea what I've done to survive? I had to stab myself to make it look like I'd been in a fight. That takes guts."

Dwight was one delusional son of a bitch. "I bet Tanner's wife and kid and Link's parents would disagree with you."

Dwight picked up the rifle he'd put down when he moved Lucas. He held it casually against his body. "I had to take care of myself. No one else would do it. And now I have to take care of you."

"There's no war here to slow down an investigation. Someone will figure out that you did this."

He shrugged. "I don't see why. I've been careful. I've never once said a bad word about you. I'm the loyal friend who sat by your bedside and followed you home to make sure you were okay. Now, Bo, he's talked his mouth off about how pissed he is. That boy can't handle his liquor. He was a might miffed you got the ranch. And I'll make sure the sheriff knows how much you embarrassed him last night at the fair. No one in these parts wants a queer in their family."

Dwight was severely underestimating this town, in Aidan's opinion. There would be some people who wouldn't accept him, but not all. Even the ones who wouldn't condone his lifestyle wouldn't want him dead. Dwight was in for a mighty big wake-up call if he managed this.

"How exactly are you going to frame my brother? That's not his gun. Everyone knows he loves his Remington Model 7. He would never use yours." Sometimes Aidan thought Bo loved his rifle and the hunting that went with it far more than he would ever love any woman. He was pretty sure Bo slept with that rifle from time to time.

"I have no intention of shooting you. I'm—well, Bo—is going to lock you in the barn and set it on fire. By the time the ranch hands see the smoke and make it back from the east pasture, it will be too late. I've already hidden the gas can in Bo's trunk. Dumbass doesn't even lock his car."

God, he prayed Lexi was still asleep. He couldn't bear the thought of Dwight tossing her inside with him and Lucas. He pulled uselessly against the ropes he'd lovingly fastened to this table for his subs. This barn was supposed to be a playroom, a place where they could be themselves and love each other however they wanted. Now it would be his tomb. The ropes bit into his flesh, tearing at his skin. He felt blood start to leak from his wrists. Was that a little bit of give?

"Hurting yourself isn't going to help." Dwight stood over him. He had the rag in his hand. He shoved it into Aidan's mouth. Aidan fought, but he gagged as the rag nearly found the back of his throat. He had to concentrate to breathe. "Can't have you screaming, can we? I wonder if they'll think you and that boy down there were playing your kinky games and Bo couldn't take finding you like that. Or, hey, maybe they'll blame Lexi. No real woman wants to lose her man to another man."

Dwight pulled out a match when he got to the door of the barn. "Don't worry too much. I poured the gas around the inside perimeter. The only window is up in the loft, and I made sure it's closed. The smoke will kill you before the flames get to you. I'm not a monster, after all."

The monster he'd been friends with lit a match and dropped it to the ground. Fire lit and raced like the tiny Matchbox cars he and Bo used to play with. It raced up the track that led all the way around the barn. Within seconds, he and Lucas were surrounded by flames. Dwight slipped out of the door, and it snapped into place. He had no doubt Dwight had locked it behind him.

He couldn't see Lucas. He had to pray that he wasn't close to the fire. Aidan struggled with the ropes. He wouldn't give up. He was too close to everything he wanted. Lucas's life was on the line. He pulled, trying to get the screws to give. He would try everything he could because he was not going to let that son of a bitch kill his loves.

Aidan pulled and pulled as the smoke began to fill the barn.

Chapter Nineteen

Lexi thought about getting up and going after Lucas. It might be fun to watch the way the Master handled getting attacked by his sub. Lucas might get a spanking. That would definitely be a sight to see. She sighed and stretched. He might be getting a spanking even as she lay here.

When had she started thinking of Aidan as her Master? Even back when they were living a very vanilla lifestyle, she'd dreamed about being able to call Aidan Master. It had been Lucas who introduced her to BDSM, but Aidan had always been everything she wanted in a Dom. His alpha nature was what attracted her to him in the first place. She and Lucas might be halves of a whole, but they needed Aidan to complete them.

She let her mind drift. She felt truly relaxed for the first time in forever. She was getting married. No long engagement this time. They were going to elope. *Vegas, here we come.* She knew her mom might be upset, but Lexi wasn't taking any chances this time. She was tying that man up.

Or would it be Lucas? How exactly did they figure that out? Her mom had married Jack, and Dani had legally married Julian, but Lucas wasn't exactly a sub in the way Sam and Finn were. *Why the hell am I thinking about this when my men are out there doing hot, dirty things to each other?*

Maybe she wasn't as sore as she thought.

She pushed the covers back and put on one of Aidan's T-shirts. It covered everything that needed covering. She would grab a cup of coffee and then go sneak a peek. Then she would sit down and write for a while. That sounded like a great way to spend the day.

She stopped at the door when she heard a cell phone chirp. Lucas's. He must have forgotten it, a sure sign he'd relaxed. She found it buried underneath the scrubs from the previous evening. Aidan had decided they would keep the scrubs for when they needed to play doctor. She glanced down at the number. Ben Dawson. Oh, she wasn't about to miss that call.

"Hello."

There was a pause. "I'm sorry. I'm looking for Lucas Cameron. Is this Lexi?"

"In the flesh. Lucas is doing things he really can't do with a phone in his hand. I'm afraid you have to talk to me."

A low, seductive chuckle came across the line. "Oh, sweetheart, I would love to do more than talk to you. Have you decided to leave those two boys you were playing around with? Maybe you would like to see how semi-psychic twins do it. I can answer that question. We do it better. Hey!" Ben's voice went from sexy to irritated in a second. "You didn't have to throw something at me. I get the picture, asshole. Fine. I'll move on. Chase wants to talk to Lucas."

Weird. Chase forced Ben to make his phone calls? Those twins were a very curious pair. "Lucas isn't here. I can have him call you back."

A slow sigh came over the line. "No, don't bother. We're coming out there. We're at the police station right now. Chase is nervous about something. I've learned to trust his instincts. He's an asshole who throws staplers at his own brother and refuses to talk on the phone because he's sure it's going to give him cancer, but he's freaky on target when it comes to stuff like this."

"Did they let Karen out?" Lexi was a bit surprised. She'd heard they were planning on throwing the book at Karen. By the time Bo had come to pick them up the night before, everyone had known that

Karen had been found drunk in her car not far from the accident.

"No, she's still in jail, but Chase is certain it wasn't her."

That was in line with what Lucas thought. God, she wanted it to be Karen. It was very disappointing. She'd been looking forward to seeing Karen in an orange jumper. "They found her in her car in a ditch. She wrecked it after she tried to kill us."

"Then why didn't her airbag deploy?" Ben asked. "According to the report, she blew a 1.6 on the breathalyzer. She was two times the legal limit. There's no way she drove that car, much less managed to drive Aidan's truck off the road. That was deliberate and took discipline Karen Wilcox simply doesn't have. But of course we can't get anyone to see that here. These cops like open-and-shut cases."

He had a point. "If not Karen, then who?"

"Chase has been looking into the firefight Aidan was injured in. He doesn't like it."

"I'm sure Aidan didn't like it, either." But she didn't see why Chase was spending his time on it.

"No, you don't understand, sweetheart. Things don't add up. The reports don't make sense. Why was Aidan hit from both the back and the front? PFC Creely explains—and I'm using air quotes here—how it all went down, but I don't buy it." There was a muffled pause as though Ben had put his hand over the phone, then he was back. "Fine, I'll tell her. Chase wants you to know that this was the sloppiest report he's ever hacked into a government database to read."

Interesting. "Does he do that often?"

"Often enough to get the FBI interested in us. There's a reason we had to go through McKay-Taggart to get this job. Some people like to watch baseball. My brother likes to hack high-security systems."

Maybe Chase Dawson would be the one in an orange jumpsuit. But that was irrelevant. "What did the report say?"

"Specialist Tanner's injuries were to the back of his neck. According to Creely, Tanner broke position and ran. But Chase checked his records. Tanner was set for Ranger training two weeks after his death. He was seasoned. He'd seen worse fighting. He wouldn't have run. Most of the men killed in the fight were taken out by M16s. Unusual, but not unheard of. Insurgents can get M16s, too.

And then there's the fact that all the weapons were recovered from the scene. All but one. PFC Creely said he lost his M16 somewhere between the scene and the hospital. That makes ballistics tests impossible."

"Who is this Creely guy?" She would like to have a talk with that asshole.

"It's Dwight Creely, Aidan's foreman."

Holy shit. Dwight, who constantly harped on Aidan to take his sleeping pills. Dwight, who got agitated every time Aidan started to remember something. "You think Dwight killed those men and shot Aidan?"

Ben hesitated, but only for a second. "Suspect is the proper word. We don't think he killed all of them, but what if he panicked? What if he accidently killed someone and shot Aidan? Big Tag is calling an associate from the Agency to see if he can find anything out. It wouldn't be the first incidence of friendly fire the US Military has covered up or just plain looked over. But we think Creely wants it buried, and it looks like he's willing to kill to keep Aidan quiet. This was never about you. This is about Aidan."

"You have to come out here. Come now." She let the phone drop. That son of a bitch was out there with Aidan. Unless Lucas had found them, Dwight was alone with Aidan, and she had no idea what Dwight had planned next. It was obvious to her now that Dwight had done what he did to get Aidan back to the ranch where he could watch the only man who could put Dwight away. Now that Aidan was starting to remember, Dwight had decided to take him out.

She stopped in the middle of the hall. She couldn't panic. Panicking would tip Dwight off. She needed to stay calm. She went to the office and pulled up the radio. If Aidan was out on the range, he should have his radio with him. She tried to turn the radio on but got nothing. She checked the cord to make sure it was plugged in, but all she came up with was a ragged end.

Someone had cut the cord to the radio. Someone didn't want the cowboys on the range to be able to get in contact with the house.

Her hands shook. Ben and Chase were on their way, but it was twenty minutes from town. She couldn't wait.

Think. Think. Think.

247

Aidan's dad kept a multitude of guns in the house. She remembered that from her previous visits. It had been years, but she seriously doubted Aidan had gotten rid of all of them. Lexi remembered that there was a gun cabinet in the closet. She opened the closet in the office, and sure enough, the gun cabinet was still there.

And locked.

Damn it. The desk. She rushed to the desk and prayed the key was there. She opened the desk drawer and found something much better than a key. Sitting right there on top of some papers was a revolver. She was going to have such a long discussion with Aidan about gun safety right after she saved his ass from the man trying to kill him. She picked up the revolver. Damn, it was a heavy son of a bitch. She found a fast load cartridge. Six bullets. Hopefully she wouldn't need them at all, but she wasn't going to go after PFC Dwight Creely with a crop, and that was the only other "weapon" she had seen in that closet.

She silently thanked her stepfathers. Jack and Sam had taught her how to use a pistol and a rifle. They had taken both Lexi and her mom to a shooting range. Her stepfathers' belief was that if she and her mom were going to be around guns, they should damn sure know how to use them. She popped the cartridge into place. The phone was sitting right there. She picked it up and dialed her mother's cell, praying she made a connection. Her mom and stepdads were twenty minutes away, too, but she was calling in the cavalry.

"Hey, baby, how are you doing this morning?" Her mom sounded cheery and awake.

Lexi didn't have time for chitchat. "I need you to send Jack and Sam out to the ranch. Do not come yourself. Matter of life and death—maybe mine, definitely Aidan's. Love you. Bye."

Lexi hung up the phone. It immediately rang again, but she let it go. She knew her mother. Jack and Sam would be on their way. Whatever happened, at least she knew someone she trusted was coming for her.

She clutched the gun at her side, holding the barrel down and away. She started back toward the bedroom. She didn't even have on shoes. She would get dressed and then go after them. It would be okay. So far Dwight hadn't done anything blatant and open. She could see now that he'd tried to blame someone else for his crimes. He would lie in wait. She had time. She would find Lucas and Aidan in a ridiculously compromising position, and they would wonder why she was running around with a gun. By that time, Ben and Chase would be here, and Jack and Sam would be hard on their heels.

Then why had Dwight cut the radio cord?

There was no rational reason to do that unless he was making his move. If he sent the ranch hands out of range of cell phones, they would have no way to call for help.

Prickles of trepidation raced along her skin. She rushed into the kitchen. She would get dressed and find them and pray it wasn't too late.

She was rushing through the kitchen when she stopped. She felt her hands begin to shake as she realized what she could see through the small kitchen window. It was a window over the sink, draped with faded yellow curtains. It framed the scene in a sort of weird normality. Dwight stood in front of the barn door. His back was to the window. He stood there casually, a rifle at his side. Why was he watching the barn? Was he waiting for Aidan to come out of the barn? Would he shoot Aidan?

Smoke. The faintest hint of smoke drifted from the barn.

Rolling nausea swept through her system as she realized what was happening. Aidan was trapped in the barn, and it was on fire. Terror threatened to swamp her. She didn't know if he was dead already. He could be dead, and she'd been lying in bed. And where was Lucas? Lucas had gone looking for Aidan. Had he found Dwight?

She clamped her free hand over her mouth to stop the scream that threatened to escape. They couldn't be dead. They couldn't. Her mind wouldn't wrap around the idea. They were alive, and they were in that barn. They were waiting for her.

They were her men, and by god, no son of a bitch was taking them from her.

Lexi forced herself to walk to the front door. Dwight would see her if she charged out the back. She had no doubt he was better with a rifle than she was with a handgun. After all, he had a lot of practice killing people. She hadn't even gotten into a fistfight before.

249

She had to do this.

She'd never in her life felt so alone or small as she did as she crept out the front door and around the small ranch house. Her heart pounded in her chest. She wasn't brave. She sure as hell wasn't fearless. She was afraid of everything, but she couldn't afford that now. She was way more afraid of losing Lucas and Aidan than she was of getting herself killed.

She reached the edge of the house. Now she could smell the smoke. How long had they been trapped in there? She was sure Lucas was in there, too. Otherwise, he would be fighting like hell. Lucas was a fighter. Aidan had already proven how hard he could fight.

It was her turn.

Tears blurred the world around her as she held the gun up in a two-handed stance. Immediately her arms ached from the weight, but she wasn't about to fail now. As quietly as she could, she walked out into the open. Dwight still had his back to her.

"Are you going to move out of my way, or are you going to force me to shoot you?" She asked the question in a clear, calm voice that belied the horror she felt.

Dwight's back stiffened and his hand tightened around the rifle. He turned slowly, one hand up. "You don't want to shoot me, girl. I can't do what you ask."

Wrong answer. She pulled the trigger.

The gun exploded, sending jolts of shock up her arm. The kickback set her on her ass and, once more, she wished she'd put on underwear. It was the theme of her life lately. Her lack of proper panties didn't stop her from jumping up. Dwight was on the ground. Lexi approached quickly, gun at the ready. His body twitched in the dirt. She kicked the rifle away. Blood streamed from the wound in his chest. A thin line seeped from his mouth. He was obviously in pain, and he wasn't dead yet.

And she didn't have time for him. He'd made his decision the minute he'd set that barn on fire. She shot him again, right in the chest. Again the recoil hurt, but she was ready this time. She stayed on her feet and immediately turned to the barn.

"Aidan!" She screamed his name, praying he called back.

Heat poured from the barn, threatening to scorch her skin. She pulled at the barn door, but something held it closed. A lock. It was a combination lock. She had no idea what number Aidan would use.

She stepped back and aimed for the lock. After this was done, if she never saw another gun again, it would be too soon. She spread her legs wide to handle the kickback better and fired. The lock exploded. She set the gun down and pulled open the barn door.

Heat blasted from the open doors. The sides and the back of the barn were fully ablaze. Smoke was everywhere.

"What the fuck?"

Lexi turned and saw Bo staring down at Dwight's body. Ike sat beside him, his chest heaving as though the dog had been running.

"Help me, Bo. They're in here. We have to get them out." Lexi yelled before she ran into the barn. She could barely see through the smoke. It billowed out of the open doors. She could make out the rack. Someone was on the slab. *Aidan.*

She raced across the floor. Her eyes were adjusting and the smoke was clearing now that it had a place to go. Aidan was tied down. His wrists were bloody from where he'd tried to pull himself free. There was a rag in his mouth. She pulled it out. God, she couldn't breathe. Aidan was so still.

Please. Please. Please. Let him be alive.

"I have Lucas," Bo yelled over the crackling of the fire.

She looked over, and Bo was pulling Lucas across the floor. He wasn't conscious. She couldn't tell if he was dead. His head rolled back as Bo dragged him by the shoulders. "Get him out of here!"

"I'll be right back." Bo dragged Lucas's body outside.

She could feel Ike beside her. He whined up at her as though begging her to free his master.

Aidan coughed. It was the most beautiful sound she'd ever heard. "Lexi?"

She started working the ropes that bound Aidan. "I'm here. We have to get out."

He shook his head. "No, angel. You have to run. Get Lucas out if you can, but Dwight's going to kill us all. You have to run."

She tugged and managed to pull his right hand free.

Bo was suddenly back in the barn. He pulled a knife out of his boot and started sawing through the ropes on Aidan's right foot.

251

"Dwight won't be killing anyone, brother. Your girl took him out. Remind me not to piss her off. And your damn dog must have known something was up. He barked right outside my window until I got my ass up."

She crawled onto the table to get to Aidan's left hand. Her lungs were burning. A piece of the roof fell beside her. They didn't have much time.

"Damn, girl. That is very distracting." Bo cut through both ropes in the time it took her to work through the first of hers. He avoided another board that fell. He was perfectly calm, given the situation. He took that wicked knife and slashed through the rest of his brother's ropes. "I'm trying to rescue my brother. You don't need to be flashing your cootchie. It's awfully pretty, though."

She huffed and jumped down from the table.

"You little prick, that's your sister-in-law." Aidan's hands were shaky, but he rolled off the table. His knees struck the floor.

"Yeah, hurt me later, brother." Bo took the left side, Lexi the right, and they got Aidan to his feet.

She nearly fell as they made it out of the barn. Aidan slumped down, but Bo took his weight, leaving her to drag air into her lungs. She coughed, her lungs aching as she saw Lucas on the grass. He was so still. She raced to him, running her hands across his body, praying for any sign of life.

"Didn't work out how I wanted it to," Lucas muttered between parched lips. "My horniness got me in trouble today."

She laughed through the tears falling from her eyes. She put her head to his chest, reveling in the sound of his heartbeat. "Let this be a lesson to you, Lucas Cameron."

"You take care of that asshole, Dwight?"

Lexi nodded. "He's gone, babe."

His hand found her hair. "That's my girl."

"Our girl." Aidan was suddenly at her back. His face was haggard, and his voice sounded three kinds of ruined, but he was alive. She sat up, and Aidan leaned into her. "Our girl saved us. We'll never hear the end of it now. And she did it all without any underwear."

Lucas gave her a tired thumbs-up.

In the distance they heard a siren sounding.

Here came the cavalry.

There was the sudden sound of gunfire. Lexi jerked up.

Bo stood over Dwight, Ike at his side. He shrugged. "You've seen those movies. Bad guy always comes back. This one ain't coming back. You know, I never did like that son of a bitch. You think anyone would notice if I shot him a couple hundred more times?"

"Don't you dare," she threatened.

She wrapped her arms around her men. Nothing in the world mattered but the fact that they were alive and well.

Two hands started to find their way under her T-shirt.

"Hey," Lexi protested.

They both snickered.

"It's my comfort object," Lucas said.

"It's my security blanket," Aidan added.

They were together, and this time it was forever. Lexi felt her heart swell. She had everything she needed.

But she was going to start putting on panties first thing in the morning.

Chapter Twenty

Six months later

"You're doing what?" Lexi asked as Dani jumped up and down in pure excitement.

Julian smiled as he sat down at the wide outdoor dining table that graced the Barnes-Fleetwood Ranch's backyard. It was a glorious day, and almost everyone she loved was enjoying a barbecue and celebrating the fact that Lexi had finished her first book. It was a romance, and she hadn't sold it yet. She did have an agent though. She'd been signed by a woman named Lara Anderson who repped a couple of Lexi's favorite authors. She'd met Amber Rose the other day and still couldn't quite believe it. They'd had lunch together and the woman had been so kind, giving her advice and tips, telling her stories of how her own career had begun.

It was a start. A slow one, but her family insisted on celebrating every little thing.

This was the first time they'd all been together in weeks. She missed this group since she'd moved fully to Deer Run. The last time they'd been together had been for Sean Taggart's wedding in Dallas.

It looked like even the wild security crew was starting to settle down.

"Danielle is opening a spa." Julian looked odd in his terribly expensive shirt and slacks, with a hot dog in his hands.

"You're opening a spa in Willow Fork?" Willow Fork barely had a beauty parlor, much less a spa. Of course, it was practically a metropolis compared to Deer Run. "I don't think Willow Fork is a spa friendly place. They look down on women wearing bikinis much less getting rubdowns and waxing their hoo haws."

"It's a destination spa." Dani's face was lit with enthusiasm. "It's an old ranch that shut down years ago. We're renovating and building it into something special. There will be horseback riding and hiking and facials and massages. We're going to have entertainment for kids so we can get families out there. I thought maybe writers could use it for a retreat or something. I'm excited about it. It's a project for a class."

She had to shake her head. The rich really were different. Most people would think of a college project as a paper analyzing different business practices. Not Dani Lodge-Taylor. Nope. When she did her business project, she opened a multimillion-dollar spa. "Well, I'll be there for the opening."

"You'll love it," Dani promised. "It was a good thing I came up with the idea since it turns out Julian owns a huge tract of land in Willow Fork. Did he ever mention he bought the land so he could shut down a development and keep my sister from profiting off the sale of our family home?"

She'd met Dani's sister. It was probably a good thing.

Julian shook his head. "Yes, I actually meant to keep that secret, but my wife turned out to be a bit nosy."

"I didn't tell her," Finn said, sitting down next to Julian. "She was pissed at me, too."

"Well, I'm not mad now. Now I'm excited. I just hired a manager. She used to run this resort in the Caribbean that catered to people in the lifestyle. Her name is Gaby, and she has two kids. She and her husband are from Texas. They thought it was time to come home. I am really excited about this project. It will bring jobs to the whole area." Dani chatted on, but Lexi found her focus shifting.

Aidan and Lucas were standing together at the swing set. Olivia and Josh were sitting in swing seats, laughing as the men pushed them. They looked perfect standing together, talking as they entertained the kids.

"Hey." Her mother curled an arm around her waist. Dani sat down with her husbands. They were arguing happily about budgets.

"Hi, Momma." Love for her mother swelled in her heart. She let her head rest against her mom's shoulder.

"I finished your book, baby girl," her mom said. "I am so proud of you. It's great. I love how much of your heart and soul you put in there."

"Thanks. I'm happy with it." It might never sell, but it did what it was supposed to do. It told her story. Oh, the names might have changed and the circumstances, but at the heart it was about the love she'd managed to find. It was about the peace she'd come to.

"One day I hope you're ready to try again," her mother said. "The best thing I ever did was have you kids."

Strange, mentioning having kids never scared her anymore. No matter what happened, this time she would lean on her family. "I thought marrying Jack and Sam was the best thing to happen to you."

"It was a great thing, but you kids, you were the expression of my soul. All three of you were the product of the love in my heart for the men in my life. I loved your father. It was a child's love, but it was love. I love Jack and Sam with everything I have. I hope one day you want kids, Lexi, because those men love you. And those kids would be something to see."

She didn't doubt it. Not for a second. She looked down at the rings on her finger. Two thin wedding bands, connected. Lucas had put the first one on her finger when they had legally married. She hadn't gotten her Vegas wedding. Nope. She'd been married right there in Deer Run and it had been beautiful. Aidan had placed the second on her and one on Lucas when they cemented their relationship at The Club. They were the O'Malleys. Lucas had legally changed his name. They were a family.

And she had no intention of it being just the three of them.

"We threw away the condoms last night, Momma."

They had made love with nothing between them. She wasn't sure how long it would take to get pregnant, but she was ready for it.

"I'm so glad, baby girl."

She stood there with her mother, the warm spring breeze playing through her hair. They each watched their men. She hugged her mom and prayed she would be as good a mother as Abigail Barnes-Fleetwood had been.

Jack declared the burgers were ready, and everyone started to line up, chattering happily about their business deals and what the kids were doing.

She stood with her mom and watched it all. They were a wild, weird, crazy bunch.

And they were hers.

* * * *

The Texas Sirens' series will continue with *Siren in Waiting*, now available.

Author's Note

I'm often asked by generous readers how they can help get the word out about a book they enjoyed. There are so many ways to help an author you like. Leave a review. If your e-reader allows you to lend a book to a friend, please share it. Go to Goodreads and connect with others. Recommend the books you love because stories are meant to be shared. Thank you so much for reading this book and for supporting all the authors you love!

One to Keep
Nights in Bliss, Colorado, Book 3
By Lexi Blake writing as Sophie Oak

Stefan Talbot likes order and control. He approaches his life with the same meticulous precision that he uses to put paint on his canvas. Nothing good comes from chaos, and that is why he has refused to allow himself to get close to Jennifer Waters. They are like fire and ice. Though she is younger, her talent as an artist is unquestionable. But she lives her life like she paints—with wild, passionate abandon. It is intoxicating and terrifying, and he can't get her out of his head.

Jennifer ran from Bliss to put Stef behind her. She had come to the mountain town seeking a mentor but found much more than she bargained for. Cool and distant, Stef was like a marble statue and no matter how hard she tried, she couldn't break through his shell. She moved to Dallas to start over, but nothing is going as planned. When the art gallery where she works is robbed and a precious painting is stolen, Jen is accused of the theft. Jen is thrilled when her bail is met, until she realizes her savior is Stef and he has a few conditions. First and foremost, she has to return to Bliss.

Against the backdrop of the Winter Festival, Stef and Jen's attraction catches fire. But the dark forces behind the robbery in Dallas have followed Jen home. A criminal syndicate believes she still has the stolen painting and they'll kill to get their hands on it.

Siren in Waiting
Texas Sirens, Book 4
By Lexi Blake writing as Sophie Oak

Bethany "Mouse" Hobbes spent her entire life waiting, especially for the love of Bo O'Malley. But for the first time in her life, she is ready to start living, with or without him. She has found her dream, restoring a rustic farmhouse on the outskirts of town.

Trev McNamara left Deer Run a high school hero and has returned, his pro football career in ruins. When Trev meets Mouse, he discovers a passion strong enough to overcome his past. But can she accept his dominant desires?

Bo O'Malley has lived his whole life in the shadow of his brother, never committing to anything or anyone. When the woman he secretly loved all his life begins an affair with the man who betrayed his trust, Bo will do anything to claim her as his own.

Transformed by their love, will Mouse be enough woman for both of them?

About Lexi Blake

Lexi Blake lives in North Texas with her husband, three kids, and the laziest rescue dog in the world. She began writing at a young age, concentrating on plays and journalism. It wasn't until she started writing romance that she found success. She likes to find humor in the strangest places. Lexi believes in happy endings no matter how odd the couple, threesome or foursome may seem. She also writes contemporary Western ménage as Sophie Oak.

Connect with Lexi online:

Facebook: Lexi Blake
Twitter: authorlexiblake
Website: www.LexiBlake.net

Sign up for Lexi's free newsletter at
www.lexiblake.net/newsletter/

Printed in the USA
CPSIA information can be obtained
at www.ICGtesting.com
LVHW051323140324
774486LV00020B/130